WHAT DOESN'T KILL HER

A THRILLER BY

MAX ALLAN COLLINS

Other Books by Max Allan Collins
Published by Thomas & Mercer

The Memoirs of Nathan Heller

Mallory Mysteries

The "Disaster" Mysteries

Other Novels

WHAT DOESN'T KILL HER

A THRILLER BY

MAX ALLAN COLLINS

The characters and events portrayed in this book are fictitious. Any similarity to real persons, living or dead, is coincidental and not intended by the author.

Published by Thomas & Mercer, Seattle

www.apub.com

ISBN-13: 9781612185293
ISBN-10: 1612185290

Library of Congress Control Number: 2013904877

Printed in the United States of America.

ACKNOWLEDGMENTS

I wish to acknowledge my frequent collaborator,
Matthew V. Clemens,
for coplotting,
forensics (and other) research,
and the preparation of a story treatment
from which I could develop this novel.
—M. A. C.

In memory of Bj Elsner
with fond remembrance of days
at the Mississippi Valley Writers Conference

If you are bent on revenge, dig two graves.
—*Chinese proverb*

There is a sacredness in tears.
—*Washington Irving*

True first love is dangerous.
—*Stephen King*

CHAPTER ONE

Ten Years Ago

Breath coming in raspy gasps, sixteen-year-old Jordan Rivera peeked out from her hiding place under her bed.

Too loud, she knew, working to calm herself, control her breathing. *Too loud.*

This had been such a typical boring evening, dinner with her folks and her older brother, Jimmy, then to her room for homework. Now the dullness that was her life had taken a terrifying turn. . . .

She'd been lying on her bed, wearing only a knee-length nightshirt, algebra book open in front of her as she daydreamed about Mark Pryor. About kissing him. About *more* than kissing him . . .

While it seemed every other cheerleader lusted after quarterback Pete Harris, Jordan had set her eyes on Mark, the team kicker. Mark was no broad-shouldered knuckle dragger—he was short and thin, like she was; but his hair was blond where hers was black, his eyes blue where hers were dark brown.

Not just a football player, either—Mark was incredibly bright and no stuck-up jackass like so many jocks. And she just *knew* those lips of his would be the softest of any guy's in the senior class—even if she hadn't found out for herself yet.

Such thoughts had sent her homework retreating to the furthest recesses of her mind, only to be interrupted by the crash downstairs.

She never jumped at the "boo" moments in scary movies, but this jarring sound, unexpected and unknown, made her jump, all right. Shook and shivered her. As she hopped off the bed, she settled herself, thinking clumsy Jimmy had knocked something over, or maybe one of her parents had tripped and fallen.

These innocent thoughts disappeared when, from beyond the door, came muffled, alarmed voices, and what sounded like someone thrashing around.

Cautious but without hesitation, she opened her door, stepped into the hallway, and had just gotten to where she could see down the stairs when she heard her mother scream, "*Run,* Jordan! Run!"

The words themselves barely registered—it was the fear in her mother's scream that seized Jordan. Fear like nothing she'd ever heard from her mother before. It stopped her like a punch, and the girl's eyes automatically shifted across the railing to the first floor . . .

. . . *where her father wrestled desperately with a man in dark blue.*

The front door was thrown open wide, a small hole in the wall where the knob had crashed into it. *That* had been the sound Jordan had heard—this man in blue had forced his way into their home!

Their unwanted guest seemed to be wearing a police uniform . . . *but why would a policeman be wrestling with her father?*

Then light glinted off something in the intruder's hand—*a knife!*—whose blade slashed down across her father's face. A ribbon of scarlet glistened on her dad's cheek as he howled like a wounded animal.

Her mom again screamed, "*Run,* Jordan!"

But there was no going forward, the stairs blocked now by the struggle between the intruder and her father. And then her brother, Jimmy, entered into the fray, coming to aid Dad, but too late to prevent a second knife blow that plunged deep in her father's chest. Dad sagged back to the floor, blood blossoming on his white shirt.

Jimmy was diving at the intruder, and she wanted to help, but Jordan's training was to obey her parents, and her mother had said "Run," and so she ran.

Back to her room, where she shut the door behind her, considered going out the window, but there was nowhere to go, just straight down to the ground, two floors below.

Should she jump?

She would almost certainly break one leg, if not both, and *then* how could she ever get away?

She looked for her cell phone, remembered it was in her jacket downstairs . . .

. . . *downstairs*, where Jimmy's voice rose in a peal of yowling pain.

Jordan shuddered, choked back tears, scoured her room for a weapon, seeing teddy bears, CDs, posters of teen idols, the mirror over the tiny dressing table. Though nothing looked out of place, nothing resembled a weapon either, unless she broke the mirror maybe. Then her eyes fell on her student desk.

Scissors inside.

She jerked open the drawer, found the scissors, and drew them out as the sounds of struggle grew closer. Someone was coming up the stairs—*more than one person?*

Holding the scissors like a knife, the points not as sharp as she wished, Jordan threw open her window to suggest that she'd fled, then squeezed under her bed.

Where she waited.

Trying to control her breathing, a ragged sound so loud that it seemed to echo throughout the room. The house. The universe. Sweat matting her hair, running into her eyes. Cold terror flowing through her veins, her heart hammering in her ears. She looked at the scissors in her trembling fist and tried to force herself not to shake. The room seemed warm, but she couldn't stop shivering.

She peeked under the hanging bedspread toward the door. Sounds of struggle had grown louder, closer, moving to the hallway beyond that door. Grunts and growls and bodies bouncing off walls.

Then Jordan heard her mother nearby, crying, "Why are you *doing* this to us? What did we *do* to *you*?"

If the intruder answered, Jordan didn't hear the reply.

Shivering, her teeth chattering now, she heard the struggle perhaps another ten seconds—then there was a loud gasp right outside her door.

Not Jimmy or Dad—her mother.

She wanted to scream, for her mother, for herself, for mercy, for no reason but to scream at the insanity that had invaded her sphere.

But Jordan managed to stay silent and even made her breathing quieter, eyes glued to the light leaking in under the door.

After what seemed like forever, the door swung slowly open and Jordan stared at a patch of hallway. An eternity seemed to pass before she saw a shoe take a drunken step in. Instantly, Jordan recognized her mother's white New Balance walking shoe. Her mother's foot hung there for a long moment, then a bead of blood plopped like a solitary raindrop on the toe.

Her mother took another unsteady step, a gurgling sound coming from somewhere. As Jordan watched, her mother's feet hesitated, then the body those feet had supported toppled.

And her mother's face came to rest just inches from Jordan's own.

Mom's brown eyes wide, staring, lifeless, blood visible at the corners of her mouth and now Jordan screamed.

The shrill wordless wail seemed to fill the whole world and even though she tried to stop, Jordan couldn't. And when need for breath demanded a stop, the scream started right back in, on and on, her mother's eyes staring at her without life, without love, without hope.

A hand closed around her ankle and pulled—*hard*—cutting off her scream. She released the scissors to try to grip the floor or the underside of the bed or *something*, but she felt herself traveling backward, her fingernails clawing uselessly at the hardwood floor as she jerked her foot, trying to free herself of the firm grip. On her tummy, she tried to twist around to see her attacker, but couldn't lift her shoulder, the bottom of the bed blocking her.

As he drew her effortlessly out from under, by both ankles now, Jordan tried to kick free, though her attacker proved too strong. She was halfway out when she stretched her right hand and managed to grasp the handle of the scissors and take them along with her.

"Let me *go!*" she yelled. It came up from her chest but sounded small and childlike.

The attacker pulled harder and she found herself out in the middle of the floor, the protection provided by the bed a distant memory. He jerked her leg to one side and Jordan was forced from her stomach onto her back, the room suddenly seeming very bright around her.

She could see him finally.

Tall, white, more muscular than Jimmy, but probably only a few years older than her brother. His blond hair stood out at odd angles, tousled from all the fighting. Sky-blue-eyed, pug-nosed, Beach Boy–looking with an awful wholesomeness. He wore a police uniform, but the badge and shoulder patch were different than those of their local Westlake, Ohio, PD. In his right hand he clenched a hunting knife, streaked with glistening red.

Releasing her foot, he leaned closer to her and she saw her chance. She thrust the scissors forward, but he responded with psychic ease, dodging her attack, slapping her arm away, scissors clattering across the floor somewhere.

As she watched her weapon twirl away, pain exploded inside her head, and as she fell back, she realized the attacker had punched her in the side of the head, which knocked her jarringly onto the floor.

The pain seemed to be everywhere and even smacking her head on the hard flooring didn't register much. Jordan blinked and fought to clear her mind. Even as she did, her attacker grabbed a hank of hair and yanked, forcing Jordan to her feet with a fresh yowl of pain.

She tottered in his grasp, trying to get her feet under her, eyes darting around the room searching for another weapon and, at all costs, trying to avoid her dead mother.

Her attacker pulled her around until they were face-to-face, only inches apart, as if they were dancing—his icy blue eyes boring into her. She tried to turn away, but he jerked her hair and made her look at him again. This time anger mixed with her terror and she took a good look at her mother's murderer. And probably her father's, and her brother's . . . who would be here helping if they could . . .

. . . if they were alive.

She doubted she'd survive this, but in case she did, she would memorize every detail about him. That he wore no mask meant he would likely kill her. She had a sudden fatalistic, even Zen-like realization of that. But if she could survive, she would *know* this bastard. . . .

Start with this: he's wearing contact lenses. Are his eyes really blue, or not?

He smells of cologne mixed with sweat from his struggle, making a pungent, sickly sweet odor.

The knife danced into her line of sight, her mother's blood glistening on the blade.

Jordan tried not to stare at the steel shaft bobbing slowly like a serpent poised to strike. What gripped her now was not fear of death—she was past that—but the anticipation of pain. The pain she *did* fear, and that sent hot tears flowing.

"This is what I do," he said, almost calm about it.

She said nothing, but her face must have registered her confusion at his too-simple explanation for slaughtering her family.

"It's what I do," he said, as if volume and repetition would make her suddenly understand his gibberish.

She managed, "You kill . . . families?"

He shook his head, obviously angry that she was too slow to grasp his meaning. "I reestablish the natural order . . . God's natural order."

"God told you to kill my family?"

His eyes flared and he smiled. "Yes. You perceive. How nice that you perceive."

"I perceive that you're *insane!*"

The eyes went cold again, as lifeless as her mother's, and Jordan realized too late that she had made a mistake. Using her hair as a handle, he whipped her around, smashing her face into the mirror, glass shattering.

She crumpled, landing atop the dressing table, fingers scrabbling for a weapon—*he'd found something to break that mirror for her, hadn't he?*—shards, or even a brush, makeup, *anything*, but he still held on to her long black hair and jerked her back to a standing position. Her hands empty, something warm and wet on her cheeks. That coppery taste on her lips was blood.

Better to keep her mouth shut.

Still using her hair like reins, he forced her to the floor next to her mother.

"Pick her up," the intruder said.

Jordan looked at the dead body of her mother and began to sob. "I . . . I can't . . . she's too . . . too heavy."

Her mother was barely bigger than her, but that was what she said to try to get out of the terrible task demanded of her.

"Then drag her," the intruder said.

"What? . . . Where?"

He squatted down and showed her the knife again. "Wherever I *tell* you to."

To punctuate his statement, he jabbed the knife deep into her mother's back, just above the kidney.

Jordan cried out, as if the knife had gone into her.

There was blood, but not very much. Maybe dead people didn't bleed.

"Now," the intruder said.

Forcing herself to her feet, Jordan bent at the knees and picked her mother up under the arms. Though it made no difference now, Jordan tried to be gentle.

"Downstairs."

The wood floor was slick with her mother's blood and even as she struggled with her burden, Jordan fought to keep her balance, tears running freely down her cheeks again, mixing with the blood from the cuts inflicted by the mirror. To her surprise, Jordan felt no pain—no fear, really. Was this what it was like to accept death? It was that moment when the dentist's drill sends you to that place where you lull yourself, *This will be over soon, this will be over. . . .*

She dragged her poor mother into the hallway, heaving for breath.

The stairs now.

The intruder preceded her, going down backward, one knife-gripped hand also holding on to Jordan's hair, the other on the railing. Her back to him, holding her mother from behind, she would take a step down, drag her mother a step, take another step, drag her mother a step. . . .

Halfway down, she let go of Mom, and hurled her weight into the man, knocking him backward, her hair released reflexively as he fell. She spun to push him again, but he had regained his balance, and slapped her.

Slapped her hard, her head twisting impossibly on her neck.

Then, with the knife at her throat, his other hand gripping her by a bicep, he trotted her down the stairs and flung her to the floor. She was pushing up groggily to see the horrific sight of the intruder dragging her mother down the stairs by one arm, bump bump bumping, like a terrible Slinky.

She began to cry and then he was shaking her, as if she had fallen asleep in the midst of an important task. He had dumped her mother on the entryway floor nearby.

He pointed toward the living room. "In there. *Take* her!"

Holding her mother from behind, the back of the dead woman's head near her face, Jordan hauled her burden, the small woman seeming heavy as a sack of grain. The smell of her mother's hair lingering in Jordan's nostrils reminded the girl of how comforting that scent had been on every other day of her life.

When she got to the living room, despite her efforts not to look, Jordan saw the bodies of her father and brother tossed like broken toys discarded by an evil child. She managed to swallow the wail of despair that wanted as desperately to escape as she did.

"Over there," the intruder said, pointing with the knife. "In front of the couch."

Jordan dragged her mother over to the sofa and rested her on the floor there.

"No. Sit her up."

Jordan glanced back at the intruder, who lifted an eyebrow and the knife.

She did as she'd been told, and when her mother was seated on the floor with her back to the sofa, Jordan instinctively reached up to brush her mother's hair into place.

"Now him," the intruder said, pointing the knife toward her father, over by the fireplace.

Darker-skinned than her mother, Jordan's father had been a successful insurance executive until this terrible night. Now, white shirt stained scarlet, vicious cut running from his left ear down across his cheek, Peter Rivera was the broken husk of a man.

Dad proved more difficult to move—half again as heavy as Mom. The living room's white carpeting had patchy blotches of crimson and pink, and the tooth of the carpet made it even harder to move her father's deadweight than on the wooden floor upstairs. At least her father's eyes were closed, peacefully unaware of these posthumous indignities.

As Jordan struggled with her task, she heard the intruder stride over and she expected him to grab her by the hair again; but instead he grabbed a lifeless arm and helped her drag her father over next to Mom. She successfully arranged Dad into a sitting position against the sofa, as well. Her parents' heads tilted toward each other, touching, a parody of a loving posture.

She knew what was coming next. Without a word from her taskmaster, she turned and faced her fallen brother, Jimmy, over by Dad's recliner. Taller than her, Jimmy shared Jordan's same delicate bone structure. He'd always been a skinny kid who got picked on for his gangly clumsiness, let alone his sexual orientation.

Only a year ago, right before his high school graduation, Jimmy's biggest concern had been coming out to their parents. Jordan had known her brother was gay for years, but their folks seemed clueless.

But when Jimmy had finally screwed up the courage to tell them, Mom's only response had been "Of course you are, sweetheart. We've known that for years." Not a trace of judgment, much less sarcasm in her voice.

Then Jimmy had said, "Please pass the potatoes," and the moment brother and sister had been dreading came and went without incident.

"Come *on!*" the intruder said. "Get *moving.*"

Now he was in a hurry?

As she dragged her dear dead brother across the room, the enormity of what she was facing—the last few minutes of her life—finally settled in on her, and like even the bravest prisoner ever ushered to execution, she found herself shaking again.

The intruder helped her prop her brother up next to her mother and she thought about trying to fight back again, but her face stung with the mirror-shard wounds, her neck ached from his jarring slap, and she decided he had heaped enough pain on her already. All she wanted now was for this to be over. Someone someday would catch this monster, and stop him. But not her. Not tonight.

"All right," he said, almost smiling, nodding, obviously pleased. He gestured with the knife again. "Now sit down next to your brother."

"What?"

"*Sit* with him."

She did it.

She joined her family, knowing she would soon be joining them in a more profound way and they would all be in Heaven together. Oddly, her sudden sense of calm was accompanied by an accelerated shivering.

She never would kiss Mark Pryor, though, would she?

The intruder leaned down over her, and Jordan's eyes fixed upon the knife. Then she decided she didn't want to see it coming, and closed her eyes.

But instead of the blade slashing across her throat or driving deep into her chest, she felt the intruder's touch, almost gentle as he lightly brushed her hair away from her bloody forehead. His fingertips were warm, soft, not rough as she'd anticipated. She kept her eyes closed tight even as she braced against the blow that would be coming any second now.

"Relax," he said. "I'm not going to kill you."

Her eyes sprang open, and a sudden fury rose up through her fear and resignation. "I should believe *you*? You murdered my *family!*"

He shrugged. "That doesn't make me a liar."

As if to demonstrate his goodwill, he moved away from her, settling on his haunches. But the knife was still firmly grasped in a gloved hand.

"Why would you kill them," she asked, tears struggling to get out, "and not me?"

"I need you alive," he said. "Now, quiet."

From a pocket, he produced a small digital camera, much like the one Jordan had pestered her parents for last Christmas. Which she hadn't gotten.

Holding the tiny camera up, he grinned, full of himself, and said, "Say *cheese*."

She lurched as the flash went off. *This couldn't be real, the killer of her family taking snapshots!*

"Sit still," he commanded.

This time she faced the flash blankly frozen.

He stuffed the camera into a pants pocket.

Then, from another pocket, he withdrew a small square foil packet. From sex ed class she knew instantly what it was . . . and what awaited her. . . .

Death was the better option. She had barely kissed any boys. She hadn't come anywhere near what this creature obviously had planned for her.

She tried to get up, but he slapped her back to the floor and crawled on top of her. He pushed up her nightshirt even as she fought to keep it down. Her sightless parents, propped against the couch, looked on.

"You're going to help me," he said, his voice as cool as a cemetery breeze.

"Why don't you just kill *me*, too?" she asked, wanting that, wanting that so bad.

"I told you. I need you. You're going to help me."

"Help you?"

He smiled at her, even as he fumbled with his pants. "You're going to tell my story."

"What . . . what. . . ."

He ripped open the foil pack, his grin goofy. "You will bear witness to what happens to families who don't follow God's natural order."

Then he was heavy on top of her and Jordan couldn't struggle anymore. He was too strong.

"Please just kill me," she begged.

"No, no, no . . . just lay back and enjoy. You'll live to tell my story. You'll live to . . . to . . . tell . . . the *world.* . . ."

And even as the terrible thing happened, as Jordan Rivera retreated to a private corner of herself and distanced herself from this violation, she made herself a solemn promise.

Tell his story?

Like hell I will.

CHAPTER TWO

Today

Dr. Donna Hurst stood in the nurses' station sporking dainty dips from a cup of peach yogurt, savoring each bite as if they were worthy of the effort. Not Donna's favorite breakfast, but with only three weeks left before her Cozumel vacation, the tall green-eyed redhead—a youthful forty-something in white lab coat over a black silk blouse and matching slacks—was still fighting off that last tenacious ten pounds, especially around her hips.

Getting on staff at St. Dimpna's Center—possibly Ohio's premier mental health facility—had been Donna's goal since she'd become a psychologist, twenty years ago. Achieving that goal had taken twelve years of moving from one facility to another, building a reputation, losing a husband, and alienating her two kids. But here she finally was on staff at St. Dimpna's, and that still mattered to her.

Nibbling another spoonful, she looked through the chicken-wire-crosshatched window into the dayroom.

Several female patients lounged there, watching TV, mingling over children's board games, playing cards, a few staring out windows on this sunny spring day. Despite a variety of ages, ethnicities, and medical conditions, the women had in common one thing: they were battling mental illness. All casually dressed—just no belts or shoelaces.

These were the doctor's patients, and she had made—to various degrees—headway with them all . . . with one significant exception.

In her midtwenties—her raven ponytail and smooth features making her look much younger—Jordan Rivera sat on a sofa gazing up in silence at the wall-mounted television. She wore blue hospital scrubs, having already adopted that outfit by the time Donna arrived here two years after the girl's admittance.

Girl, Donna thought, catching herself. *That's how I think of her. Not woman—girl.*

Doctor and patient had spent countless hours in one-on-one sessions, and to this day the only voice Donna had ever heard in those sessions was her own. Group sessions found the girl . . . *the young woman* . . . equally unresponsive. There and in all situations, Jordan Rivera remained mute.

Not medically so—nothing physically wrong with the patient's vocal mechanism. Hers was apparently hysterical mutism, resulting from the trauma of the crimes committed against her and her family, a decade ago now.

The layperson might mistake this patient's silence for catatonia, but of course the doctor knew better. While Jordan might sit, unmoving, for hours at a time, she didn't display any of the rigidity of a true catatonic patient. Though catatonia could be caused by post-traumatic stress disorder, which surely made Jordan a candidate, Dr. Hurst would never classify Jordan as clinically catatonic.

Still, in addition to not speaking, Jordan Rivera often spent her waking hours virtually immobile, as if every emotion had been silenced, stuffed into some deep, dark recess of the young woman's mind—a private place that Donna had not yet been able to reach.

Yet in other key respects, Jordan was a normal young woman. Since she had been admitted to St. Dimpna's, shortly after the tragedy, Jordan had kept to herself, but she was no human slug. She stayed fit, working out as best she could in the dayroom, doing laps around the yard when allowed outside, and reading books and magazines from the selection provided to the patients, a limited variety to be sure, since all reading matter was carefully screened. No use of computers was allowed. Television channels were monitored, too, although screening their content wasn't always possible.

Jordan's solitary ways were such that she rarely had problems with other patients. A significant exception involved Kara McCormick—an incident about nine months ago, in group.

Jordan, several other patients, and newbie Kara sat in a loose circle. All but Kara were accustomed to Jordan sitting silently throughout. Toward session's end, Donna turned to Kara, whose only comments thus far had consisted of smug grunts and snorts as other patients spoke about their issues.

"Kara, as the newest member of the group, would you like to introduce yourself to the others?"

A reedy blonde with pink-and-blue streaked bangs, eighteen-year-old Kara had been sexually abused by her stepfather until she had finally resorted to slitting her wrists. She still wore the gauze bandages.

"Kara," the girl said sullenly.

Donna waited, but Kara stared at her bare legs as if the answers to her problems might be found on her kneecaps.

Gently, the doctor asked, "Would you like to tell the others why you're here?"

Kara exploded from her chair, bisecting the circle to loom over Jordan, finger-pointing. "Why doesn't *she* have to talk? Everybody else has to, what's so special about *her*?"

Before Donna could speak, Kara was leaning in at Jordan, fists balled. "Too *good* to speak to us? And how come you're wearin' *scrubs*? You're no goddamn nurse! You're just another loony tunes like the rest of us!"

Donna knew at once Kara was deflecting the attention from herself and her own troubles.

Jordan sat placidly, eyes on Kara. The doctor noted that not even verbal abuse brought this one out of her shell. It was almost as if Jordan didn't hear Kara, although her eyes on the new girl's face said otherwise.

"Kara," Donna began, putting some edge into her voice, "Jordan is—"

"She's *what?* Your frickin' *pet?*"

Donna was rising, to put herself between the two patients, but Kara beat her to the punch, literally—launching a tiny fist at Jordan's blank face.

The mute girl rose, blocking the punch with a martial arts move, then grabbed Kara in a hug, pinning the girl's arms to her sides. The two patients were looking right at each other, Kara wild, eyes and nostrils flaring, Jordan as placid as when she'd been sitting there.

The mute patient was not fighting back, just stopping, containing the attack, though the skill of that kung fu–style move (*where had* that *come from?*) indicated Jordan could have done the new girl damage.

Kara was going berserk, flailing as best she could, even trying to head-butt Jordan, who continued to hug her, as calm as a monk at prayer, even if the string of epithets spewing from Kara would have made a real monk blanch.

And still Jordan maintained her embrace.

Donna stood frozen at the sight, not willing to enter in and turn this confrontation into something even more physical. Like the rest of the group, the doctor gaped as Jordan hugged Kara until the girl's rage ebbed, her energy sapped, and finally Kara was reduced to tears.

As Kara's rage melted, Jordan released her grip. Kara did not throw a punch—she was way past that. Instead, she threw her arms around Jordan, the embrace reversed now, and the two remained that way until Kara was cried out.

Dr. Donna Hurst had witnessed some amazing things in group sessions, but nothing to top this. And despite Jordan still remaining mute, she and Kara had developed a friendship and some means of communication all their own. Kara would talk to Jordan, and manage to find enough response in Jordan's face to constitute a reply.

Before long, Kara had even adopted Jordan's uniform of light blue scrubs.

In subsequent group and one-on-one sessions, Donna had intensified her own attempts to communicate with Jordan; but no discernible progress had been made. Today would be like the hundreds of other sessions, Jordan sitting silent, listening politely, Donna talkative, sick of her own voice by the end of the hour.

Ditching the yogurt container, then taking a quick hit from her coffee, Donna prepared for another bout of frustration. When she opened the dayroom door, the noise level went up—patients talking to others and themselves, chairs scraping on the tile floor, the professional voices of the morning show on the TV that Jordan watched from the sofa.

Sitting beside her patient, Donna said, "Good morning, Jordan." She had long since stopped asking this patient, "How are you this morning?" It only emphasized the one-way nature of their conversations.

In any case, Jordan did not acknowledge the doctor's presence, continuing to stare at the television.

Well, Donna thought, *at least she's engaged. . . .*

Following Jordan's line of sight, Donna said, "*Good Morning Cleveland,* huh? Wonder if anything interesting's happening in the Mistake on the Lake today."

Jordan, of course, shared no opinion on this subject. On the medium-sized flat-screen television, the host was saying something about breaking news.

"Jordan, maybe we should—"

The girl raised a hand.

That gave Donna a start—this was a direct reaction. Rare from this patient. . . .

On screen, a perfectly coiffed female reporter stood in what appeared to be a middle-class neighborhood, saying, *"Valerie Demson for WCLE Channel Seven News, reporting from Strongsville, where last night tragedy struck. An anonymous 911 call brought police to a house down the street . . ."* She gestured with the hand that was free of a microphone. *". . . just behind me . . . where they found a family inside their home . . . victims of homicide."*

"Jordan," Donna said, "I'm going to have to turn the channel. . . ."

The nurse in the glassed-in office had the remote, and Donna cast an eye in that direction, but the desk was empty.

The reporter was saying, *"The murder victims were Arnold and Angela Sully and their teenage daughter, Brittany. Viewers may recall that Brittany Sully received national attention when she and another senior girl at Strongsville High went to the senior prom as dates. Police would not respond to speculation that a hate crime aspect may pertain to this tragedy."*

Donna rose to go switch off the television herself.

"We will follow this breaking story as it develops," the reporter said. *"This is Valerie Demson for WCLE* Channel Seven News.*"*

After hitting the switch, Donna turned to see Jordan staring at her. Approaching the patient, the doctor said, "I'm sorry, Jordan. I know it must be difficult for you to hear about that kind of unpleasantness. . . ."

The young woman continued to look at her, but not blank faced—wheels obviously turning behind those dark eyes . . . *but what was Jordan Rivera thinking?*

Raising her hand for silence was more direct communication than Jordan had made with anyone, with the possible exception of Kara, in a decade.

Donna sat next to Jordan again. "I'm sorry I didn't get that turned off sooner." *Wheels were turning.* "Obviously, there's no way we can monitor everything that's aired, and we don't want to deny everyone the simple courtesy of being able to watch—"

Jordan's head swiveled. Her eyes were narrow.

Donna reared back a little—the intensity of the woman's gaze was like a door had been opened on a blast furnace.

Woman, she thought. *Not girl. Woman. . . .*

"What do I have to do," Jordan Rivera said evenly, in a low husky voice unknown to her stunned doctor, "to get the hell out of this place?"

CHAPTER THREE

"You know what's weird?" Kara McCormick said, grinning, running a hand nervously through her pink-and-blue bangs.

"No," Jordan said. "What's weird?"

"How your real voice sounds so much like the one I used to hear in my head."

"You hear voices in your head?"

"No! I mean, the voice in my head I heard when you didn't talk out loud."

"You heard me when I wasn't talking?"

"Kind of. That so hard to believe?"

"No. But then, Kara?"

"Yeah?"

"You're fuckin' nuts."

Kara bubbled with laughter while Jordan just smiled as her mental-ward inmate pal punched her lightly on the arm.

"Well, maybe so," Kara managed through her laughter, "but *you* are fuckin' nuts *and* a bitch."

That made Jordan laugh, too, though not as raucously as Kara. Around the sunroom, other patients were staring at them.

Like the dayroom, the sunroom had chicken-wired windows. This smaller area, though, was as good as its name, streaming as it was with springtime rays, and serving as a literally sunny place for patients to meet with visitors.

Jordan and Kara sat on a secondhand sofa against the wall, while a few other patients were scattered at the room's far end, most sitting at tables with relatives who were often anxiously providing most of the talking. Jordan wore a blue T-shirt and jeans, while Kara remained in the scrubs she'd adopted.

"I never thought of myself as a bitch," Jordan said, still smiling a little. "I'm not sure I mind it."

"Hey, it's a pretty good trick for a deaf-mute."

"Hey—I heard that. Who's the bitchy one now?"

When she was with Kara, Jordan allowed herself to cut loose, a little, and flash the occasional smile—but only with Kara.

Of course, Jordan's mom would have blanched at her language; but ten years in St. Dimpna's, and making friends with Kara, had added more than a hint of salt to her vocabulary.

Kara's laughter trailed off into a thoughtful silence. "You mind answering a question?"

"Try me."

"What's it like out there?"

Jordan thought about it. Yes, she was speaking again, but she still kept most everything to herself. Said no more than she had to, to anyone.

Anyone but Kara.

The therapy that had worked best for Jordan came not from any doctor, not even Donna Hurst. And it hadn't been just the shock of that newscast that brought her out of her decade-long funk. Her return to the world, to herself, had begun when she had made a friend. Kara.

Who was saying, "I mean, not living here, that's gotta be great. But it's also gotta be . . ."

"Scary," Jordan said.

Kara nodded, and said, very tentatively, "Because of . . . what happened to your family?"

"No. I'm not afraid of that son of a bitch."

"Not afraid?"

"No. He can come back and have another shot at me anytime he likes."

Kara was just looking at her. "Uh . . . honey. You never said that to Dr. Hurst, did you?"

"Hell no. You think I'd be living off campus if I did?"

They laughed again, not so raucously.

"Anyway," Jordan said. "It hasn't been so long since you were out there. You remember what it was like."

"I remember. And I remember winding up in here, too."

"Well, it's not jail. You didn't do anything."

"If . . . if that killer isn't what you're afraid of . . . what *is* scary about it?"

Jordan shook her head. "Just being out there. Outside these walls."

"I hate these walls."

"Who doesn't? But they do protect us."

"True that."

Jordan shrugged. "I don't know if I'm smart enough to get by on my own."

Kara drew back, a skeptical smile tickling her lips. "And *I'm* fucking nuts?"

This time Jordan didn't laugh. "I'm serious."

"So am I!" Kara said. "You're as smart as anyone in this dump. And I include the docs."

Giving her friend a sideways glance, Jordan arched a brow.

"Them and the nurses and everybody. Come on, girlfriend. You're smart and you know it."

"Yeah? I didn't even finish high school."

"You got your GED in here, didn't you?"

"Whoopy do."

Kara met Jordan's eyes and held them. "Don't try those moves on me. I'm not Hurst. You left here for a *reason*, right?"

Jordan managed a tiny nod.

"You wanted something more than this . . . this medicated *cave* we all hide in."

"Fancy talk. Maybe you're the smart one."

"Bullshit. Get off your ass, girl! Go out there and fucking *get* it. Whatever it is you're after. College, the right guy, a fat job, whatever."

Her friend's pep talk was actually working—Jordan could feel herself bucking up. She managed a tight smile, unusual for her without humor to prompt it. "Thanks, honey."

"You know who's got your back, right?"

"Yeah."

"And once you get your shit together, outside? There's one more thing you need to do."

"What?" Jordan asked.

"Bust my ass out of this hellhole," Kara said.

Jordan laughed, nodded, said, "Gonna happen," and the two girls bumped knuckles.

That was about as close as Jordan liked to get to touching another human. For these two, that simple gesture was the equivalent of a long embrace between dear friends who hadn't seen each other for years.

"First off," Jordan said, "I'll round up some Dimpna Dust and sprinkle it all over you."

Kara grinned at that, but sadness was in it.

Dimpna Dust was the mythical magic powder Kara had invented, to sprinkle on the air on those rare occasions when someone got released.

Jordan had gotten her dust—Kara was still waiting for hers.

After walking Kara back to the dayroom, Jordan retreated down the stairs to the ground floor. For the last decade, Jordan had seen only the top floor of the three-story facility. Having the freedom to leave that floor behind was both exhilarating and—as she had admitted to Kara—terrifying. As the stairwell door clicked shut behind her, the real reason for her return to Dimpna's hit her like a practical joker's bucket of cold water dumped from overhead.

All she had to do was go to the damned meeting, sit there for an hour, and keep her mouth shut. God knows, she had remained mute for a decade with no real problem. Now, just sitting in a room with people who were, presumably, in the same boat as her scared the living hell out of her.

Why?

She had no idea.

The corridor before her stretched endlessly, doors on either side, and if she just kept going, down to the far end, she could walk right out. No one stopping her. But she couldn't allow herself that luxury. And it was more than just that she'd promised Dr. Hurst—this was a condition of her release.

Ignore it, and she could be back inside with Kara, *not* visiting.

Two people, a man and a woman, both middle-aged, came through the door at the far end of the hall and hustled toward her, or at least that's what it seemed like. She was wondering why the hell they would do that when the pair veered through an open door to her left.

From within the room, she heard the man's slightly echoing voice say, "Sorry—we didn't mean to be late."

Jordan heard Dr. Hurst's rather loud but friendly reply: "That's all right—we're just getting ready to start."

If group had already begun, it would be rude for her to interrupt. She would just slip by. Maybe next week. That should be fine. She couldn't avoid the Victims of Violent Crime Support Group meetings forever, but skipping just one meeting couldn't hurt. . . .

Picking up speed, Jordan sneaked a glance as she reached the closing door. She smiled to herself. She'd ducked the bullet.

Then standing right there, just inside the room, her hand on the knob, was Dr. Hurst, smiling out at her. "Well, Jordan. Hello."

"Hi."

"I was hoping you'd make it today. You're just in time. Come on in, come in."

Busted.

Forcing a thin smile, Jordan said, "Lost track, visiting Kara. Sorry."

The doctor's smile never wavered. "No problem. Come find a chair. How is Kara?"

Don't you *know? You're her doctor.*

"Fine," Jordan said.

The room was the size of a high-school classroom, but instead of desks, fifteen folding chairs were arranged in a circle.

Across the room, a dozen or so people mingled around a small table with a coffee urn and three plates of cookies. The room had the aroma of coffee mixed with disinfectant and floor wax.

Yum.

"Help yourself," Dr. Hurst said, pulling the door shut.

"No thanks. Watching the sugar and caffeine."

"Not a bad plan." Dr. Hurst moved toward the circle of chairs. Again she spoke loudly. "Okay—shall we get started?"

Slowly, the attendees began taking seats, chairs scraping. Most seemed older than her, but two young women were close to her age. As the group took seats, Jordan managed to snag the only chair with an empty space on either side.

She waited anxiously as the last few stragglers left the coffee table and joined the circle. The last thing she needed was somebody plopping down beside her, bringing along the sort of vapid small talk she so wanted to avoid.

Finally, the man she'd seen rush in sat down across from her, and she let out a little sigh of relief.

"All right," Dr. Hurst said. "First off, we have a new member today."

The psychiatrist turned to Jordan with a nod, making her wish for invisibility as all eyes swung her way.

"This is Jordan," Dr. Hurst said.

Most group members said, "Hi, Jordan," in a mix of mumbles and confidence and everything in between. *What was this, a kindergarten class welcoming a new student?* A few just nodded in her direction, and Jordan summoned up a nod for all of them.

"Now," the doctor said, her expression pleasant yet businesslike, "who would like to start today?"

Jordan sensed the doctor turning to her, the others following that example; but she sat stoically, eyes cast downward, as if the only acquaintance she hoped to meet was the polished tile floor.

As the silence asserted itself, Jordan felt her cheeks flush, yet still could not bring herself to speak. This was in part a remnant of her silent decade, but there was more to it than that. Part of her *wanted* to talk. But she simply had no idea how to explain why she was here to a roomful of strangers.

Because that would mean acknowledging, even sharing what had happened to her and her family in the only home she had ever known. St. Dimpna's hadn't been her home—it was just a stopover, like an airport between flights.

Eyes pressed down on her.

So did her own muteness, a burden she not only endured but embraced. Still, a part of her ached to let it out, all of it. But the promise she had made herself ten years ago was stronger than she was. *Giving in,* something inside her said, *telling these people, means the intruder has finally won.*

So she would not tell his story. She would never tell his story. Her pulse slowed as she retreated to that place where she had spent the last ten years. The weight lifted, the silence sheltering now, not oppressive. Her parents' house *had* been home. But now, this place within herself—this was home and here she could remain . . . as safe as in her mother's womb.

As her eyes came up to meet Dr. Hurst's, the door flew open and Jordan nearly leapt from her chair into a combat stance.

Everyone had turned from her to the sound, and she too stared at the dark-haired young man in the doorway, about her age, bangs brushing his eyes. Tall, skinny, wearing jeans and a faded Foo Fighters T-shirt, he reminded her slightly of her brother. Of course, Jimmy wouldn't have been caught dead in the holey Chuck Taylors that the young man wore.

Caught dead . . .

"Sorry I'm late," the latecomer said, shutting the door and turning to the group. "Stupid damn car croaked again. Had to get it jumped. Kindness of strangers kinda thing."

Dr. Hurst said, "That's all right, Levi. Stuff happens."

"Doc, stuff doesn't happen. Shit happens."

That got a few laughs. But just a few, and not loud.

"Levi, please. Come, join us."

Jordan's anxiety returned—the only place for the interloper to sit was in an empty chair on her either side. He was going to talk to her, she just *knew* it, and she wanted no part of talking to him or any other guy, any other human, for that matter.

And if he hit on her . . . ? She would hit on him, all right, and not in a way he would enjoy.

As Levi pulled out the chair on her right, she looked up, and he gave her a nod and a quick smile. Was there a leer in it? Was he flirting with her?

Asshole. If he so much as *whispered* in her direction. . . .

As the new entry got settled in next to her, Jordan was dismayed to see the faces in the circle slowly turning back her way.

She sent her eyes to Dr. Hurst, begging not to have to speak.

Across from her, someone said, "Why don't I take the plunge?"

She looked up to see the middle-aged man who had come in ahead of her. The woman he had come in with sat half a dozen chairs to his left, approximately halfway around the circle from Jordan. Not a couple, evidently.

"I'm David," the man said.

At least no one said, "Hi, David," like it was an AA meeting or something. They just sat and waited.

For the first time, Jordan really looked at him. Tall, slender, his dark hair showing some gray, David wore a three-button navy polo and jeans. His black New Balance sneakers looked like they had just come out of the box. With his prominent cheekbones and well-carved if sharp nose, he might have been handsome, but his hollowed-out cheeks made that a nonstarter. He wasn't much older than Jordan's dad had been when he died, though his dark blue eyes seemed about a hundred.

Finally, looking up almost shyly, David said, "Jordan, welcome to group. These are nice people here. But we're *all* messed up. Or Levi, if you prefer? Fucked up."

David smiled and so did Levi and some of the others. Some.

"We're none of us here for our amusement. We're here for a reason. Mine happened six years ago."

The room, despite the circle of people and metal folding chairs, became so quiet, the sound of her own breathing made Jordan self-conscious.

"I was still writing then," David said. "Belle . . . my wife . . . was expecting, our second daughter on the way. We were home that night with Akina . . . our other daughter. We weren't doing anything that special. It was like . . . a thousand other nights, with the possible exception that Belle, pregnant and all, was getting these cravings. Like, she would look up and announce suddenly that she simply *had* to have a sardine and peanut butter sandwich, or a grape Popsicle, or . . . or a Canadian bacon and pineapple pizza, from Salvatore's."

A few people nodded at the latter—indicating Salvatore's pizza was worth craving, even if maybe that combo wasn't. *Why,* Jordan wondered, *did this white guy have a daughter with what sounded to be an African-American name?*

"Belle was having a difficult time with her pregnancy, and I was doing everything I could to make it go easier. Hey, if she wanted Salvatore's, Salvatore's it was."

Jordan's eyes drifted to a dark-haired man seated halfway between Dr. Hurst and David. This group member had obviously undergone some serious plastic surgery. *What was his story?* she wondered. *Was he a burn victim?* Whatever the case, he was watching David raptly. Everyone else in the circle did likewise, if without that intensity.

"Didn't matter that Salvatore's was clear across town," David said, "and didn't deliver. She wanted what she wanted, and I wanted her to have it. Called in the order and drove to pick it up."

He drew in a deep breath, let it out, and looked toward the doctor, the way a guy on the wrong side of a lifeboat views somebody with a spare life jacket. What he got was an encouraging nod.

"When I got back . . ." David stopped.

The group sat silently. A thirtyish brunette woman sitting next to David touched his elbow. When he turned to her, she patted his arm.

"When I got back, they were dead, Belle and Akina—shot. And . . . mutilated."

No one moved.

"I still don't know whether the killer had been waiting for me to leave, or whether he would have killed me too, if I had been there."

Silence.

"I wish he had killed me."

Dr. Hurst said, "Do you, David?"

". . . No. Not really. What I wish is that I had been there, too, to defend them, to stop him or die trying."

The doctor nodded and smiled a little. Apparently arriving at this place had required a long journey for David.

"But I wasn't there," he said. "I wasn't there to defend them *or* to die. Except . . . he did kill me, in a way." He let out something that might have been a laugh, but wasn't. "And there hasn't been a David Elkins novel since."

David Elkins. *The thriller writer!* Jordan had never read him, but his books had often rested on the nightstands of both her parents. And hadn't there been movies?

She knew nothing of the loss he'd suffered. Was it a famous crime, out in that world she'd withdrawn from? Certainly David had been famous. Or famous for a writer, anyway.

And now Jordan spoke: "Did they catch who did it?"

Every eye turned to her, and it knocked her back.

"I'm sorry," she said.

Dr. Hurst said, "Jordan, that's all right. Usually we don't ask questions until we're sure the group member is done speaking, but . . . I didn't give you the protocol. My bad."

"No, I'm sorry," Jordan said again, weakly. "None of my business."

The doctor said, "We're *here* to share. . . ."

"It's all right," David said, looking at Jordan, but his smile died somewhere on its way to his lips. "No, they . . . the police . . . never did."

"I'm sorry," she said yet again.

"I've never been able to understand why he picked my family. Was it the nature of what I wrote? Was I spared? Or was my survival just a fluke?"

I was spared, too, she thought. But didn't say it.

The brunette woman was squeezing David's shoulder now. He had the expression of a crying man, but no moisture came.

Too cried out, Jordan thought. She knew all about that.

Dr. Hurst said, "David, I know how difficult that was. I would never have asked you to put yourself through that. Why did you?"

He made a tiny hand gesture in reference to the much grander one he'd just made. "I thought our new member should know that she wasn't the only one here . . . the only one in the world . . . to have lost everything."

She hadn't known of David's tragedy, but he seemed aware of hers.

"This group has done me good," he said to Jordan, "and it can do good things for you, too. But it starts with you *letting* it. You can't allow this thing to fester inside of you. Or it will kill you."

"What doesn't kill ya," Levi muttered.

Jordan turned to him sharply.

"Makes ya strong?" He held up his hands in surrender and returned to silence.

She supposed he was just trying to help. But what Levi had said—did that mean this long-haired goof knew who she was, too, and what she had gone through? How much did they *all* know about her?

Dr. Hurst said to David, "I understand that you're writing again."

David gave up a halfhearted shrug. "If you can call it that. Certainly nothing that's worth a diddly damn."

"Are you working on something now?"

While the writer stammered for an answer, Jordan felt a tingle at the back of her neck. She knew she would want to talk to David, and away from group. The crime against him and his family bore at least vague similarities to her own family's tragedy, despite some jarring differences. She and he had both been spared. In her case, at least, it had been intentional. Had the same been true in David's?

Glancing up, she noticed that the group was wrapping up with David, eyes again slowly turning her way.

Jordan tried to think of how to say that she had *nothing* to say when the man bearing signs of plastic surgery spoke up, in rescue.

"I'll go next," he said in a measured baritone. "My name is Phillip. This is my second meeting."

Heads swiveled in his direction. Phillip had short brown hair and, unlike the other more casually attired members, wore a white shirt and red tie under a navy blue vest, with navy slacks and black loafers. He sat square in the chair, both feet on the floor, his hands folded in his lap.

Then there was his face. . . .

Angular, with high cheekbones and a pointed chin, his skin unnaturally white, his eyes light brown, his nose little more than nostrils, like two holes poked in snow. Lips virtually nonexistent. Though his speech was relatively normal, his breathing between words was clearly audible.

"I didn't speak at the last meeting," he said, "but now the time seems right for me to share my story."

Everyone watched him expectantly. Though the damage to his face made it hard for Jordan to estimate his age, he must be somewhere in his thirties.

"Go ahead, Phillip," Dr. Hurst said.

"I was walking my dog in Rockefeller Park," Phillip said, sitting woodenly on the metal chair. "Near Wade Avenue Bridge."

Knowing nods; a well-known area.

"What kind of dog?" someone asked.

Dr. Hurst said, "That's really not of any—"

"English bulldog," Phillip interrupted. "Named Cromwell." He smiled and it was fairly ghastly. "I named him after a hero of mine."

This elicited a few impressed smiles and nods, but Jordan had no idea who Phillip was talking about.

"Anyway," Phillip said, "I was walking with Cromwell—this was two and a half years ago, winter. Cloudy, getting dark, but we'd walked that route, oh, hundreds of times before."

Jordan allowed herself to be drawn into the man's account. She knew what he had to say would be terrible, and rather than bother her, it made him seem an ally.

"Cold evening," Phillip said. "Snowing earlier, but wasn't when we were walking. I saw a man coming toward me with a shovel in his hands. I assumed he was a park employee, who'd been out clearing the sidewalks."

Phillip paused, inhaled, the sound resonating, punctuating silence that sat among them like another member of the group.

"As we neared each other, I nodded at him," Phillip said, eyes flicking around the circle. "When we were almost even with each other, the man swung the shovel, hitting me in the face."

Two members, a woman, a man, shuddered, as if feeling the impact.

Unconsciously, a hand rose to brush his wounds. "It felt like he hit me with his car, but only in my face, my head. Everything went black, not in the sense that I lost consciousness—just vision. My feet went up and my head went back."

Phillip's hands moved behind him, miming his effort to break his fall.

"I felt my balance go, but I couldn't get my hands down fast enough to brace me. When I hit, I cracked my head on the sidewalk."

"My God," the woman halfway around the circle said. Then she covered her mouth, as if to prevent further comment.

"Still, I didn't lose consciousness. I was awake, seeing flashing lights—seeing stars, as they say—with blood running into my eyes. I knew what he was doing, though. Every single thing. He stole my wallet, my watch, my dog."

"He stole your *dog*?" someone asked.

Phillip gave a weary nod. "I'm afraid Cromwell wasn't much of a watchdog. I like to think he looked back at me with regret, as my assailant dragged him off. But I heard no whines, much less barks. Canines can be fickle."

Next to Jordan, Levi blurted, "Did they catch the jag-off?"

"Cromwell or my assailant?" Phillip said with dry humor. "Neither, I'm afraid."

"Did you see your . . . your assailant's face?" someone asked.

Phillip shook his head. "He wore a hoodie, up, and it was getting dark. It all happened so fast. And yet I remember it in slow motion. . . ."

There was a long silence.

Finally breaking it, Phillip said, "But I learned one thing, at least, on that cold winter night."

They looked at him the way a disciple might at Christ or maybe the Dalai Lama. Would the secret of life be revealed?

"I can take more than I ever dreamed I could," Phillip said matter-of-factly. "And I learned that you have to focus on what's important in life. Which is two things, come to think of it."

But what, Jordan wondered, *if you didn't have anything important in your life?*

Directing his comment to the stalled writer, Phillip said, "You have to do what you were put here to do."

By whom? God? The same God who allowed terrible things to happen to damage these people?

Dr. Hurst asked, "And what is that for you, Phillip?"

He smiled, and this time it wasn't ghastly at all. "I'm a teacher."

As they shuffled out after the meeting, Jordan mulled it all. Among the people she had met here, one was still trapped by what had happened to his family, while another had managed to turn an attack on himself into something positive.

David Elkins was a survivor, but one who had been absent at the time of the crime. The survivor Phillip, like her, had been personally attacked—perhaps not to the extent she had, but certainly violently assaulted.

Two survivors—one positive, one negative. She felt close to both men, in their misfortune.

But closer to Elkins.

Was she crazy, thinking his family's intruder might have been hers?

She was well aware that she was posing herself this question while walking on the grounds of a mental institution.

CHAPTER FOUR

Mark Pryor sprinted up the alley, the material of his Men's Wearhouse two-for-one suit pants straining, suit jacket unbuttoned and flapping, tie flapping too, his white shirt cool with underarm sweat, his Florsheims scuffing on the concrete.

"Freeze!" he yelled, but why did he bother?

The kid he was chasing, on this warm spring day—white, maybe twenty, surfer-blondness undermined by the dopey dragon tat running down his left arm—was way out in front, running as effortlessly as a track star among wannabes. This was probably due in part to the perp's better aerodynamics—after all, he wore only Reebok running shoes and a red leather thong.

Mark had ten years on the freak, but even so was still the youngest detective on the Cleveland PD, only recently promoted. Right now, he felt like the oldest, lungs burning, legs aching, as the mismatched pair entered block three of the pursuit. The detective had his gun in hand, but that was mostly just a threat, and might have been a baton he was hoping to pass to a relay runner.

Charging hard, Mark entertained the thought of shooting the perp—he was barely closing the distance between them—but that was only a fantasy. The paperwork and condemnation that would follow, even if he just winged the guy? Not worth it. Not close to worth it.

Anyway, Detective Mark Pryor had never shot anybody.

Ahead, the alley came to a T and his only real chance to catch Perry the Perv, as the youthful perp was known to the neighborhood, was anticipate which way the kid would go and beat him there.

"Left," Mark said between gasping breaths. A command, though Perry couldn't hear him. Almost a prayer.

Perry's nickname, incidentally, came from everyone knowing that he collected jars of his bodily fluids in his rathole apartment and applied their contents in various unspeakable ways to, in, and on various mentally challenged teenage boys, who he also collected.

Right now Perry was lathered in sweat, and the last thing the detective wished to do was lay hands on this noxious sex offender, and shooting the creep would prevent that. But how could you explain it to a shooting board? Bringing down a guy armed only with a thong.

Mark picked up speed and cut a diagonal line toward the left corner—if Perry went right, then he was in the wind, good and g.d. gone. But the young detective was betting on left, because Perry hadn't done anything *right* in his whole pathetic life. . . .

True to his nature, Perry veered left, where Mark was coming up fast. The detective launched himself, his shoulder driving into the Perv's ribs. He'd been the team kicker back in high school, but he knew how to tackle, all right. As much as he despised having to touch this lowlife, Mark hugged him tight and together they flew.

"Mother*fuh* . . ."

That was as far as Perry got before his nearly bare body skidded into the pavement, Mark on top of him, and the air whooshed from Perry's body like a balloon a fat kid sat on.

All that bare flesh had made a body's worth of skinned knee of Perry, and the pebble-and-trash-strewn alley put up more fight than he did. Mark could imagine how painful that was—his knee burned where he had skinned it on the concrete and torn his pants. At least he had another pair at home. Of course, the jacket was filthy now and a mustard stain decorated a sleeve.

He cuffed Perry's hands behind him, then stood, brushing alley crud off as best he could. Perry lay on the ground, blood leaking from cuts and scrapes, wheezing like a fish on the deck of a boat, whimpering, trembling.

"What were you chasin' me for anyway?" Perry finally managed pitifully, as Mark hauled the scraped, bleeding, living carcass to its feet. "I wasn't doin'—"

"You have," Mark interrupted, "the right to remain silent," and continued to Mirandize the Perv, who continued to insist he'd done nothing wrong.

Mark said, "Nothing wrong? You were in your bedroom getting ready to rub God only knows what onto Cleotis Redington."

This in reference to a mentally challenged teenager Perry had violated on more than one occasion.

"That was strictly consexual."

"Consensual, dipstick."

"Consenting, consexual, whatever."

"Perry," Mark said with a sigh, "I already told you, you have the right to remain silent. Do us both a favor and *do* so."

Perry shut up and this gave the prisoner a chance to take stock of his situation. "Hey, man," he said. "I hurt. I'm really hurting."

"Then you shouldn't have run."

And Perry started to cry, the way a little kid does who had skinned his knee. In this case, all over. . . .

A heavyset guy in a cheap suit lumbered up next to Mark and stopped, hands on his knees as he sucked air. Detective Robert Pence.

"Good . . . good . . . good," Pence panted. "You . . . you . . . caught . . . him."

Six-three, near three hundred pounds, a few months from retirement, Pence had been assigned to keep an eye on the rookie detective. But to Mark, it sometimes felt the other way around.

Out of shape or not, pretty much over the hill maybe, Pence remained a good, smart cop.

"We got him all right, Bob."

"The helpless twerps of Cleveland can rest tonight," Pence said. "But it's your bust, Marky Mark, not mine."

"Your snitch's tip led us here."

"Yeah, caught the Perv in the act, and isn't that one for the memory books? But kiddo, last thing I need in what's left of my career is another bust. What are they gonna do, add another five bucks to my pension? *Use* this, sonny boy—take it to Captain Kelley. Get on his fuckin' radar."

Mark winced.

"I know you don't like that kind of language, kiddo, but this'll get his attention. And then we—*you*—will have his attention on that *other* little matter."

"Think so?"

"I know so."

"He shrugged it off last time."

"That's because you insisted *I* take the lead. To him, I'm yesterday's news, and he's not wrong. This will be your show. I'll be long gone, kiddo. Do it. Convince him."

An hour later, as the older detective booked Perry the Perv downstairs, Mark rapped on Captain Kelley's pebbled-glass door.

"Come," Kelley said.

Mark went in. He had not bothered to clean up, let alone change out of the filthy, torn suit. He stood there for a long moment while Kelley studied the screen of the laptop on his desk and continued typing.

Captain John Kelley—rail-thin, titanium-hard African-American with close-cropped salt-and-pepper hair, a pencil moustache, and a hawk nose where half-glasses currently perched—had a reputation for being consistently hard and occasionally fair.

After an eternity that was perhaps thirty seconds, the captain looked up. "Well, don't *you* look like shit? Tell me the other guy looks worse."

"Yes, sir, he does," Mark said. "Bob's booking him now."

"Good. Very good." He waved dismissively. "Go take a shower. You have spare clothes here?"

"I do."

Kelley returned to his laptop, then glanced up with a frown. "Is there some reason you're still here, Detective?"

"I knew taking this lowlife down was a priority for you, Captain, and I thought you'd like to know we got him cold."

"I gathered that. Congratulations. Go take your shower."

Mark risked a smile. "I thought I might have bought a little . . . goodwill."

"You did, huh?"

"Maybe . . . five minutes worth?"

"Try three. As long you aren't hoping to sell me that crackpot theory again."

And now Mark took an even greater risk. He sat in the chair opposite his captain. "It's not a theory, sir. There's nothing crackpot about it."

Kelley removed the glasses and pinched his nose. This meant the captain was getting a headache, and Mark knew his time here would be less than five minutes.

"You believe," Kelley said with zero enthusiasm, "that a serial killer is operating in Cleveland."

"I do, Captain."

"You *do* understand, that despite what the movies and television might have you believe, there is not an epidemic of serial killing in this nation. That it is in fact rare. And that on the rare occasion it does turn up, it is not our business—it's FBI turf. You do know all that?"

Mark nodded. "I would be happy if we could convince the FBI to take over."

"To take over what? There is no investigation."

"Sir, the killings in Strongsville follow the MO."

"MO," Kelley said, and closed his eyes. Whenever Mark used a term that was commonly heard on TV, the captain closed his eyes like that. Finally he opened them. "The FBI doesn't feel there's a serial killer at large here, which means there is *no* modus operandi. No 'MO' for a killer that doesn't exist."

"Sir—the Strongsville murders—"

"Are not our jurisdiction, FBI aside. The father in that slain family was an investment banker. You don't think he destroyed enough families that somebody couldn't have gotten a little payback?"

"But, sir, it's a *family* again. . . ."

"Christ on a crutch, Pryor, *years* separate these murders, which only have vague similarities and many differences. That's not the makings of a serial killer, especially in a city of this size."

Mark got to his feet and leaned his hands on Kelley's desk. "I've done some digging on my own, Captain. On my own time. I don't think he's killing just here."

Kelley gave him a long, cold look.

The thing for Mark to do right now was say, *Yes, sir, thank you for your time, sir,* and go clean up as requested.

Instead, he said, "I think we're just the perpetrator's home base. I've found other murders, following a similar pattern, in several other parts of the nation."

The captain said nothing.

"They all take place *between* the murders here in the greater Cleveland metro area. It's almost like the killer traveled for a period of time, committed one of these atrocities, then traveled some more, committed another, then eventually, would complete the circle with another instance here in Cleveland."

Kelley shook his head in slow motion. "You don't even hear me, do you, Pryor? You know the feds keep track of such crimes. They gather statistics, using sophisticated algorithms that are beyond our capacity. This allows them to focus on patterns like you're talking about. If what you're saying was the case, they would know."

Mark shrugged. "That leaves two possibilities. They already know and are working without our support, for some reason. Or . . . they missed one. They may be sophisticated, sir, but it's not an exact science."

"Pryor. . . ."

"At the very least we need to alert them. But what we really need is a citywide task force, spanning all the suburbs and surrounding towns."

Kelley's clipped laugh was a pit bull's bark. "I wonder if the FBI will appreciate the free advice? The way I appreciate being told how to operate courtesy of a rookie detective."

"Not my intention, sir. Just providing input. The day you welcomed me to the detective bureau, you said my input was always welcome."

"That was one 'welcome' too many," Kelley said. "I must have been in a really good mood. I *was* in a good mood, briefly today, when you told me you'd bagged that pervert. But do you think I'm in a good mood now?"

"Possibly not, sir."

Kelley smiled, or anyway pretended to. "All right, rookie—you want a task force? Fine. You think we have another Mad Butcher? Okay."

The Mad Butcher of Kingsbury Run, Cleveland's most infamous serial killer, had murdered at least a dozen people in the nineteen thirties. The Butcher had worked for years, undetected, before police realized the scope of their problem. In the end, though suspects emerged, no arrest was ever made.

"Now," the captain was saying, "how are we going to pay for it? And what cases are we going to pull detectives off, what crimes do we have them ignore, all so they can hunt a monster that no one on the planet but you thinks exists?"

That was a lot of questions, but Mark knew enough not to answer any of them.

Kelley let out a long breath, pushed back in his chair, away from the desk a little. "Look, son . . . you're smart. That's how you went from uniform to plainclothes so quickly."

"Thank you, sir."

"But are you smart enough to know what I need, to be able to take your theory upstairs?"

"Evidence," Mark said.

"And what do you have?"

"A pattern."

"That overstates it. I'd call it . . . a hunch. You *think* you *might* have a pattern. And you know you have no evidence yet."

"But I've uncovered information, facts, that may lead us to actual evidence."

"I should hope so. Or do you think the chief or the mayor or God almighty is going to let me set up a task force based on a rookie detective's hunch?"

Dejection washed over Mark, mingling with the mustard, crud, and pervert's sweat that stained what was left of his suit. "Sir, this is the third time I've brought this to you."

He nodded. "Actually the second. Last time you let that poor bastard Pence risk his pension on it. And frankly, that you sold Bob Pence on this thing is probably why this conversation has gone on as long as it has."

"People are dying. Someone has to care."

The implication of that, of course, was that Kelley didn't care. Mark felt the way he had as a kid and had overstepped with his dad. An explosion would likely follow, and it wouldn't be pretty.

But Kelley was only looking at him, hard and unblinking. It took forever for the words to come, but they came: "You've got two days to get your shit together, then bring it in to me, Detective. I'll look at it and if you've got something, we'll kick it upstairs."

Elation flooded through him. "Yes, sir."

"But if you don't convince me that there's something to do, you're never going to bring this up again. Understood?"

"Understood, sir."

A bony finger pointed itself at him. "And, Pryor, that goes for even efforts on your own time. If there's nothing there, you will leave this shit alone, forever. Otherwise, you'll drive yourself crazy with this kind of shit, or worse . . . *me*. Agreed?"

"Agreed, sir."

"Now, get the fuck out of my office."

Mark did so.

Driving home, Mark was on automatic pilot, his mind racing. He was exhilarated by the opportunity he had practically forced from his captain. But he knew he lacked objectivity. He knew that he had . . . what was it, a blind spot? A sore spot? Whatever it was, it dated all the way back to high school, and a girl he still loved though they'd never even kissed.

He had been working up the courage to ask Jordan Rivera out on a date when his hopes and dreams were interrupted by her family's slaughter. Those brutal, tragic deaths had sent her to St. Dimpna's as a mental patient. High school senior Mark had felt helpless, unable to do anything but follow the unsuccessful investigation in the newspapers.

Somewhere along the way, he must have said to himself, *I could do better than this.* But he had no conscious memory of it. Still, he knew very well that the Rivera tragedy had sent him down the path to law enforcement.

He had stayed close to home after high school, enrolling at Case Western Reserve University in downtown Cleveland. During Mark's senior year, the famous thriller writer David Elkins had suffered a tragedy similar to the Rivera girl—the rest of his family shot, then mutilated.

The case made national news, though only the local papers covered the police efforts to find a connection between the Rivera and Elkins homicides. Captain Kelley may have thought Mark picked up *MO* from TV, but actually the press coverage had provided him that—the differing modus operandi having discouraged investigators from continued pursuit of any link between the crimes.

Jordan's family had been knifed while the Elkins family had been executed by gunfire, the latter victims disfigured by knife slashes almost as an afterthought. The Riveras' door had been forcibly thrown open, but at the Elkins residence there had been no sign of illegal entry. Elkins had, in a later magazine interview, gone so far as to mention unlocking the door when returning home with a pizza.

In his early days on the PD, Mark was discouraged to find he still had no access to either the Rivera or Elkins case files, and no way to investigate either. He approached the detective who was in charge of the still open Elkins case and had been told to ef off.

But now he was in plainclothes, a detective, and he could do things and go places denied to a uniformed cop. Still, if he were to call the Strongsville PD, and ask to talk to the detective there, Mark figured Captain Kelley would hand him his butt.

The Strongsville murders—the closest he had come to a fresh crime scene—were just the latest in a string of such crimes that were not several cases, but one collective case—*his* case.

A year and a half ago, a family had been killed in O'Fallon, Missouri. Again, similarities—family murdered, one survivor, a son this time. Like the Riveras, Frank and Carol Northcutt had been stabbed to death, and as in the Elkins killings, the pair had been slashed postmortem. But no shootings, and the surviving son, Lyle, was in his twenties and hadn't lived with his parents for several years.

But that surviving son was why the case had attracted Internet notoriety—Lyle Northcutt, "Buck Knife" to his friends and fans, was bass player in a cult-favorite metal band, Throbbing Meat Whistle.

Speculation ran high that Buck Knife's music had played a major role in the slaughter of the musician's parents. Long before the killings, such songs by the band as "Fuck 'Em All" and "Kill the Bastards" had inflamed the debate about metal music, and post-tragedy, brought out self-appointed arbiters of popular culture who insisted that Buck Knife had no one to blame but himself for the deaths of his parents.

Internet stories provided a look into the musician's parents, who apparently were white bread, All-American, churchgoing. Their only sin, their only break from Middle American conformity, was their pride in their son's music and success.

Even Lyle had been a normal kid. Frank had coached Lyle's Little League team and Carol had run the concession stand at those games. Members of the PTA, Frank and Carol helped organize the

Planned Parenthood book sale every year and volunteered weekly at the local food bank.

Unlike the Elkinses and Riveras, who were very well off, the Northcutts had been firmly entrenched in the lower regions of the middle class—they were both retired teachers.

The Northcutts of Missouri, along with half a dozen other families scattered across the United States, had made it into Mark's growing printout folder and expanding computer files.

Funny, or perhaps odd or even ironic, but the name *Lyle* summoned a memory of an event that had been minor in the great scheme of things but had a major impact on Mark's formative years.

Elementary school bully Kyle Underwood, a mean-hearted little son of a biscuit, was responsible for Mark's enduring aversion to swearing. The kid had sworn like a fourth-grade sailor himself, and maybe that's where Mark had heard the words. He sure hadn't heard them at home.

Bully-boy Kyle had prodded and picked on Mark, day after day, making a habit out of stealing the boy's lunch money, and that of many of his friends. One day, after school, Mark had simply snapped.

Balling up his fists, he stood up to the bully and snarled, "Fuck you, Kyle! I'm not taking your shit anymore!"

But instead of fighting, Kyle had simply started laughing and pointing. When Mark turned, his father had been standing there. Usually Mom picked him up, and she always waited in the car. But here Dad was, frowning.

"That'll be enough, boys," Dad had said, and dragged Mark off.

Kyle Underwood would get his comeuppance another day, at the hands of another kid. This day was a black one in Mark's memory. He thought maybe his dad would understand, even compliment him, for standing up to injustice. But all Dad did was ground him for a month, accepting no explanations or excuses, making Mark swear to never swear again.

For some reason, that took . . . and Mark got a lot of kidding over the years, even to this day, for having such a goody-two-shoes vocabulary. Had he learned anything from the experience? Maybe that fighting injustice wasn't a license to otherwise break the rules. Or maybe he had just been so ashamed at disappointing his dad that he was still trying to make up for it.

Even though Dad had been gone, for how many years?

The houses around Mark now were part of the suburb of Strongsville. He knew little about the Sully family, who had lived in a nice white house on Cypress Avenue, just west of I-71 and the Mill Stream Run Reservation.

As he pulled to a stop in front of the Sully residence, Mark noted the police tape still X-ed across the front door. He got out of the car, trying to get a feel for the neighborhood. At dusk, the lights were on in neighboring homes, a breeze promising a cool night, with not another soul on the street except for a middle-aged woman walking her corgi two houses down on the other side.

A predominantly white neighborhood, where everybody on the block knew everybody else, yet a killer had managed to infiltrate, murder the Sullys, and take his leave. And all the while, no one heard or saw a blessed thing.

Why this house, when they all looked so much alike?
Why this family?
Why this street?
Why, why, why?

Mark asked himself those and a thousand other questions, not getting one g.d. answer.

CHAPTER FIVE

Jordan sat barefoot in the lotus position on the hardwood floor in the middle of her studio apartment. Wearing a plain white T-shirt and gray sweatpants, black hair ponytailed back, eyes shut against the sun filtering through the venetian blinds, she endeavored to clear her mind.

The past two weeks had blurred by, leaving the young woman exhausted, and not just physically. So much had been heaped upon her since seeing that news broadcast in the Dimpna dayroom that she had been able to do little more than simply cope.

Dr. Hurst had been a big help, especially those first few days, going well beyond doctor/patient counseling and group therapy—no denying that—even driving Jordan to see her parents' attorney.

Family friend Stephen Terrell might have been intimidating with his barrel chest, Brooks Brothers suit, and severe gray-framed glasses. But the warmth of his smile and that sprinkling of salt in his pepper-colored hair made him at once accessible. Of course Jordan remembered him younger, though the twinkle in his brown eyes made him seem like your favorite uncle.

When Jordan had first entered St. Dimpna's, Terrell had visited frequently, but that trailed off due to her lack of communication. His last visit had been probably eight years ago. Now, as his secretary opened the door for Jordan and gestured her in (Dr. Hurst waiting in the outer office), the attorney beamed in a manner usually reserved for long-separated family members.

It touched Jordan so much that she actually smiled at him.

But when he came around the desk with his arms extended for a hug, she backed away, smile vanishing. The attorney clumsily held out a hand for her to shake, as an alternative, and when she didn't take it, he clasped his hands at his chest and bowed slightly. Such a big Buddha of man, making that little awkward gesture, made her smile again. Briefly.

"Jordan, wonderful to see you," he said, as he nodded toward one of his two client chairs. "I think of your folks every single day." He got himself seated behind his big mahogany desk. "It's a tragedy that none of us will ever get over."

What could she say to that?

"But I was thrilled to learn," he went on, "that you're out under God's blue sky again, ready to meet whatever life brings."

That had a rehearsed sound and she couldn't compete with it. So she just gave him a curt nod.

He raised his eyebrows, and his smile asserted itself for just a moment before disappearing, as if to say, *So much for small talk. Down to business.*

Flipping open a waiting folder, he said, "I don't have to tell you that your parents were good people."

Then don't.

"But more than that," he said, "they were *conscientious* people. Jordan, you should be proud—your mom and dad, they provided very well for you."

She said nothing. This was his show.

The attorney's forehead frowned while his mouth smiled. "Jordan, what I'm trying to say is . . . you're a very wealthy young woman."

Her eyes tensed. "My parents were doing all right, Mr. Terrell. But we sure weren't rich."

"Jordan, your father carried extensive life insurance policies on himself, your mother, and both of you kids."

"News to me."

"It's not something he would have talked to you about, not until you were a little older."

"I was in high school."

"Your grandfather on your dad's side died of heart disease in his early sixties. And your grandmother, your dad's mother, died at fifty-seven of breast cancer. That family history made your father, an insurance man himself, cautious."

She said nothing.

He plowed on. "With the payouts for your parents and your brother, the interest accrued over the last decade, and the sale of the house—"

She sat forward and sharpness entered her tone. "Our house was sold?"

He swallowed and nodded. "With you in St. Dimpna's, in a state of mental health that precluded your participation, I—as executor of your parents' estate—had to act in your best interests. I had no way of knowing when . . . or even, *if* . . . you would ever get out of that hospital."

"So you sold our house?"

"Maintaining the place was a financial burden you didn't need. Indicators were that housing values were going down, so I acted while you could still benefit from a relatively friendly marketplace."

"You sold it."

He nodded. "At almost twice what your father bought it for. And the mortgage had already been paid off. Your dad had a windfall about fifteen years ago—"

"I can't go back to my room."

Do I want to?

"With taxes and insurance, and utilities, Jordan, it was a financial drain. I discussed this with Dr. Hurst and she agreed that the money could be better used for your future, whether in St. Dimpna's, or . . . out in the world. And, frankly, I didn't imagine you would *want* to go back there."

"It was our home."

The intruder had taken their lives. Now added to that was their home.

Terrell looked decidedly uncomfortable. "I apologize if I have done anything that contradicts your wishes. But, frankly . . . and I mean in no way to be unkind, Jordan . . . but for two years I came to visit you, and you never made eye contact with me, let alone expressed yourself in words. As someone entrusted, by your father and mother, with your welfare, I had to use my own best judgment."

Tears were flowing, warm and wet on her cheeks. *Damnit!*

Terrell opened a drawer, produced a tissue, and half rose to hand it across the expanse of the desk.

"Thank you," Jordan said, dabbing her cheeks.

"I know this is difficult," Terrell said. "It's difficult for me, too. Is it all right to discuss the specifics of your financial situation?"

Jordan nodded.

She had never really thought about having a "financial situation." Never even wondered who had paid the freight at St. Dimpna's—the state, she supposed. Now she realized it was more like her parents' estate.

The attorney, who looked as shaken as she felt, was saying, "Your parents left you in a very comfortable position, monetarily speaking."

Not really caring, wanting to hurry this up so she could get out of this office and be anywhere else, she asked, "How so?"

"Well," Terrell said, "your net worth is not quite three million dollars."

"... What?"

"You heard right, young lady."

"But how?"

"Mostly insurance," Terrell said, glancing at the folder on his desk. "A million-dollar policy on your father, half a million on your mother, plus another hundred thousand on James. Just under four hundred thousand, after closing and various other costs, on the sale of the house. The rest is from interest and dividends from existing investments. With no other relatives, it's all yours now."

Jordan shook her head slowly. Though the money meant nothing to her—she would gladly trade it to have any one of them back, Dad, Mom, Jimmy—the size of the sum was staggering.

"I would not blame you," Terrell said, "if you considered me negligent for not maximizing these funds. I am not a financial planner, and your parents obviously could not have anticipated a situation where they would be gone, and you would be hospitalized and out of communication for a decade."

She stopped listening. He was saying something about having put the funds into CDs at an unfortunately low rate, and how after all this time, her father's investments would need a hard look from a financial advisor for updating, and that he hadn't felt he had a right to gamble with her money without her input, and so on and so forth.

"I know it's a lot to digest," Terrell said, wrapping up.

"No shit," she said.

The attorney's eyes widened. "Ah ... a very understandable reaction. I have all the materials here, bank books, stock certificates, everything ..." He handed a packet across to her. "... We can go over that now, or—"

"Or later," she said, getting up. She nodded at him. "Thanks, Mr. Terrell. I'll do some digesting."

And try not to choke on the way down.

"Good, Jordan. Thank you. Really glad to see you looking so well. So fine. A regular young woman."

She *was* a young woman—that much she knew. Not a girl anymore. Not a high school girl with hopes and dreams, but a woman, a young woman.

Just not a regular one.

Now, still in the lotus position, as she opened her eyes to look around her efficiency apartment, she knew she could live in a condo or a house at least as nice as their old one, but what good would it do? Funny thing was, when she began thinking about the possibilities of a new, nicer, much bigger place, right away she knew that Jimmy would be the perfect guy to help her pick things out and really decorate the place.

Jimmy, who she appreciated a lot more now that he was gone. At St. Dimpna's, thinking about her family, it was Jimmy who she had missed the most, surprisingly. How she wished she could tell him what a really good older brother he'd been.

But there would be no bigger, better living quarters for her. She had only a GED earned in a mental institution, but she knew how to do this math: *the less she spent on herself, the more she'd have to track down the killer of her family.*

Dr. Hurst had helped her find this simple single-room apartment, not far from St. Dimpna's. Blue-collar, ethnically diverse, the historic Ohio City district was far removed from her experiences in suburban Westlake. She might have been dropped on Mars. But she had already adjusted.

Getting this apartment meant she was an easy walk from St. Dimpna's—she not only had no driver's license, she hadn't even finished driver's ed yet when her life was yanked out from under her. This way, she would be close to her support group, and Kara.

The white-walled apartment was as spare as it was small, its kitchen little more than one wall with a few cupboards, an apartment-sized refrigerator, a small stove, a minuscule microwave, a single well sink, and a black-topped table with two chairs. This galley setup should be more than sufficient. Her mom had been a terrific cook, and Jordan had picked some of it up; but her menu would be salads and fresh fruit supplanted by microwave and boiling-bag cuisine.

The wall opposite was home to a laptop computer (the newly rich girl's first major purchase), which—with its Internet connection—was the closest thing to a luxury in her monk-like existence . . . and even that was a tool for her investigation.

Under the windows, near the door to the tiny bathroom, a mattress and box spring crouched on the floor. She would never *ever* hide under another bed.

No television, no radio, no pictures on the wall. The only personal item was a photo of her family on a small plastic table near the head of the bed where it shared space with an LED alarm clock. An artist's sketch pad on the dining table rested next to a box of colored pencils.

She had always been good at sketching. In another life, drawing had been a release, a simple pleasure—now it was a skill to be utilized. Just this morning, she had begun drawing. When she was finished, she would have a distributable picture of the man she sought. Recalling him vividly was not difficult—those ten years could be blinked away.

The alarm clock beeped. She uncurled, rose, and strode over to turn it off. Two hours until her next meeting with the Victims of Violent Crime. Funny—she would have expected a politically correct euphemism for the group—Survivors' Support Group maybe. As if they'd all been on a dumb reality TV show and got voted off.

No, somebody at Dimpna's, maybe Dr. Hurst, understood that what she had been through, what David and Phillip and the rest had experienced, would not be soothed by soft language.

Just enough time to dress, get to St. Dimpna's, then visit Kara beforehand. Normally, she would walk, but today, she would take her little green-and-white Vespa scooter (her other big investment), the only thing she could legally drive to get around. That way she could spend some extra time with Kara.

In the week since her first group meeting, Jordan's existence had been almost as silent as before she'd seen that newscast. She left the apartment only to go to the grocery store. Her kung fu exercises were a twice-daily routine.

This was a self-taught, largely self-created form of martial arts training built upon what she'd learned five years ago from a Chinese kid who'd had some kind of breakdown. On his road to recovery, he shared with her what he called "the beneficial health maintenance" of Tai Chi. No one at Dimpna's had objected, because she and her friend—one of the few friends she'd cultivated other than Kara—were really just pursuing an alternative form of exercise.

Upon this she had built a self-defense system amplified by books and videos she'd been able to obtain through inter-library loan. Whether its application would be practical or not remained to be seen.

Her modified Tai Chi and yoga kept her centered and calm. She had a goal and was working toward it. She was, however, wrestling with the contradictory nature of two promises—one to Dr. Hurst that she would participate in group, and the other to herself—that she would never tell the intruder's story.

She would not give her attacker that satisfaction, even in the relatively private forum of the support group. Still, Jordan felt that she owed Dr. Hurst something. She had promised to talk, but about what? This distracting thought was not enough to interfere with her mission, and merely provided a backdrop to her digging.

The Google search started simply enough, Jordan typing the phrase *family murdered.* That got her eight million hits, some of which had mentions of her family. Adding quotation marks narrowed the scope to 731,000, but by adding the phrase *Cleveland, Ohio* she knocked the total down to zero. Removing the quotes sent the total back up to over six million. Two steps forward, one step back. . . .

Her Net search was less a simple linear progression and more a process. Each step was more about trying something that got her more information without overwhelming. In this endeavor, patience wasn't just a virtue, but a necessity. And it had been a slow go, at first, since she'd had no access to computers at St. Dimpna's, and had to get computer literate on her own and in a hurry.

She hadn't read any of the copious Internet stories about her family—she just couldn't make herself go there. Not yet. That would be easy enough to track and no doubt there was information that would be new to her. She had no knowledge of the police investigation. Just an intimate acquaintance with what had happened in that house on that night. . . .

And, so far, there was precious little information online about the newscast murders, the slain family in Strongsville. She had learned the names of the family members, but not much else.

Looking into the Elkins case gave her an uneasy feeling—David had shared the tragedy with the group last week, freely; but as Jordan read articles from the *Plain Dealer* and other Internet sources, she felt somehow that she was invading his privacy, viewing pictures of his wife Belle and daughter Akina.

Belle had been a beautiful African-American woman, and—though Jordan had never heard of her—was evidently a well-known writer herself.

Jordan could see similarities between the crimes, but not between her family and the Elkinses'. The writer was almost wealthy, the family lived in a different part of the metro area, the couple only had the one child (although Mrs. E. *had* been pregnant), and Akina had been much younger than either Jimmy or Jordan.

When Jordan entered the disinfectant-scented sunroom, Kara was already sitting on the couch.

As they bumped fists, Jordan said, "You're looking good, girl. Healthy, even."

"You, too."

Jordan shrugged. "Stepped up the workouts a little, but what's your excuse?"

Kara yawned, stretched, fists clenched, giving Jordan a glimpse of her friend's scarred wrists. "Haven't been having nightmares lately."

"Cool."

"Yeah. Haven't dreamed about my stepfather fucking me for weeks now. Just him *trying* to fuck me."

"Well, it's a start."

"Plus, I've been talking to Dr. Hurst. Doubled up on the sessions. Kind of . . . opening up a little. You must be a good role model."

"A role model for opening up? Maybe not."

Kara lifted a lecturing forefinger. " 'The secret to life is not surviving the storm, but learning to dance in the rain.' "

"This is the kind of bullshit Dr. Hurst is telling you?"

Kara shook her head. "Fortune cookie. They ordered takeout for us last night, special treat. Kinda seemed like good advice. How is your rain dance goin'?"

"If you mean me and Mr. Google, I'm mostly getting my toes stepped on."

"How so?"

She told Kara about the first meeting of the group and how afterward she had added the Elkins case to the Net search mix.

Kara frowned. "You aren't reading up on your own case?"

"No. That'll come."

"Okay, baby steps, I get it. But look how you're limiting yourself, honey."

"I just got out," Jordan said defensively.

"Yeah, I remember. Who sprinkled the Dimpna Dust on who, anyway? Have you talked to this Elkins dude yet?"

"No."

"Well, you must know that everything the cops have on a crime like that isn't gonna be on the web. They always hold back some shit. Like maybe they're working on how these two family killings are linked."

Jordan frowned in thought. "I guess that is something they might keep back."

"Damn straight. So the only place you might find *out* what the cops already know is—"

"By talking to them?"

"The cops? Hell no!"

"Oh." Jordan nodded. "Elkins, you mean."

"Actually, there's one other place."

"Yeah?"

Kara tapped a finger on Jordan's forehead. "*You*, sweetie. How long have we known each other? And you never talked about what happened. Granted, you were playing mime games most of the time."

"Mime games. Bad joke."

"Good advice, though. Comparing notes with Elkins? Couldn't that maybe get you someplace?"

"You mean . . . those similarities between the cases that the cops held back?"

"Like they say in the geezer wing, bingo! Plus, it might jar some stuff loose from the back of both your brains."

"Huh?"

Kara shook her head and her pink-and-blue bangs bobbed. "It's like my therapy with Dr. Hurst. Some things that I remembered, I only *thought* I remembered. When the doc and me started digging into it, she found what she called *false memories*."

"Yeah?"

"It was my mind trying to protect me from something even worse than what I remembered."

Jordan shook her head, once. "Believe me. I'm not doing that."

Kara held her hands up, and the scars showed again. "Okay, but the only way to *really* find out is to start looking at what's going on under all that black hair."

Jordan's eyes tightened. "Trust me, Kara, I know enough already."

"You think so? You're probably right."

Jordan forced a smile as she got to her feet. "Appreciate the advice. Gotta get to group. I was late last week."

Kara ignored that, looking up at her, a child with an old woman's eyes. "Why did you suddenly want to get out of here? What made you finally break your . . . your vow of silence?"

Jordan pointed toward the nearest door and spoke evenly, softly, wanting no one but her friend to hear. "There's a monster out there killing families. And if I don't find him, and stop him, he'll kill again and again."

"*You're* gonna stop him."

"Yeah."

"You're gonna . . . kill him?"

"Oh yeah."

Kara studied her for the longest time. "Nothing means more to you."

"Nothing."

"Honey, it sounds to me like you haven't really broken that silence at all. Time to look back, and speak up. To yourself."

". . . Not that easy."

"Hey, it'll be easier on you than the next family that butcher singles out."

Then Kara bolted to her feet and hugged her friend, so quickly there wasn't anything Jordan could do about it. Then Kara was gone from the sunroom, as if Jordan were the one still imprisoned here.

Glancing at a wall clock, Jordan realized she really was almost late, and headed downstairs, fast as she could without running. When she arrived at the classroom-like space, most of the group was already seated. Luckily for her, David Elkins was still over by the coffee urn, chatting with last week's late arrival. What was that kid's name?

Levi, Dr. Hurst had called him. Like last week, the youngish man wore jeans and the holey Chuck Taylors. This time, the Hives were in for the Foo Fighters on his T-shirt, while the thriller writer had exchanged a black polo for last week's navy one.

As she approached, Jordan ignored the younger man, hoping he would take the hint and buzz off, and said, "Mr. Elkins—I just wanted to say how sorry I am for your loss."

He gave her a slight nod. "And I'm sorry for your loss, too. We all have that in common here. Expressions of sympathy are appreciated, but not required."

Jordan wasn't sure how to interpret that—had she committed another breach of protocol?

Still, she risked saying to him, "If you don't mind, Mr. Elkins, when we're through here? Might I have a moment of your time?"

"Certainly. And it's David."

She nodded. "And Jordan, please. I *would* like to talk to you."

Levi, who hadn't taken the hint, interjected, "And I'd like to talk to *you*, Jordan."

Spinning to the guy, she said, "*Really*, jackass? Lookin' for a date at group therapy? Pathetic."

David stepped between them.

"It . . . it's not like that," the young man said.

Her teeth were bared. "You just keep your distance or we're going to have a problem."

David, still standing between them, held up a hand like a referee and said to her, "It really *isn't* like that."

"Jordan," Levi said gently, a little afraid but summoning strength, "there's no problem, really. I'm gay, all right?"

David turned to her and his eyes held hers. "Levi wants to talk to you for the same reason *I* want to talk to you . . . and you want to talk to me. His family was murdered, too."

"Everything okay over there?" Dr. Hurst called from her seat in the circle.

"Just fine," David said. "We were just making plans for some after-group socializing."

"Well then," the doctor said, "if you'll join us, we can get started."

Jordan turned her back to David, and to Levi, to the whole group. Flushed, she worked to hold back tears. She had just unleashed some of her rage on some poor gay kid, who, like her brother Jimmy, had already suffered way enough shit in his life. What was *wrong* with her?

Like she didn't know.

She turned to the refreshment table, selected a chocolate chip cookie and a napkin, and went over and took the seat next to Levi.

She gave him the World's Record smallest smile and a nod that was smaller than that. And he grinned and nodded back.

David was next to her on the right. Across the way, Dr. Hurst was flanked by Phillip and an attractive but dowdily dressed middle-aged redhead—the woman who'd come in with David last week.

Glancing around the circle, Dr. Hurst asked, "Who would like to start this time?"

No one said a word.

Turning to the redhead, Dr. Hurst asked, "Kay?"

Before Kay could speak, Jordan heard herself say, "I'm Jordan Rivera, and I'd like to talk about what happened to my family."

CHAPTER SIX

That Captain Kelley had scanned every page, if quickly, of Mark's file was encouraging. That he had been frowning, his eyes so slitted behind the half-glasses riding the hawk nose, boded less well.

The sharply dressed senior detective took off the glasses, opened his eyes wide then tightened them again, closed the file, and flung the glasses on top of the inch-thick manila folder, sighing in the manner of a father whose wayward child had brought home a D-minus report card.

"That's it?" he asked. "That's all you got?"

"So far," Mark said, feeling like he'd been kicked in the stomach. Years of work were in that folder.

"Not much to it, is there?"

"Captain, all due respect, there *is* something to this."

Kelley stared at the young detective blankly. Then a small, sly smile revealed itself. "You know, there just might be. Not a bad job, son, for a side project."

Relief flooded through Mark, but he didn't allow himself to smile. He wanted to present a businesslike demeanor, not an eager-beaver one.

Kelley leaned back and rocked in his chair. "Nothing yet that I can take to the FBI, or even kick upstairs . . . but you've done a lot of digging, Pryor, and maybe, just maybe, you're gonna hit somethin'."

Now he couldn't hold back the smile. "Thanks, Captain."

No sooner had Mark's smile emerged than Kelley's disappeared. "You're still on your own time. I can't assign this to you, not yet—there's too much else on the docket around here. But if you want to keep at it, on your own? I'm down with it."

"I'm happy for that much, sir. And I'll keep you up to date on my progress."

"Start now. Tell me about this suspect of yours."

"Basil Havoc," Mark said. "Of the several possible suspects I've considered, he's number one."

"Saw his name in your files—remind me."

Mark shifted in his chair, sat forward. "When David Elkins didn't talk to the media right away, after the murders of his family? Reporters started zeroing in on the people around him in his life. Somehow they found out Akina Elkins, not long before she was killed, had started studying gymnastics under this guy Havoc. Guy was quoted in one of those stories. 'She'll be missed, sweet girl . . .' "

"The typical twaddle. But how does that make him a suspect?"

"It doesn't, but you see—I *knew* Jordan Rivera when we were kids, and I remembered that she used to study gymnastics. Turns out she studied with Havoc."

"You *knew* her?"

"Yes. We were in high school together."

Two hands came up in a stop-right-there gesture. "This thing better not be personal, Pryor. Was Rivera your steady or some shit?"

"No! No. She was just a classmate." Not exactly a lie.

"So knowing her a little made it possible to talk to her?" Kelley asked. "And she told you about Havoc? What, at the nuthouse?"

"No, no sir. The last I heard she was still in St. Dimpna's, and essentially catatonic."

"Then how . . . ?"

"I reached out to some mutual friends from those days, and they say she studied under Havoc. Just briefly. She quit the lessons, in fact, not long after starting them."

"Why?"

"That I don't know. Yet."

"So what's the gymnastic coach's story?"

Mark sat back. Crossed an ankle over a knee. Suddenly he was feeling damn near at ease with the captain. "Havoc has a pretty darn impressive background."

"How impressive?"

"How about '92 Olympics impressive?"

"Olympic star, huh? From the USA?"

Mark shook his head. "United Olympic team."

"What the hell is that?"

"After the Iron Curtain fell, the nations in the Russian bloc couldn't get individual teams together fast enough, so they joined forces. Havoc is from Moldova, one of twelve countries that made up the United team. He got a silver medal, then came over here. It wasn't long before he settled in Cleveland and started his gymnastics center."

Kelley was nodding slowly, clearly interested. "Where's Havoc now?"

"His school is still going here in Cleveland, but Havoc himself travels quite a bit."

Kelley rocked awhile. His eyes were moving in thought. Mark said nothing. Waited for his boss to process the information.

Finally the captain said, "So, your suspect knew both families. I like that. Did he have any connection to the Sullys in Strongsville?"

"No, sir. Not that I've found so far."

"You got anything else suggestive about him?"

Mark nodded, and gestured toward the file. "In 2008, the US

Women's Gymnastics Championships were in Boston. Around that time, a family was murdered in Providence, Rhode Island."

"Boston's in Massachusetts," Kelley reminded him.

"Yes, but Providence is only about an hour's drive from Boston."

Kelley frowned. "Do you know for *sure* that Havoc was in Providence?"

"No," Mark admitted. "I've seen footage from the championships, definitely putting him in Boston during the week the Rhode Island family was killed."

"Have you talked to the Providence PD?"

Mark wanted to be careful here. He was about to admit contacting another jurisdiction for information that might pertain to at least two, now maybe three, local cases, none of which were his.

Finally, he said, "Yes, sir. I realize I may have overstepped, but yes."

Kelley grunted. "We'll skip me tearing you a new asshole and go straight to what you found out."

"Okay. The detective there said they wrote it off as a home invasion gone south. The parents and a fifteen-year-old adopted son were shot with a nine mil."

"Were they mutilated?"

"The Providence guy didn't say so, and I didn't ask."

"Why the hell not?"

"I figured he would have mentioned it had they been. Or if that was the case, and they were holding it back, I didn't want to send up any alarm bells."

"That might ring back in Cleveland, you mean? And let your captain know you're 'overstepping'?"

Mark swallowed. Uncrossed his legs. "Something like that, sir."

But Kelley had already moved on. "What kind of gun was used in the Elkins murders?"

"Nine millimeter."

"Possible connection, then."

"Possible connection, yes."

"A lot of nine mils in the world." The captain nodded toward the general world outside his office. "There's a jungle full of fuckin' Glocks out there, you know."

"Oh, I know, sir."

Kelley nodded toward the file before him. "I just skimmed this. Is there anything else that ties Havoc in?"

"Well, in 2010, when the US Women's Gymnastics Championships were in Hartford? Havoc was there, too."

"Why, was a Hartford family murdered?"

"No, but a family in the Bronx was."

"Yeah, and getting from Hartford to the Bronx isn't exactly from the earth to the moon. I get the drift. Go on."

Mark did: "Family of six, all shot, the adults mutilated."

"Slashed?"

Mark nodded. "Two hours from Hartford, an easy drive."

"Nine mil?"

"Yeah," Mark said. "The parents dealt in illegal substances, so it got attributed to them angering the wrong crowd."

Kelley rocked some more. Gently. Eyes moving again. Then: "So none of these bullets has ever been compared with another?"

"No, sir. No one's connected these crimes."

"You would think the FBI computers would have done the job."

"You would think. But that doesn't seem to be the case."

Kelley chuckled dryly. "And that's why you keep pesterin' my ass? Be-cause you have connected these crimes."

"Right, sir. And, well . . ."

"Spill it."

". . . you are in a position to ask for comparisons of the bullets in these cases. Whereas I am just—"

"A worthless shit-for-brains rookie, yes, I know, with the weight of a gnat that just landed on an elephant's ass."

"I was just thinking that, sir."

That actually made Kelley chuckle.

The pair sat silently for a while as Captain Kelley mulled his options.

"The foundation you're pouring for this house of horror isn't strong enough to hold up an outhouse, you know. And don't tell me you were just thinking that."

"Not strong enough yet, sir, no."

"Well, let's just say, for the sake of argument, that you turn out to be Sherlock the Fuck Holmes and you've uncovered a serial killer that the FBI, in all its power and prowess, missed. If those bullets match, they'll take over all these cases so fast, you won't know whether to shit or go blind."

"I don't have any problem with the FBI taking over for me," Mark said, raising his palms as if in surrender. "They are certainly better equipped for it than a crap-for-brains rookie."

There was a somber aspect to Kelley's expression that reminded Mark, improbably enough, of a minister or priest. "You just want this guy caught."

"And stopped." He sat forward again. "If I'm right, Captain, this monster has killed over a dozen people in the last decade, and that's just the ones I've been able to find. There's no telling how many there are, really."

For perhaps thirty seconds, the only sound was the squeak of Kelley rocking in his chair as he thought. And of Mark's heartbeat in his ears.

Finally, Kelley said, "Okay, kid. I'll try to get the bullets sent here for ballistics examination."

At last, *at last*, someone was taking him seriously on this thing.

Kelley jerked forward, sat with his elbows on the desk. "Keep looking at this Havoc character, but tread the hell lightly, okay? Low profile, you understand me?"

"Yes, sir."

"If this turns out to be nothing, I don't want this blowing up into a lawsuit against the city, follow?"

"Yes, sir."

Kelley made a dismissive gesture with his right hand, as if shooing away a stray dog. "Meantime, on your own time only, for now. And till I say otherwise, this stays strictly between you and me."

"Yes, sir."

"Now, get the fuck out of my office."

Mark did.

In his car, hours later, Mark was still riding the high from his sitdown with Captain Kelley. They had spoken almost as equals . . . well, as members of the same species, anyway. After the meeting, he and Pence had closed down three twerps who had been stealing equipment from a local recording studio. Those three were now sitting in the slam and the studio owner was happy that his equipment would eventually be returned. All in all, a pretty good day.

Now, with darkness creeping up on the city, Mark sat in a credit union parking lot on Emerald Parkway, just north of Interstate 480—next to Basil Havoc's generically titled American Gymnastics Center.

Mark had the window down on his Chevy Equinox, letting the warm spring air drift over him. The breeze brought soothing sounds of birds and insects, and the gentle rustle of tree leaves, if occasionally disrupted by the roar of jets—he was not far from Cleveland Hopkins International Airport.

Soon kids were piling out of the gymnastic school into waiting parental minivans and SUVs. The next wave out, maybe ten minutes later, was instructors. Evening settled in and muted traffic noise banished the nature sounds, the jets seeming distant now, and a little forlorn as day surrendered to night.

Finally, half an hour later, Basil Havoc exited the school, locked the door behind him, then strode to his Escalade. Lit only vaguely by a streetlight at the lot's far end, the gymnastics instructor—tall, fit, fortyish—was easily recognizable, from his jungle-cat gait if nothing else.

Mark had neglected to tell Captain Kelley that he'd been staking Havoc out for weeks. Why risk his boss's wrath? And anyway, there was nothing to report as yet. The gymnast seldom varied from a few set routes—after leaving his school, he would go home or to the bank depository; if the latter, he would either go directly home or first stop at one of two nearby restaurants (one Chinese, one Italian). He varied this on two occasions, when he went to two other Chinese and Italian restaurants.

As usual, Havoc's Escalade went south on Grayton Road before turning onto I-480 east. And as usual, Mark's Equinox entered the highway two cars back.

They merged onto I-71 south, separated now by a semi. Mark cruised behind the big rig, swinging toward the shoulder to get occasional glimpses of Havoc's vehicle. He settled in for the long drive down to Medina, the suburb where Havoc shared a nice home with a Great Dane and an absentee daughter, mostly away at boarding school.

The Internet made it easy to learn all kinds of things about people who had gained any amount of celebrity, and Basil Havoc— a frequent subject on gymnastics blogs and in articles posted from sports magazines—certainly qualified. Apparently Havoc was a stern taskmaster with a temper, which made him a good candidate for violent behavior. Which helped make him a good suspect.

Havoc's Escalade veered right onto the ramp for Royalton Road, a change from pattern, and the same exit Mark had taken the night before, when he stopped by the Sully home in Strongsville. A spike of excitement accompanied the young detective up the ramp.

On Royalton, Havoc soon turned left onto Howe Road, just past the Samurai Sushi Steakhouse. Mark hung back, breathing hard. No cars between them now—Havoc seemed to be mimicking Mark's route from last night.

Would he turn right onto Cypress Avenue, the block where the Sully home sat, now silent and vacant?

They skirted the east boundary of the SouthPark Mall, crossing Polo Club Drive. Havoc continued south—if the man stopped at the Sully home, would that constitute probable cause? How Mark would love to have an excuse to haul this creep in. They passed Pomeroy Boulevard on the west, then Tracy Lane on the east, the Escalade obeying the speed limit, Mark doing his best to hang back and not be spotted. They passed Shurmer Road on the west and, despite the row of houses on the east side of Howe Road, Mark could hear the faint echo of traffic back on I-71.

The Escalade continued south, passing Canterbury Drive. *Just two blocks to go*—Mark was practically holding his breath now, wondering if (*almost praying that*) Havoc would make the turn.

Glendale Avenue streaked by and—as they passed the houses, most with their lights on, families enjoying an evening together (*something the Sullys would never do again*)—Mark's excitement was replaced by a cold, anger-tinged resolve.

When Havoc's turn signal came on, Mark felt almost that he had willed it, that he now controlled the Escalade, that he was making it go to the house where that family had been so savagely murdered. . . .

As they eased west on Cypress Avenue, Mark closed the gap some. Would Havoc stop, or slow, or even just look over at the Sully house as they passed? In the darkness, it was impossible to tell the latter.

Then at the corner, Havoc turned left onto Park Lane Drive, heading south. *Was Havoc just screwing with him?* Had the gymnastics coach made him somehow? He wasn't driving a department car, and his tailing technique had been by-the-book—how could the g.d. guy have gotten onto him?

Havoc turned right onto Drake Road, going west again. No way Havoc could know he was a cop! Much less realize that Mark had been investigating him.

Another left, and they were heading south again, this time on Pearl Road, Havoc leading, just under the speed limit—*where the heck they were going?* They passed through the major intersection with Boston Road.

Flummoxed, Mark was not exactly riding Havoc's tail, but with limited traffic—they'd been the only two cars on Cypress Avenue—the guy surely would make him soon, if he hadn't already. Mark could always pull off onto one of the side streets, which led to nothing more than a forest of cul-de-sacs. . . .

But if Havoc stayed on Pearl, as far south as Center Road, in Brunswick, Mark could simply peel off, get back on the interstate, and head home. No harm, no foul.

At the inappropriately named Beverly Hills Drive, Havoc turned east, then again, into the parking lot of a strip mall. Mark followed. He'd come this far.

The single-story mall had five outlets, one out of business, three closed for the night, with Apollonia's Italian Restaurant, at the far end, blinking its red OPEN sign.

Havoc parked.

So did Mark, half a dozen spaces over—when Havoc went inside, Mark would just pull out. His excitement, his anger, had fizzled into frustration and embarrassment. Still, a part of him wanted to just march over to Havoc's car and confront the creep.

Then, watching the Escalade out his open window, he realized that just the opposite was happening—Havoc had climbed out of his Escalade and was approaching Mark's Equinox with that easy gait of a jungle beast. My lord, the man moved quickly! And with seemingly no effort.

Mark scrambled for something to say as Havoc came up to the driver's side door. The man had a mop of dark hair and a Tom Selleck mustache, his well-developed musculature obvious beneath a dark polo emblazoned with the name of his business. His face was wide and flat with a small, flattened nose. Dark cold eyes peered out from beneath heavy eyebrows. Displeasure radiated off of him, as he leaned down like an angry carhop.

"You following me for a reason?" Havoc asked, his middle-European accent less than pronounced but more than apparent.

"Sorry, I thought you were somebody else," Mark managed with a nervous laugh. "Friend of mine." Lamely, he held up his cell phone. "I tried to call but when he didn't answer, I assumed it was 'cause he was driving."

Havoc let out a long breath and his displeasure seemed to go with it. "Your buddy has an Escalade, huh? Seems like everybody does these days."

"Or an Equinox," Mark said, with a strained smile.

Nodding at the detective's blue vehicle, Havoc grinned. "Yeah, I see these everywhere."

Was he playing with Mark?

As the two men exchanged shrugs and pleasant expressions,

Mark wondered: was this the beast that killed Jordan Rivera's family? The Elkinses? The Sullys? A knot in Mark's gut tightened itself.

"I was starting to think my buddy was leading me on a wild goose chase," Mark said, thinking about the Sully home. "Ya don't mind my saying, kind of a roundabout route to get here."

The big man nodded, the breeze ruffling his dead-looking hair. "Brunswick exit might be easier, but with all that damn construction on the interstate? Makes it one lane most of the way. I hate getting stuck in traffic. And there's always traffic."

I-71 did have its share of construction and frequent traffic jams. "I don't know if I was ever on Cypress Avenue before," Mark said with a grin.

"It's a quiet part of town."

Was this guy messing with him?

Jerking a thumb toward the restaurant, Havoc asked, "You know Apollonia's?"

Mark shook his head.

"It's damn good," Havoc said. "You should try it. Osso buco to die for."

He gave Mark a little wave and nod, then turned and headed to the restaurant.

Was he letting a killer walk away?

Yet what else could he do? Mark had no evidence to speak of, and he had just come close to giving himself away. If Kelley knew about this botched-up episode, all the ground Mark had gained with the captain would be lost.

He thought about going in that restaurant and ordering a meal, and sitting where Havoc could see him, and maybe getting under the skin of this monster. Give the guy something to think about, something to worry about.

Then he drove home.

My love for Italian food is, I'm afraid, one vice I just can't resist. I'm afraid I tend to lose control, eating too much and too quickly, and while gluttony is, perhaps, a minor sin, it is still a sin.

So this evening, this very special evening, I force myself to eat slowly, to savor every bite of a single delectable portion. I will savor tonight's task, as well. After a satisfying repast, there is nothing quite like doing God's work to boost the metabolism. My deed for tonight is doubly delicious. Not only will I be doing His work, passing His judgment down on another unrepentant sinner, but I will be sending (rather graciously, if it's not ungracious of me to say so) a gift to my reward, my prize, my Jordan.

Now that she's back in the world, my world, it's time I reintroduced myself to her, to let her know that I've been waiting for her, for such a very long and lonely time.

I have just the thing to welcome her back. I've been keeping track of a sinner who has an apartment at Archwood and 32nd Place. I could have dealt with her at any time, but there are too many sinners for me to address each and every one—I am but one simple man, after all. Once I started studying her, however, He showed me The Way. First, she bears a striking resemblance to my Jordan—the same long, black hair, same facial structure, same body type. One who didn't know better might suspect them of being sisters.

This sinner is a fornicator. Fornication has its place, in the repopulation of God's green earth. But this fornicator seeks only pleasure and self-gratification and, most of all, is an unrepentant, even casual *killer. Do I exaggerate? She killed her own* child *by having it aborted. It is hard to imagine such brutality.*

Or such shameless sinning. Mere weeks after committing the abomination of killing one of God's children, she has lain with men who are not her husband. This woman (her name is Clare Deems) I have come to think of as the anti-Jordan. Please understand that any resemblance between this sinner and God's Reward to Me Whose Name is Jordan is physical only. Clare is harlot-like whereas Jordan is pure, filth where Jordan is purity. Still, in a symbolic sense, Clare might be seen to represent the old Jordan. The Jordan before I came into her life to rescue her from a sinning world. (In Jordan's defense, this was the world she was born into, and she did her best navigating it, and let us not forget she delivered herself to me as a virgin.) So Clare represents the past, and must be eliminated so that the new, the purified Jordan can take her rightful place.

At my side.

I've been watching this sinner for a while now. She is one of many that I check on from time to time, knowing they won't change their wicked ways, knowing that sooner or later I may be called upon to visit them as a manifestation of the metaphorical Grim Reaper, to mete out His will for them. I can't be everywhere. I can't do everything. I have a lot on my plate, especially now that Jordan is back in this sinful place. Suppose she were corrupted before we could come back together? But no, such thoughts must not deter me. Keeping her close is a priority, but not my only responsibility. I am still busy with God's work. After all, who was it that said, "Idle hands are the devil's workshop"? It's not in the Bible, although Matthew 12:43–45 comes rather close.

Tonight, I'm standing in the shadows at the north end of the half-block-long apartment building where Clare Deems lives. I am in a raincoat, though there is no sign of rain. An inveterate sinner, Clare must be commended for her work ethic and regularity of habit. When her shift

ends at ten, she will pull into the parking lot before ten thirty. The restaurant where she works stops serving at nine and, even if she picks up
one of the male customers for purposes of fornication, she will manage
to get home by ten thirty. It's actually very impressive, but a well-orga-
nized sinner is still a sinner.

I check the lighted time on my cell phone—ten twenty. Any minute
now. I glance east, looking for headlights, but nothing yet.

He will provide. I have faith. I have stood here several nights and
kept vigil for Clare and every night, without fail, she has arrived on
time. Now, it's just patience that is required of me. And it doesn't take
long before I am rewarded. The headlights of her Kia Soul appear in
the drive and I watch as she swings through the lot to her usual parking
place.

As soon as she puts the car in park, I'm moving fast, but not running.
I've rehearsed this a hundred times in the theater of my mind. She will
turn off the lights next. There, good girl. She'll open the door and when
she gets out, her back will be to me. It will be the only mistake she needs
to make. The last she ever will make. . . .

She is as accommodating to me as she would be with any of her
many lovers. She gets out of the car, yes, her back to me. She never hears
me coming. From behind, lit only by the streetlight at the lot's far end,
she looks like Jordan. Though I know His will, I am tempted to do more.
She reminds me so much of my prize, My Reward, that I feel myself
having impure thoughts. Even as I do, my hand snakes out, wraps around
her flat belly, and I pull her to me as my other hand covers her mouth
with the cloth. I've soaked it in chloroform and it will render her unconscious quickly. In the meantime, she bucks and fights, rubbing against
me, multiplying my impure thoughts, but she is no match for my strength
much less my spiritual resilience. My face is buried in her neck and she
smells good, but not like Jordan, who smelled so fresh and clean that
sacred night. Clare's scent is a combination of sweat, spilled beer, and

some cheap perfume mixed with a sale brand shampoo. Earthly scents that one must admit have their carnal appeal.

Just as I wonder if I'm going to be exposed too long in this lot, she goes limp in my arms. Working quickly, I hit the unlock button on the key fob as I drag her around to the passenger side, tuck her in, as if she were slumbering or slumped drunkenly, and close the door. I walk back to the driver's side, start the car, put on my seat belt, and pull away. Check my watch. Elapsed time, not even two minutes.

I could have dispatched her right there, but I have better plans. As we drive through the night, I glance over. She's really not as pretty as Jordan—even with only the passing streetlights as illumination, that much is clear.

Twenty minutes in a car with an unconscious female might be dangerous, but she is important in my plan to remind Jordan of our time together.

When I get to the Ohio City Historic District, the neighborhood where I know Jordan now lives, I can't resist driving by her apartment. I reduce speed as I pass her building, look up at the light barely visible through her closed venetian blinds. I smile as I suppress the urge to alert Jordan that I am so close.

But no. I am no hormone-rattled teenager, honking for his date to come join him. She and I will have a much more meaningful relationship than that, our bond already formed but soon to be forged into something eternal. And it will happen soon enough. Tonight, I have God's work to do.

I consider leaving the body near her door, but that seems too obvious. While I want her to know I'm thinking of her, there's no reason to be boorish.

Fairview Park is less than a mile from both her apartment and St. Dimpna's. Close enough to make my point, and nice and quiet at this time of night.

I pull to the curb, extinguish the lights, then the ignition, before sitting and watching. The neighborhood is quiet. These are working-class people and will be up early to get to work. By now, nearly all of them are asleep. My only concern is the lonely soul out walking a dog or the insomniac who thinks a stroll in the cool air may make him drowsy.

Once I'm satisfied that Clare and I are alone, I get down to business. She has moaned softly once, and she may be close to coming around. I doubt she will regain lucidity before it is too late to matter for her. God has passed his judgment on her already—mine is simply the duty to carry out that sentence.

I get out of the car, go around to her side, and remove her from the passenger seat. Still no sign of another soul as I walk into the darkness of the small park, Clare slung over a shoulder. When I've reached the tiny grove of trees that passes for nature in this area, I drop her to the ground. She lands on her back, a tiny whimper emerging, but no movement.

Even in this darkness, it's clear this is not Jordan. For tonight, she'll do. Kneeling next beside the unconscious sprawl of her, I wipe stray strands of her dark hair from her face. In a cheap way, she is pretty. My arousal is returning, so I concentrate on my work. Removing the hunter's knife from its scabbard in my waistband, I close my eyes, picturing the exact pattern of stab wounds I lavished upon Jordan's mother. That should provide resonance, and a nice reintroduction. Showing Jordan I haven't forgotten how cooperative her mother was, sacrificing herself. The woman thought she was protecting her daughter, when in reality what she did was deliver her to me.

Just as I raise the knife, Clare's eyes drift open. They seem hazy and I can't tell if she's aware or not, though her body heaves at the first blow, ejaculating blood, then jerks a little thereafter, spurting more blood, but soon it is like stabbing a bag of grain, and bags of grain don't bleed. The knife follows the pattern of Jordan's mother. It performs its duty with divine guidance, as He works through me to hand down his justice. Technically, I suppose, I have taken her life. But He has taken her soul.

After, I lean over her, panting, unaware I had worked so hard, and from my exhilarated exhaustion, one might think I had followed my worst instincts and committed fornication upon this creature. But I have maintained control. To be with anyone but Jordan, from here on out, would be a sin, and I stay on the other side of sin.

I wipe the blade clean on Clare's clothing, then put it back in its scabbard in my waistband. I take off the latex gloves I have been wearing since arriving at Clare's building and wrap them and the chloroform rag in the raincoat. This package I will drop in a sewer or Dumpster later.

For now, it's time to go.

But not until I've said a prayer for Clare.

Amen.

CHAPTER SEVEN

"Jimmy was just about the best older brother a girl could hope for," Jordan said. "I could share any feelings, any secrets with him. He kidded me, sure, but he'd been through so much himself."

Tears welled and Jordan stopped, swallowed, glancing around the circle at the encouraging smiles and nods of the Victims of Violent Crime Support Group.

"He'd been through a lot," she said, " 'cause, well, 'cause he was gay. It was something he hid for a long time, and I was the first one in the family that he . . . came out to. He was so afraid I'd be disappointed in him. But I didn't care. And neither did Mom or Dad. He was just Jimmy . . . kind, loving. . . ."

A box of tissues was passed her way and she used them, dabbing her eyes, blowing her nose, everyone just waiting.

Finally Levi asked, gently, "Did you see him?"

Jordan's head jerked up. "Huh? What?"

"The killer. Did you *see* him?"

It had all been so positive, so shockingly easy, talking about her mother, father, and brother. As if she and a girlfriend on a sleepover were in her darkened bedroom, on a comfy bed, leaned back talking about wonderful times, the way you might before drifting off to sleep after a fun day.

But the door to the rest of the house was cracked open, the light a bright vertical slash, and what was waiting out there, the horror of all that, she couldn't face, much less share.

She could not open that door.

Chin lowered, Jordan said, "That's all I have to say right now."

Dr. Hurst's expression was kind and so was her voice as she said, "Jordan, I know it's difficult. You've done very well, sharing the positive memories. But we need to push past those, and face—"

Jordan shot her a look that melted the doctor's pleasant expression into pale blankness.

Before the situation could deteriorate, the woman who seemed to be friendly with David, and was now seated across from Jordan, spoke up: "I've been trying to make myself talk about *my* family, too. Thank you, Jordan, for giving me the courage."

All eyes turned to her.

"I'm Kay," the woman said.

A little taller than Jordan, her naturally red hair with some streaks of white, Kay was about the age Jordan's mother would have been. What had once very likely been a striking figure had plumped up some, and her pretty face bore lines that gave it a perpetually melancholy expression that smiling didn't entirely erase. Her eyes were big and blue behind bifocal lenses with dark-blue plastic frames.

"My sister, Katherine, and brother-in-law, Walt Gregory, died two years ago."

The group listened in respectful silence, the keen interest and sympathy of everyone quite obvious to Jordan.

"I went over to their house for dinner," Kay said, "but when I got there, no one answered. The doorbell just rang and rang . . ."

Though she occasionally glanced around the circle, her eyes briefly drifting past Jordan, Kay didn't seem to see any of them. Her voice never changed pitch. She might have been reciting a poem or sharing a recipe.

"When I tried the door, it was unlocked. I didn't think anything of it, really—Katherine might have been in the kitchen, using a noisy appliance or something, and Walt could have been watching the TV in the den. So I just went inside. But Katherine wasn't in the kitchen, Walt wasn't in the den, they weren't anywhere downstairs."

Next to Jordan, David fidgeted. *No one else here had heard this story,* she felt, *but* he *had.* The toe of the writer's sneaker was grinding at the tile floor like he was trying to stub out a cigarette butt.

"I called and called, but no one answered," Kay said. "Just my own voice a little bit. They had a huge great room with a vaulted ceiling and the echo just seemed to bounce around in that big empty space. But after that . . . just silence. There had to be an easy explanation. They'd forgotten I was coming over, maybe, or got called away. No reason, really, to be uneasy, or scared. But I was. I was."

This woman had felt the same kind of fear that Jordan had, on her own terrible night.

"Finally," Kay said, swallowing, "I worked up the nerve to go upstairs. . . ."

The tissue box made its way around to the speaker. She nodded thanks, took one, and instead of using it to dab at tears, wound it around her index finger, unwound it, and wound it again as she continued.

"They were on the bed, holding hands. They each had a single bullet hole in their temple, and a pistol was on the floor, next to Walt's side of the bed."

Kay was shaking a little now, the tears coming, the tissue finally finding its purpose.

"The police called it murder slash suicide," Kay said, then, with a nervous, embarrassed smile, seemed to have found her composure. A moment later, she began weeping uncontrollably.

Jordan rose and crossed to the woman, vaguely aware that all eyes were on her, but for the weeping woman's, whose face was buried in her tissue-held hands.

"Jordan . . ." Dr. Hurst began.

The sound of the doctor's voice caused Kay to look up. When she did, the younger woman bent over and awkwardly wrapped her arms around Kay and held her close.

The older woman, still crying but less savagely now, clung fiercely to Jordan, who hugged her back, even harder.

When the tears subsided, still in the young woman's embrace, Kay looked up at her. "That was . . . was very kind, dear."

After a tiny smile and tinier nod, Jordan straightened and walked back to her seat and resumed her previous rather stiff posture, as if nothing had happened.

Dr. Hurst said, "Jordan, as Kay said, that was a very kind gesture . . . no, not gesture, but impulse. What prompted you to . . . express yourself in that way?"

The look Jordan gave the doctor was a withering one. "If I knew, it wouldn't be an impulse, would it?"

This seemed to momentarily stun Hurst, but a few small smiles blossomed in the circle, including David and Levi.

Later, outside in the sunny coolness of the early spring afternoon, David—with Levi tagging along—approached Jordan. Kay was lingering nearby as well, but didn't join in.

"Sometimes Hurst just doesn't get it," Elkins said.

"Yeah?"

He nodded. "Not everything has to be discussed. You saw somebody crying, it touched you, you showed a little support, end of story. Not everything needs to be analyzed."

"Or," Levi said, hands in his jeans jacket, "*psycho*analyzed."

"I guess she's just trying to help," Jordan shrugged, not quite believing she actually said that.

"We're gonna get some coffee," Elkins said. "Wanna come?"

"I don't think so. Thanks."

Levi said, "Aw, come on. You kind of owe me one."

"I do?"

"Yeah. You scared the ever-lovin' piss out of me last week. I thought you were gonna tear my head off."

Jordan smiled a little. "Sometimes I overreact."

"Not that you aren't cute enough to hit on. If I was into that."

David gave her half a grin. "Come on, kid. You'll love the place."

The coffee shop, a couple of blocks away, had been renovated from an old bakery. The counter where Jordan ordered her coffee was a display case that dated back to that original purpose, filled with baked goodies that once upon a time would have called out to her. She used to have a terrible sweet tooth. The night she lost her parents, it left. Jordan figured Dr. Hurst would have some windy explanation about the meaning of that; but to her it just meant empty calories she didn't have to worry about.

She took her coffee over to David and Kay, who were already sitting at a high-top table near the shop's front window. The writer gave her a nod, and Kay added a warm smile, as Jordan sat down. Of the dozen or so tables and booths, maybe a third were full. Levi had been just behind Jordan in line, and caught up with them.

David, she assumed, wanted to talk to her about the similarities between the murders of his family and hers. Maybe not tonight, maybe this would be socializing to lead up to that, but she felt that was what this was about.

She didn't know anything about Levi's situation—*similarities between his tragedy and theirs,* she wondered?—but she assumed that Kay was joining them only because David seemed to be her ride.

Jordan was glad they had avoided a booth. Sharing a side with somebody might make her uneasy. Having her own chair, her own space, made this easier. The skinny skater boy sat down next to her, the aroma of his caramel-Frappuccino-whatever invading her space in a much more welcome way.

Levi managed to find room to open his laptop on the small table and fire it up.

"First, let me introduce myself," he said. "Levi Mills."

There were no last names in group—she only knew David's was Elkins because of his status as a best-selling thriller writer.

Levi was holding out his hand.

Jordan didn't take it. "Sorry. Germaphobe. But my last name's Rivera, if that helps."

Kay said, "Isenberg is mine," and nodded and smiled.

"I think you know who I am," the writer said.

"Right." She bounced her eyes from David to Levi. "We've been in group together three weeks. Let's skip the b.s. What's this about?"

Levi, his fingertips resting at the bottom of his keyboard, said, "I think you know. Your case."

"My case? You mean, my family getting butchered?" The words came out with a little more attitude than was probably necessary.

He held up a hand in a stop gesture. "*Case* is just a way to reference the crimes. It doesn't really speak to the greater impact those crimes had on you. Or the ones that impacted me . . . or David . . . or Kay."

These three people, like her, had been through ten kinds of shit. Chagrin flushed her.

Jordan said, "You'll have to excuse me for being such a complete bitch. I haven't been on the outside very long. I have the social skills of a biker on meth."

David grinned at her. "What would you know about a biker on meth?"

"Oh, I saw half a dozen brought in at Dimpna, over the years." She turned to Levi. "What *did* happen to you? I know their stories. What about yours?"

Levi gave her a smile that had nothing to do with the conventional reasons for smiling. "My family was killed two and a half years after yours. I was even younger than you were."

"I don't mean to sound cold," Jordan said. "But were there any similarities . . . ?"

He shook his head. "Not direct ones."

"How . . . ?"

"My parents . . . the word the papers used was *perished* . . . in a house fire."

Jordan flinched at the thought. "That's terrible. I'm very sorry, Levi. But that doesn't sound like murder."

"Oh, it was murder. The police think someone broke into the house, drugged Mom and Dad, then set the house on fire."

"Jesus," Jordan said.

"Yeah," Levi said, and the non-smile returned. "It's pretty fucked up, all right."

"They were dead before the killer set the house fire?"

The young man shook his head. "The fire wasn't even that bad—the house was actually saved, can you believe it?"

Kay's eyes were lowered. She already knew this story. David watched Levi with quiet sympathy.

"My folks . . . they couldn't get out because of the drug the killer gave them. How exactly he managed it, no one knows. But it was by injection, in fact a drug used in lethal injection. They were paralyzed and died of smoke inhalation. Succinylcholine, it's called, what he drugged them with. Causes temporary paralysis.

Mostly used to euthanize horses, or immobilize them for surgery."

Jordan said, "I'm so sorry."

Levi shrugged. "I was even a suspect for a while. Then the cops checked my story and found I was playing video games at my friend Rick's house. Spent the night there. Didn't know anything was wrong, till Rick's mom got a call from one of our neighbors. Rick and I had heard the sirens, but didn't think anything of it. You hear sirens at night sometimes."

The young man cracked his neck, yawned, then took a long swig of his coffee.

Jordan leaned in. "What makes you think our . . . our *cases* are connected?"

Levi shrugged. "I don't know that they are."

"But it's *families*," David said, lightly bumping a fist on the table. "Your family was first, in Westlake, ten years ago."

Like she needed to be reminded?

"Then," David went on, "two and a half years later? A family is murdered in Ashtabula—Levi's family."

Jordan frowned. "Ashtabula? How far is that from Cleveland?"

Levi said, "Sixty-two miles up I-90."

Not really a suburb, the town sat just off Lake Erie, northeast of Cleve-land.

"Then two years later," David said, "*my* family was killed."

"That," Levi said, "is when I really started putting the pieces together."

"Pieces of what?" Jordan asked. "Three families murdered, but three different places, years apart, different methods, and excuse me, but nobody *else* here got raped, did they?"

Kay's hand shot to her mouth. David had the expression of a slapped man, but Levi remained calm. He was almost smiling again.

"The police kept that fact to themselves," David said, in a hushed voice.

"They always hold something back," Levi said, pleasantly.

"Actually," Jordan said, "I never told the police."

The others took a few moments to digest that.

"Maybe that's why he left you alive," Levi said.

Jordan blinked at him. "What do you mean?"

"David and I were spared, too, if that nice little word can cover something that big and awful." He glanced at the writer, then brought his gaze back to Jordan and continued: "We weren't home. But you were in the house when your family was killed. And I always wondered why he didn't kill you, too."

"You seem convinced that it's the same son of a bitch," Jordan said coldly.

"Damn straight."

Why wasn't she pissed off at this kid's calmness about the most traumatic event in her life? Instead she appreciated it.

David touched her arm and she jerked it away.

"Please," the writer said, misreading her silence. "I know this is hard. It's hard for all of us, but Levi has found some things that make me think that despite all the differences between our 'cases,' maybe, just maybe, we *are* dealing with one murderer here."

She said nothing. She was thinking. Her plans for finding and dealing with the intruder had not included bringing anybody along. This was *her* fight, *her* responsibility. . . .

"Maybe you just want to move on," Levi said. "I mean now that we know what happened to you . . . what sent you into a catatonic state for ten years."

"I wasn't catatonic."

"No?"

"I just didn't have anything to say."

Levi studied her for a few moments, then said, "Did you know there's been another crime, a family in Strongsville? Pretty similar to your situation. It would have hit the news just about the time you suddenly decided you *did* have something to say."

Was she *that* transparent? Skater boy seemed to know which buttons to push.

Her eyes swept the people around the table. "So," she said. "What have you naughty children been up to?"

Levi grinned, a real smile this time, and David smiled a little, too. Only Kay remained impassive, her eyes on Jordan.

"Levi was way out in front of this," David said, nodding to him. "Levi?"

The young man nodded back, then turned his attention to Jordan. "At first, all I did was dig into what happened to my parents. But when what happened to David's family hit the media, I saw enough similarities to start me looking—looking deeper. For a pattern, for commonalities."

Jordan asked, "And you found . . . ?"

"When I added in your family, I had a kind of line of three, on the map. You in Westlake, David in Cleveland, and my family in Ashtabula. You were first, then me in the north, then David in the middle. But now Strongsville? That's south and east of you. They were all in the greater Cleveland area, but there was no apparent logic to the locations, otherwise."

Jordan nodded. "So it's not geographic?"

David said, "Probably not."

Levi shrugged and said, "That was just the first thing I looked at."

"What about you and my brother?" Jordan said. "Both gay. Hate crime?"

"A real possibility," Levi said. "The Sullys in Strongsville strengthens that notion. Brittany Sully, the daughter who died along with her parents? She actually made some headlines in the local media for asking another girl to be her date for the prom this year."

Jordan had known that. "So Brittany was gay, too," she said.

"Actually, no—her brother in the army is. He's in Afghanistan. She wanted to show solidarity with him, so she asked a girl to prom. Seems her boyfriend was in college and not allowed to attend prom with her. So she asked a friend of hers, another girl, who *is* gay, and . . . it was really no big deal, but it made the news, and, of course, the Internet."

Turning to Elkins, Jordan asked, "Meaning no offense, you're not a gay man who had a straight wife and a family, are you?"

The writer gave her a wry smile. "No. Nobody gay in my immediate family. I don't think there's any family in America that if you look hard enough, you won't turn up a gay cousin or aunt or whatever, but . . . no."

Levi said, "Add to that, when my family was killed, I didn't even know I was gay yet."

Jordan said, "Really?"

"Well, not in any real way, I mean I hadn't even come out entirely to *myself* yet, so how the hell did the killer know?"

"Sometimes the people around you know before you do."

"But only somebody really close to me."

"How about a teacher, or a counselor?"

"I don't think so. But we do have another commonality—the Sully brother in Afghanistan is a survivor."

"Four families murdered," David said. "Each with a single survivor."

Jordan said, "He said he wasn't going to kill me because he wanted me to tell his story."

Levi's grin was a little crazy. "Only you clammed up on him. Sweet."

"But," David said, "maybe that's what he thrives on. The crime, the atrocity he's committed, lives on . . . because the survivor carries it on. And, he hopes, shares it with the world. Of course, Jordan, you cheated him out of it."

They all sat and thought about that.

"We each bring something to the effort," David said, with a general gesture. "Levi is a computer whiz, I've researched crime intensively as a backdrop to my fiction writing, and Kay has a way of providing keen insights, from the sidelines, that we might miss."

Finally, with a bit of a smirk, Jordan asked, "What do you think I can add to your little Serial Killer Support Group?"

"Information," David said.

Levi added, "The more we have, the easier it will be to determine if there's a pattern or patterns . . . and maybe even how to catch the guy."

"I like the sound of that," Jordan admitted.

"Obviously," Elkins said, "when we know enough, we take it to the police."

That she didn't like the sound of, but kept it to herself.

"All right," she said. "I'm in."

David and Levi exchanged smiles, both saying, "Good," and Kay nodded. So far Kay hadn't offered any of those "insights" that David had mentioned, and really just seemed to be along for the ride. Literally. But what the hell—every team needed a mascot.

And every survivor of violence had to find meaning. . . .

Jordan checked her watch. "I've got to go now, but after the next meeting, we'll dig in. Hard."

They said their goodbyes and the others stayed on in the coffee shop. Outside, she unlocked her scooter, started it up, then headed home, the cool air bracing, her mood upbeat.

As soon as she rounded the corner, Jordan knew the black Ford parked in front of her building didn't belong there.

She came up from behind the Ford, on the driver's side. As she neared, she caught the reflection of the driver's face in his rearview. A middle-aged African-American male, kind of good-looking for his age.

Jordan didn't look at him, but she didn't exactly look away either, as she rode by. She checked her mirror. He was noting her passage. As she glided by her building, she saw another man, white, in a rumpled suit and an unconvincing hairpiece, showing something in his billfold to the building manager. Streetlight glinted off that something.

A badge?

She turned the corner and pulled over. She supposed she knew that someone would come sniffing around at some point. The murder of her family was very old news, but her release from St. Dimpna's was *new* news, and maybe enough to get the police to revisit the case, in a perfunctory way probably. All it meant to her was more questions she had no desire to answer.

Screw it, no reason to avoid these guys. If she did, they would just keep coming around. Gunning the scooter, she went around the block and came up behind the Ford. The white cop in the rumpled suit was back in the car, obviously waiting her out.

She stopped the scooter directly beside the driver's door, leaving him no room to get out. Raising the visor of her helmet, she smiled at the detective, who actually jerked a little when he realized who had him pinned inside his car.

His window came down.

"Ms. Rivera," he said in a deep voice that seemed to start somewhere around his shoes.

She just looked at him. Did they know she had started talking again? Probably, but no reason to hand it to them. She just stared at the man. He had kind brown eyes, a short Afro, and a tidy goatee.

"I'm Detective Grant."

Silence.

He nodded toward his partner. "This is Detective Lynch."

The detective with the obvious hairpiece leaned over so she could see him, giving her a weak smile.

"We'd like to ask you some questions," Grant said. "How about inviting us inside?"

"No."

Grant frowned, more confused than irritated. "Ms. Rivera, this is important. It has to do with the death of your parents and brother."

"Has there been a breakthrough in the case?"

That took Grant by surprise. He managed to say, "No, no, it's just that we'd like to talk to you about your family and—"

"If you have new information to share, I'd be happy to hear it. Otherwise, no."

"Ms. Rivera, we never had the chance to interview you after—"

"It's still too painful. I'm in therapy. Check with my doctor—Dr. Hurst? At St. Dimpna's?"

"We understand, but if we're going to apprehend whoever killed your family—"

She sharpened her voice. "What part of 'it's too fucking painful' do you not understand?"

The detective gaped at her as Jordan gunned the scooter and rode off, fast enough to earn herself a ticket, practically daring them to come after her. But when she'd rounded the block and turned the corner, the Ford was gone.

She turned down the alley, pulled into the compact parking lot behind her building. Spaces were at a premium, but there was a light post on one side that she could lock her Vespa to.

The scooter's still-coiled chain was in one hand when two men stepped from the shadows of the storage shed behind the lot. One, a skinny Hispanic kid, had a knife that caught the dim light, the long slender blade pointed toward Jordan, like an accusing finger. The knife wielder wore black jeans and a black T-shirt, his curly hair combed back—it looked wet, like he'd just climbed out of a pool. His face had angular features and he would have been a good-looking kid if his close-set eyes hadn't made him look so stupid.

The other one, a rangy white kid, was also in black jeans and a black T-shirt, though his bore the phrase DON'T BE SEXIST—BITCHES HATE THAT.

Staying consistent with his shirt, he said, "Gimme your purse, bitch."

She held out her free hand, open palm up. "You see a purse?"

The pair traded frowns, and the white kid said, "Then your *wallet*, bitch."

Jordan let one end of the balled chain slide out of her hand with a metallic rattle. "Say *bitch* one more time."

"Ooooo, she got balls," the knife wielder purred, apparently amused by the sight of the three-foot length of chain dangling from her hand.

The white kid blurted, "I said your wallet, you lezzie cunt!"

She shook her head. "Just fuck off, fellas, and we'll be fine."

The kid with the knife took a threatening step closer, and the big one gave her a wide-eyed, sneering look that she guessed was supposed to scare her.

He said, "And the keys to that shitty little bike, too, bitch."

With a flick of her wrist, the end of the chain whipped out, whapping the white kid in the face, his nose breaking with a sharp little *crack,* sending him windmilling back, yowling, hands coming up to cover his nose where blood was erupting with scarlet insistence.

The skinny Hispanic lurched forward, thrusting with the knife, and she sidestepped, grabbed his arm, and dropped to one knee as he went by. With considerable force, she bent the skinny arm backward, then slammed into it with her shoulder. The arm snapped, the kid screamed, and the knife fell from splayed fingers to do a little hop, skip, and jump on the concrete, spinning when it landed. Rising, she backhanded his face with a fist, which shut him up momentarily as he spit blood and teeth. As he was staggering up to a half-standing position, she spun and kicked him hard between the legs and he crumpled to the cement where he alternated moans and sobs.

The bigger one charged her now, in a mix of fear and anger, his eyes white in his red-streaked face. Her chain lashed out and wrapped itself around his lower leg and she gave a sharp tug and his leg did a chorus-line kick before he dropped with a *whump*.

Jordan leapt, landing with a knee on his chest that sent blood and spittle flying from his grunting mouth. She twirled her hand and the chain wrapped itself around that hand, which became an iron fist with which she battered him, pounding him in the face, stopping when she was looking down at a blinking scarlet mask, not wanting the trouble killing him might cause.

She got off him.

The white kid lay on his back like an overturned bug. He was moaning and a tooth she had freed was sticking through a cheek.

She was breathing a little hard, but nothing extreme.

"Yo, bitches," she said. "Come dance anytime."

They said nothing, just moaning there on their backs. She went to each of her attackers and kicked them twice in the ribs—they responded with *"Unh! Unh!" "Unh! Unh!"*—and then she went over and found the knife and collected it. A switchblade. Old school.

She was chaining her bike to the lamppost when the Hispanic, his broken arm swinging like a busted fence gate, stumbled over to his friend and helped him to his feet and they hobbled into the dark, whimpering like the kicked dogs they were.

In her apartment, she put the switchblade in the silverware drawer as if it were a butter knife. She doubted those two would ever be back, but if so, she would be ready. Nice to know that what she'd taught herself could be put to practical use. Stepping to the fridge, she shadowboxed with the picture of the male face held by a magnet to the door.

She felt ready for what lay ahead.

Smiling, she stripped, went into the bathroom, and turned on the shower—hot as she could take. As the mirror started to steam, she stepped under the spray, the hot needles feeling just fine; she still felt exhilarated. She started to reach for the soap, but her fingers faltered.

Her stomach did a little back flip and her knees went weak. Slowly, she sagged and slid down to a sitting position, the hot water still pounding her. She just sat there, for quite a while, huddled in the corner in a fetal position. Maybe she was crying. Maybe it was just the shower spray. She would never tell.

Not even herself.

CHAPTER EIGHT

After his encounter with Basil Havoc, Mark would have to play things much closer to the vest. No one besides his partner Pence and Captain Kelley himself knew of Mark's investigation into the apparently·related "family" murders.

Yet somehow Havoc had made him. Had either Pence or Kelley told somebody else, a trusted reporter or another cop maybe, about Mark's homicide-investigation hobby? That seemed unlikely, but either the guy got tipped off or he maybe was even smarter than Mark had imagined.

And Mark didn't take this man lightly. If Havoc *was* the killer, that made him one resourceful son of a buck. You couldn't kill as many people as Havoc apparently had, over all those years and jurisdictions, and avoid capture without a Mensa-level IQ and a certain jungle cunning.

At work, Mark stayed focused and intense, as always. He and Pence had been busy as heck trying to track down a burglary ring, where the clues and witness interviews just wouldn't mesh. After some digging, it became clear *two* somewhat similar such rings were operating in the same area.

Either one or both of these crews had been at it for the better part of a year now. Sooner or later their luck would go south, and either somebody would be home, or would walk in on them. *Then what?* Home invasions, no matter how carefully planned, could erupt into violence.

Or as Pence colorfully said, "What if these crews find out about each other? I mean, *we* did. And suppose they don't cotton to havin' competition? Further suppose they turn up to burgle the same building, the same time? All of a sudden, we got two simple robberies turnin' into one great big fuckin' O.K. Corral."

How serious was the situation? Serious enough for purse-string pincher Kelley to green-light overtime. In this economy, that put these burglaries on a par with bank robbers.

Or maybe a serial killer.

Nearing midnight, they would normally have still been at HQ, pushing papers, sifting for clues; but Pence had gotten a lead from a snitch of his. Right now they were sitting surveillance outside the back door of Gold Medal Pawn, a rundown shop in an equally rundown neighborhood.

The snitch had told Pence that Robert Slowenski, owner of Gold Medal, was up to his old fencing ways and clearing goods for a burglary ring. This would appear to be one of the two such rings the Pence and Pryor team were seeking to bust.

In his seventies, darn near wide as he was tall, the nearly bald Slowenski was known by his colleagues (and the cops) as "Slowhand," a nickname the pawnbroker claimed dated back to when he'd once sold a Stratocaster guitar to Eric Clapton. While Clapton had indeed performed in Cleveland from time to time, the story was likely fanciful, because the nickname actually related to Robert Slowenski's reputation for being slow to pay.

Though the front of the store was dark, a dim bulb extended over the back door in the alley, with Slowhand's dodgy-looking Lincoln Town Car parked not far away, barely allowing passage for any other vehicle.

Farther down the darkened alley, Pence and Mark (behind the wheel) sat in their unmarked Crown Victoria, right where they had been for the last three hours. Mark had wanted to be a detective for a very long time, but he wondered if he'd have gone into this line of work had he known about the dulling boredom of a stakeout.

Each detective had a penlight in one hand—Pence had a newspaper in his lap, the light shining on a Sudoku puzzle that was a mystery the seasoned detective would never solve, while Mark examined a clipped newspaper story about Brittany Sully and the dust-up she had caused at Strongsville High School when she asked another girl to the prom.

Pence grunted, "How the hell are you supposed to work these dumb things? My old man helped beat the Japs. Is this their fuckin' revenge?"

Mark said, "It's all logic."

Pence threw him a look. "And *I'm* not logical? You think I broke all those cases by bein' not logical?"

"You're logical enough, but you're trying to do one square at a time. You need to see the whole puzzle."

They stayed at their individual tasks for a while, each occasionally glancing toward the pawnshop's dimly lighted back door to make sure Slowhand wasn't going anywhere. In Mark's mind, the old song "I Shot the Sheriff" kept playing, unbidden.

Finally, Pence doused the penlight, tossed the newspaper onto the dash, and announced, "Fuck it! They win. First they sink the *Arizona*, now my ancient ass."

Mark grinned, shook his head, but kept going over the newspaper story.

"What the fuck are you up to?" Pence asked. "Readin' the clippings of all your triumphs on the force? Oh. I forgot. You haven't had any."

Sticking his newspaper above the visor, Mark clicked out his penlight, and said, "Not doing anything."

"Don't shit a shitter," Pence said. "I saw that story when it first came out. About that gay girl, who got murdered in Strongsville. Her and her whole fam-damly."

"Actually she wasn't gay," Mark said. "And the whole family wasn't killed."

"No? Could've fooled me, all those dead bodies."

"Her brother is gay, and she was just showing some solidarity. And he's still alive, overseas, in the military."

"Like you care."

Mark glanced at the older cop sharply. "What?"

"You don't care about that family any more than I do. Don't know them from Adam. Or Eve or my hairy left ball. This is about you still moonin' over that chick from high school days, right? The one you never even dated?"

Mark said nothing. He tried to keep the irritation from crawling up his neck in a red rash. He knew Pence liked to pull his chain, and he also knew there was no real malice behind it.

"Marky Mark, ain't you never gonna let that go? Why don't you do what I do, when I wake up at night, thinkin' about Betty Lou Miller who wouldn't look at me sideways in high school?"

"What do you do?"

"I get out of bed real quiet, so as not to wake the wife, and pad down the hall into the john and beat my meat, hummin' the old school song."

"Must you be so crude?"

"No, it's a lifestyle choice. You *do* know we're a couple of Cleveland detectives, and not Mormon missionaries goin' door-to-door, right?"

Tightly, Mark said, "She deserves justice."

"The Jordan girl? Sure she does. But that doesn't mean she's going to get any."

"She might. She may."

Pence sighed, like Atlas switching shoulders. "You know, kid, every cop's got that *one* case that nags him, way after he's put in his papers. So I get where you're comin' from."

"Do you?"

"Yup. But you had your white whale before you ever got to be a cop. You don't learn to let that shit go, my son, it will eat your ass alive."

"I'll keep that in mind."

Pence looked sad suddenly. "No you won't."

Then they both saw headlights coming down the alley toward them. A van.

Why should a van, a simple ordinary vehicle, make his sphincter tighten and his mouth go immediately dry? When he had first teamed with Pence, the older cop had told him that the job was ninety-five percent boredom and five percent sheer freaking terror.

Tonight Mark was getting the full one hundred percent. . . .

Working to keep his breathing regular, Mark waited. Next to him, Pence was doing the same thing. They slouched in their seats down far enough that no one in the van might spot them. At least not from a distance. Maybe a half a block away, the van's headlights switched off as it pulled in.

Without really thinking about it, Mark let his hand rest on the butt of his pistol on his hip.

The van stopped on the other side of the pawnshop's back door, beyond Slowhand's parked Lincoln. That gave Mark and Pence a slight advantage. They had Slowhand's car between the van and their own.

"You remember to click the dome light off?" Pence whispered.

"Yeah," Mark whispered back. "I'm not an idiot."

"We'll discuss that later."

The van's front doors opened and two African-American males climbed out. In the dark it was hard to see much, and the dim bulb over the pawnshop door was little help. The guy on the passenger side was a head taller than the driver, and they wore jeans and cutoff sweatshirts; but from this distance, Mark could determine little else.

The African-Americans walked to the back of the van and opened its rear doors. While the pair was back there, blocked by the vehicle, Mark and Pence slipped out of the Crown Vic, neither shutting his door tight. Using Slowhand's car for cover, they crept closer.

Mark stayed on the driver's side, hanging back by the Lincoln's bumper, just in case the two guys came around the van's passenger side.

On the other side of the Lincoln, Pence—despite his bulk—was all but invisible in the alley's inky shadows. Grunts came from the back of the van, where the doors closed, and then the two men shuffled around the driver's side, lugging something awkwardly between them.

As the pair got closer to the light above the door, Mark could see that they carried a massive flat-screen TV, fifty-inch screen anyway. The shorter man, the driver, led the way, going backward, his taller associate bringing up the rear.

Mark already had his gun out and at his side, barrel pointed straight down, ready to come up fast.

When the pair got to the door, the driver used his foot to give it a couple of solid kicks.

Then they waited.

Mark and Pence, staying low, edged alongside the Lincoln.

After a moment, the taller guy hissed, "Where the fuck he at? He slow keepin' *time*, too?"

Still cradling his end of the TV, the driver managed a tiny shrug. "Fuck do I know? Maybe he's takin' a dump. Do I look like that John Edward dude?"

Then he kicked the door three more times, rattling it, making his partner almost lose his grip. More general profane bitching followed for maybe thirty seconds, then the door swung open and bald squat Slowhand himself filled the frame.

"You're late," he said to them in a low, gruff growl, small dark eyes darting up and down the alley, like bugs looking for a place to land.

"*We* late?" the driver said. "We been knockin' for half an hour, man! You slow in the hand or the head?"

"Just get that fucking thing in here," Slowhand said, stepping out into the alley to clear the doorway.

Pence popped up next to him. "Raise 'em, Robert!"

Mark stood and, in a voice much calmer than he felt, said, "Hold it right there, fellas."

The driver did so, but his taller pal dropped his end of the TV and took off down the alley like a sprinter after the starting gun.

Unable to juggle the big TV from one end, its weight and awkwardness conspiring against him, the driver watched with wide helpless eyes as the expensive electronics item tumbled from his grasp and smashed onto the concrete alley, bits of the screen shattering and scattering everywhere, like ice breaking up.

"Fuck it!" the driver said, and put his hands up.

"You goin' after him?" Pence asked, nodding toward the tall guy, who was already nearing the alley's mouth.

"No," Mark said, then eased toward the driver. He wasn't going to leave Pence with two suspects to deal with. He told the driver, "Grab some wall."

The driver assumed the position, hands flat on brick, feet spread. He'd been frisked before.

Patting the driver down, Mark asked, "Care to tell me the name of your homey? Cooperation is a beautiful thing."

"Snitches get stitches," the driver said, not even bothering to look over his shoulder.

"If that's the way you want it," Mark said, and read him his rights.

As he cuffed the man, Mark looked over and saw that Pence already had Slowhand cuffed, as well. The cop may have been old and fat, but he could still handle himself—with an equally old and fat perp, anyway.

Soon patrol cars rolled into the alley and the detectives loaded in the two suspects, who both wore the glum resignation of the career criminal who knew such indignities would occasionally occur.

Then Mark and Pence went in through the pawnshop's open back door. The interior was only slightly better illuminated than the alley. Three of the back-room walls were lined with shelves, most of the two-by-four and plywood variety, filled with every kind of cheap merchandise imaginable. The fourth was home to a desk, atop that a computer whose screen saver consisted of beautiful naked women (this would seem as close to them as Slowhand was likely to get), and next to the desk a tiny table supported a small flat-screen TV. Whatever Slowhand was up to back here, it wasn't immediately apparent. The crime scene team would be combing through this junk for days, and that didn't include the stuff in the shop's larger front end.

While Pence thumbed through the messy stacks of paper on the desk, Mark strolled along the shelves, shining his penlight into the darkness. Televisions, computers, portable hard drives, Blu-ray and DVD players, stacks of DVDs (predominantly porn), power tools, musical instruments, and one shelf's worth of piled clothing.

The latter turned out to be costumes—Indian chief, firefighter, policeman, power worker, leather guy. Had the Village People hocked their wardrobe? This was apparently the inventory of a costume shop. He just shook his head. Pawnshops were amazing places—people would pawn anything, from a screwdriver to a samurai sword.

"Take a gander," Pence said, and Mark left the shelves and crossed to the desk.

Pence pointed to the computer monitor, where Slowhand's eBay page was displayed. The pawnbroker was selling a lot of stuff online. Not unusual, this day and age.

"There was a screen saver going," Mark said. "You touch something? Crime scene unit wouldn't appreciate that."

His partner shook his head innocently. "You stompin' around must have vibrated the desk or something."

"Oh-kay."

Ignoring Mark's skepticism, Pence said, "Item here you might like to add to your eBay watch list."

Mark leaned in. "That's the Lladró sculpture from the Mohican Avenue job. In Collinwood."

Pence nodded. "How about this one? Catch your fancy?"

"Hah. That upscale grill from the North Royalton burglary."

"Yeah. Which tells us what?"

They had already determined that while the two robbery crews overlapped, some territory appeared unique to each.

Mark gave his partner half a grin. "Either this bunch of turds is invading the *other* ring's turf or . . ."

Pence said, "Slowhand is fencing shit from both rings."

"Detective Pence—nice going."

The bigger man puffed up. "Back atcha, Detective Pryor. Now, shall we go interview a certain scumbag pawnshop owner?"

Mark gave him the rest of the grin. "We shall indeed."

As they were walking out, Pence asked, "Turds? Do you kiss your mother with that mouth?"

Mark's grin turned silly and embarrassed.

"Are you blushin', kid?" Pence grunted a laugh. "You are one of a fuckin' kind, my boy, one of a freakin', fuckin' kind.' "

In the interview room, they found Slowhand sitting at the scarred table, drumming his fingers—nerves or boredom? In any case, the pawnbroker said nothing when they entered. In fact, he didn't look at either cop, as Mark took the chair opposite him and Pence remained standing, prowling like a big anxious cat. Up in the corner, a video camera captured everything, and Mark knew Captain Kelley was on the other side of the one-way glass behind him.

Pence took the first swing at the little round pawnbroker. "In all my many years on the force, I have had the misfortune of dealing with some dumb sorry fucks, Robert my man, but *you* might well be king of the dumb sorry fucks. My apologies we ain't got no throne available for your royal ass." He shook his head, then leaned in, getting right in Slowhand's face. *"eBay,* for shit's sake?"

The truth of that hit Slowhand hard enough to make him cringe; but he said nothing.

Prowling again, Pence added, "And fencing for two burglary crews at the same time? Two competing crews, workin' the same basic area, who probably like each other the way a couple of street gangs would? Bold, imaginative thinking, Robert . . . or maybe the kind of greedy shit that could get you fucked up if one crew thought they were getting the short end of the stick."

His fingertips making small circles, Slowhand massaged his forehead. If this was a nervous habit, maybe it explained his baldness: he'd simply rubbed his hair off.

Pence's comment had struck a jarring chord not only with the pawnbroker, but with Mark, too. Slowhand was just one of many fences for high-end goods in a city the size of Cleveland. Dealing with two competing crews put him seriously in harm's way, not wise for a man not as fast on his feet—or with a gun—as he once was.

Why would an experienced crook like Slowhand risk courting this kind of trouble?

Unless . . .

"You weren't just *fencing* for them," Mark blurted. "You were *running* both crews."

Slowhand's cool evaporated, and he sat there gaping at the young cop. Pence gaped at Mark, too.

"That's why you could risk working with two crews, working the same territory," Mark said, running with his theory. "*They* were working for *you*."

Slowhand shook his head, *no, no, no,* and his trembling hand seemed about to rub away the flesh above his eyebrow.

"We have two suspects in custody," Mark said. "One of them is going to get a heck of a deal tonight. The other isn't. But this is your lucky night, Slowhand, because we talked to you first. You get first shot."

Pence, keeping up, smiling to himself, no longer pacing, said, "Your lucky fuckin' night, Robert. What say? Or should we go talk to the mope next door?"

Slowhand sat there twitching like a dog with fleas, but he did not respond, did not look at either detective.

"Looks like it's somebody else's lucky night," Mark said, and started out, Pence falling in behind. The second Mark's hand touched the doorknob, Slowhand said, his voice firm and loud: "*All right!* All right."

Pence turned and said casually, "All right *what*, Robert?"

". . . All right, I'll talk."

The two detectives returned to the table. Mark took his chair opposite Slowhand, and now Pence sat as well, next to the pawnbroker.

Slowhand said nothing for a while.

Mark said, "We're listening."

Finally Slowhand said, "It was about . . . retirement."

Pence frowned in confusion. "Retirement?"

Frowning back but in irritation, Slowhand said, "I'm seventy-eight years old, you dumb cluck—y'think I wanna work forever? I meet these kids, they're already into the burglary thing, but they're strictly smalltime." He used his thumb to tap himself in the chest. "*I* taught 'em how to make some real dough. How to choose where they hit, and what kind of swag to score."

"Fagin," Mark said.

"Hey, fuck you, I'm *straight*!" Slowhand yelped. "Watch your mouth, kid."

Mark started to explain but Pence waved him to quiet. Slowhand seemed about to continue.

"Me, I figured to bank some dough," Slowhand said. "Take my ass down to Florida to live out my golden years. Learn to play fuckin' shuffleboard, maybe."

Pence said, "I'd pay to see that, Robert."

Shaking his head slowly, painting a picture in the air with two hands, Slowhand said, "I had this place *all* picked out. Little town on the gulf side, where the water's warm . . . not like the Atlantic, where you freeze your nuts off even in August."

Pence couldn't resist. "Where is this little piece of heaven, Robert?"

"Place called Yankeetown."

Mark said, "You almost made it."

"Huh?"

"You'll be going to Youngstown."

Home of Ohio State Penitentiary, where Robert Slowenski would *really* spend his golden years. . . .

Between Slowhand and the van driver—from whom words spilled like a rapper who didn't know how to rhyme, once he knew ratting out his pals might pay off—Mark and Pence got the names of the members of both burglary rings. The day shift would stay busy, rounding 'em all up, but Pence and Mark were through for the night. They got pats on the back from Captain Kelley, which were harder to earn than Medals of Valor, then went their separate ways. Pence would head for some all-night fast food joint, no doubt. Mark had a date with some cool, clean sheets.

When Mark walked out to his Equinox, a middle-aged African-American male was leaning against the vehicle. This was no robbery suspect, not hardly.

This well-dressed goateed detective was Sergeant Morris Grant, "Mo" to his friends, which Mark was not. The big-time homicide specialist hadn't deigned to pronounce ten words in Mark's presence since the younger man had earned his gold shield.

As Mark neared, Grant said in his resonant baritone, "I hear you did some nice work tonight, Pryor. Did some real good out there tonight."

"Thank you," Mark said, leaning against the fender next to Grant. "I appreciate that. Really thoughtful of you to hang around to tell me that at three thirty in the morning."

Grant smiled, his teeth very white under the nearby streetlight, glowing, feral. "I heard that about you from people."

"What?"

"That you weren't dumb."

Looking around, Mark said, "Which people? Point 'em out, and I'll set 'em right."

Grant's chuckle was almost a growl. "I like you, Pryor. People also say you're a good detective, who's going to be working homicide one day. That where you think you're heading? Office next to mine?"

"Why not?" Mark said, maybe a little too eagerly.

The homicide cop was sizing him up, testing him; but for what, Mark had no idea.

"What would you rather do, Detective Pryor? Catch bad guys all your life for no credit, or become police commissioner?"

"Is that a trick question?"

"You tell me."

"Well, I don't want to ride a desk, no matter how big or important it is. I want to be a cop."

"Like a kid wants to be a fireman?"

"Like a man who wants to take bad guys off the street."

The homicide detective's gaze remained appraising. He laughed softly, then said, "All right, here's the deal. My partner and I are looking at a cold case that has some vague similarities to another case we're working on."

"Yeah?"

"There's a witness in that cold case that we need to talk to. She's not cooperating."

What was this about?

Grant was saying, "We need you to talk to her and pave our way, or even just talk to her for us."

"Well, of course," Mark said. "Captain Kelley's still inside—he's been working these hellacious hours, too. We can clear it with him now." He stepped away from his Equinox, but Grant's arm stopped him.

"If we go to the cap," Grant said, "it's a damn near certainty he won't let you in."

Mark frowned. "Why?"

"He'll say you're too close," Grant said.

As if Grant had dialed the last number of the combination of a safe, the tumblers falling in line, the door swung open for Mark.

Mark said, "You mean Jordan Rivera."

Grant gave a curt nod. "I mean Jordan Rivera."

Somewhere a siren screamed. A long ways off, but distinct.

"I knew her in high school," Mark said. "Ten years ago. I doubt she remembers me. Anyway, she's been in St. Dimpna's for ten years and she's not talking to anyone about anything. She's some kind of catatonic or something. Detective Grant, I wouldn't do any better than you would."

"Call me Mo." He smiled again and it was awful. "She's out. And she's talking. Just not to us."

The words slapped Mark. "What? *What?*"

"Been out for a while now. Month or so. She's got an apartment not far from that mental hospital."

Somehow he always thought he would know when she got out, or be informed about it or something. But that was a ridiculous notion. Why would anyone do that?

He said, "You've tried to interview her?"

"And failed," Grant said. "Lynch and me, outside her apartment. She wouldn't talk to us, said it was 'too painful.' Pretty much told us to fuck off."

"I see."

"We thought . . . *I* thought . . . maybe you, having known her, could reach out to her. Get her to sit down for an interview with us. If not us, then maybe she'd talk to you. Old school friend kind of deal."

Emotions roiled within the young detective. "You're asking me to do this behind Kelley's back?"

Grant said nothing, which spoke volumes.

Of course, the homicide man had no way of knowing that Mark was already looking into the Rivera murders on a sub-rosa basis with the captain's blessing. And he wasn't about to reveal it.

What would seeing her again be like, after all these years, and so much pain?

Suppose she did consent to talk to him, and had some small sense of who he was, who he'd been, back in high school days. After she found out what he *really* wanted to talk about . . . well . . . *then* what? Would she still talk to him? Or would she tell *him* to ef off, too? And, if she did, could he stand it?

He sighed. Only one way to find out. He looked at the other detective with a steady, unintimidated gaze. "Captain Kelley finds out, you step up, understand? You don't leave me with my tail hanging out with my boss."

Grant's nod was solemn.

Then he offered a hand and Mark shook it.

The older detective and his partner were drifting off and Mark had his car door open when Grant turned and called, "Oh. One other thing. . . ."

The pecking order meant Mark would have to close his car door and walk over to Grant. He did.

"We caught a homicide," Grant said, reaching in his inside suit coat pocket, "a brutal thing in the Rivera girl's neighborhood. Waitress. She got around, did some hooking."

Grant handed Mark the photo, a morgue shot. She'd been a nice-looking woman, a little hard maybe, dark hair.

Mark asked, "How was she killed?"

"Multiple stab wounds. We're looking at a married guy she was seeing. She had an abortion not long ago. Maybe it was his, or maybe it was one of half a dozen other guys'."

"And?"

"You think our dead waitress looks familiar?"

Mark studied the photo. "Maybe . . . vaguely like Jordan. It's not striking."

"Her part of town. Could there be a connection?"

Not his man's style. Not even vaguely the MO.

"No," Mark said, handed it back, and went on his way.

CHAPTER NINE

Though a skimpy eater, Jordan found herself making frequent trips to the neighborhood grocery store. She could only manage so many bags on the Vespa, so every couple of days she went to Alvaro's Market.

She was in the produce aisle, trying to find the perfect shallot, when he just seemed to appear out of nowhere, like he'd popped out of her memory—*Mark Pryor*. Same perfect blond hair, a little shorter, clear complexion but with the shadow of shaving, a few lines starting around the blue eyes, the sensitive mouth maybe just a touch fuller, but still, there he was—the boy she had dreamed about in high school. And there was that wide, white smile of his! Flashing at her as he approached.

Like they were in the high school hallway and he'd spotted her and now was smiling at her, coming over to say hello, with the promise of a relationship that had never had a chance to even get off the ground.

Only they were both in a grocery lane pushing carts, his with just a few more items than hers—was he a light eater, too? As Mark neared, Jordan regretted having piled her long black hair in a loose bun under an Indians baseball cap. For the first time in ten years, wearing no makeup made her feel self-conscious. And couldn't she have thrown on something better than loose sweatpants and a Maroon 5 T-shirt?

Annoyed with herself for such girly thoughts, she felt her smile fade as Mark pulled almost even with her cart, coming the opposite direction. He was casually dressed, too—white sneakers, jeans, and a navy blue T-shirt with the letters CPD stenciled in gold across the chest, defined below as CLEVELAND POLICE DEPARTMENT.

Suddenly this didn't feel like a happy accident.

"Jordan," he said. "Hello."

"Mark, isn't it? Pryor?"

"Yes. High school. You haven't changed."

He had that much wrong.

"Nice to see you," she said coolly, and began rolling off, but he reached out and stopped her cart. She frowned at him.

"Sorry," he said, but his grip on the steel grillwork of the cart remained. "Couldn't we talk for a minute? It's been a long time. Ten years."

"We're blocking the aisle."

He gestured. "Let's go over to the coffee shop area, by the deli counter. And catch up."

"I don't think so."

"Please," he said, still holding on to her cart.

There something urgent and needy in that, his eyes begging her. She swallowed. Nodded.

She allowed him to buy her some apple juice and he had a soft drink, and they found a booth near the front window.

"I heard you were . . . back," he said.

"Released from the nuthouse, yes."

"Are you . . . adjusting okay?"

"You know, Mark, we really didn't know each other all that well. We *almost* went out for a date. If you're thinking about picking up where we left off, we missed homecoming."

He shook his head, averting her stare. "I'm sorry this is so awkward. I really don't know what to say, Jordan. But I want to help."

"Really? You're not going to pretend this is a coincidence?"

"What?"

"Running into me. Grocery shopping." She raised her can of apple juice as if in toast, but was indicating the CPD on his chest. "You're on the Cleveland PD."

"I am."

"The T-shirt's a nice touch. Casual way to let me know and maybe help keep my guard down."

He shrugged, sipped his soft drink. "You don't have to keep your guard down around me, Jordan. We're old friends."

"No. Not really. I covered that. Weren't you listening? That black cop—what's his name . . . Grant? *He* sent you, didn't he?"

Mark lowered his gaze again, but this time his eyes still met hers. "Yeah."

"Figured as much. What makes you think I'll tell you anything I wouldn't tell him?"

"Grant prompted this, but I would have come looking for you, anyway. He's how I found out that you weren't in St. Dimpna's anymore."

"So he's using us both, then. Send Pryor, why don't we? *He* knew the fucked-up little ditz back in high school—maybe *he* can get her to talk."

"It's not like that," he said.

"How *is* it then?"

He frowned.

She grunted something that was not quite a laugh, then sipped her juice. "High school was a lifetime ago, Mark. Let it go."

He touched her hand. Her spine stiffened, but she didn't draw away. His was a light touch, gentle, warm, not grasping, just fingers on the back of her hand.

"I wanted to see you," he said, holding her eyes despite a shyness in his. "You must think I was horrible, not coming to see you, after what happened to your folks and your brother."

Now she withdrew her hand, but in a fashion as gentle as his touch had been.

"But I was just a kid," he said, with an embarrassed shrug. "I was afraid. You're right—we didn't really know each other that well. But I *knew* there was . . . something between us, or that maybe there could be. When I tried to visit you at St. Dimpna's, I got turned away, 'cause of my age."

"You got older."

"Yeah. I got older, and went to college, and . . ."

"You got busy. Life went on. You moved on."

"There's truth in that. I won't deny it. But I never forgot you, Jordan, or what happened to you. How . . . helpless I felt, not being able to do anything for you. My parents found out about your . . . condition. You're, uh . . . cured? You're not catatonic anymore, obviously."

"I was never catatonic."

"You didn't talk for ten years."

"I didn't have anything to say."

Then, for several moments, neither did they.

"I was weak," he said quietly, "not coming to see you. Not dealing with you in the . . . state you were in. I let you down."

She had some more juice. "Mark, really. How many times do I have to say it? We weren't a couple. We were two kids who nodded at each other in the hall."

He smiled, just a little. "I know. This is the longest conversation we ever had."

She smiled, just a little, too. For a moment.

Mark sighed, seemed to be summoning courage, then said, "Yes, I came here to see you today, to see if you would talk about what happened. No, *not* what happened—but about the case."

"How did you know I shopped here?"

"Grant gave me your schedule. They've been watching you."

"Are they still?"

"I don't think so. They're not really investigating your case as much as they're looking into a similar crime in Strongsville."

She didn't say that she was very aware of that crime. Instead she asked, "Why aren't the Strongsville police handling it? Grant's a Cleveland cop, like you, right?"

"Right. But Grant's a big-time homicide detective, and Strongsville's a bedroom community and they requested the help."

"What kind of cop are you?"

He frowned, wondering if that was sarcastic or an insult, perhaps. "Pardon?"

"A detective, like Grant, but newer to the force? Maybe you're in uniform when you aren't stalking old high school girlfriends in grocery aisles."

He frowned deeper, not sure if she was kidding him or giving him a dig. She wasn't sure herself.

"I just made detective." He swallowed, flicked a smile, then his expression turned sober. "Jordan, I became a cop because of what happened to your family."

Jordan tried to find words to respond to that, but couldn't.

"So this meeting up with you today," he said, "is more about me wanting to help than doing some kind of favor for Grant, who I barely know, frankly." He had a gulp of the pop. "I'm just a newbie nobody to him. If it wasn't for the coincidence that you and I knew each other in high school, I would never have been on his radar."

"But you did come to see me to talk about the case."

"Yes. But I'd also like to reconnect, get to know you as an adult. Not to pick up where we left off, no, but—"

"Not going to happen," she said.

". . . Why?"

"Not right now, anyway. I'm just trying to get to know myself. I'm still in therapy. It's a day-at-a-time thing for me. After what happened, I don't have any desire to have any man in my life. Even my old high school crush."

The latter had put a small smile in the midst of a largely sad expression. "And you're not going to talk to me about what happened to your family, either, are you?"

"I'm not," she said. "I don't talk to anybody about that. Not even my shrink."

He nodded slowly. "I can understand that. But like you said: 'right now.' Things will change for you, Jordan. They *are* changing. I'd like to be a part of that, even a small part."

She just shrugged. She began to rise, saying, "Thank you for the apple juice."

He took her gently by the arm and this time she did jerk away, and glare at him. Then he motioned calmly, with both hands, for her to sit back down.

For some reason, she did.

Glancing around, not wanting to be overheard, he almost whispered, "Jordan, I think what happened to your family was just one of a number of terrible crimes committed by the same monster."

"You do."

"I do. It sounds like something from TV or the movies, I know, but serial killers are real, from Jack the Ripper to Ted Bundy. I believe a serial killer took your family from you, and I think he's still out there . . . worse, I think he's taking other families and leaving a single family member behind. To suffer, maybe. Or to keep his horror alive somehow. . . . I'm sorry. I know this must be disturbing to you. . . ."

She was sitting there frozen. Had he read her mind? How much did he know? Did he somehow know her intentions? Nothing she'd said could have tipped him.

"I studied the case all through high school and college," he said. "The deeper I dug, the more crimes I found that were similar to what you and your family suffered."

"You *studied* us?"

"Not in any kind of . . . clinical way. I care about you and your family. From the start, I was just trying to understand something that seemed incomprehensible."

"Go on."

"The deeper I dug, especially once I was on the force, the more I became convinced a serial killer was responsible for what happened to your family—one that had not yet been identified by the FBI, who are in charge of such things."

She cocked her head, as if hearing that were difficult. "So the Cleveland PD is looking into it, until the FBI can be convinced—is that right?"

"Not exactly. As I said, Sergeant Grant is helping out on the Strongsville homicides, and there are enough similarities with your case to attract his attention."

"Then who is looking into the possibility of a serial killer being responsible?"

A sheepish look crossed Mark's face. "Uh . . . right now?"

"Well, of course right now."

". . . Me."

"You."

He leaned forward. "I've shared my views with my partner, who's a veteran detective, and he sees merit in my theory."

"Theory?"

"That's all it is right now, and I've also told my captain about it, and he's authorized me to work on the case, too."

"Full-time?"

"No. Very much part-time. Actually . . . on my own time."

"I can't believe what I'm hearing."

He raised his palms to her as if in surrender, but that wasn't what he was doing. "Jordan, it's a start. And with your cooperation, I can put enough together to get the Cleveland PD onboard, and then the FBI."

She wasn't sure she wanted that. All she knew for certain was she wanted the intruder for herself. For her own justice.

Nor did she feel like telling Mark about the serial killer offshoot of group, though if he was working on a similar theory, maybe he'd have information they could use. "I'll think about it," she said.

"Okay. Can't ask any more than that."

She rose. "You have a card or something?"

He fished out his wallet, removed a card, then got up and handed it to her, their fingers brushing. The thought of any man touching her had been revolting to her, for a very long time. This was . . . all right.

"If I decide to do this," she said, "I'll call you."

"That would be great."

She raised an eyebrow and lifted a lecturing finger. "*You* don't call me. Bother me about it, your chances of getting any cooperation out of me are nil. One thing I don't need is a stalker."

"Understood," Mark said. "If I haven't heard from you in, say, a week . . . ?"

"Then you won't be."

"All right," he said. "I'll respect that."

"That would be wise."

She started to move away, and he said, "You *were* interested, then, back in high school? I thought you had a thing for our quarterback."

She looked back at him. "Pete Harris? Just another dumb jock. I was into smart boys. Guys who used their heads for something besides sticking a helmet on."

He looked so disappointed, hearing that, and his face was the high school kid's. She felt a rush of warmth for him, not love and certainly nothing sexual. More sympathy.

So she made herself smile and said, "Kickers are kind of the intellectuals of the gridiron, don't you think?"

And she turned her back on him and walked away, after getting just a glimpse of his grin. Oddly enough, her smile lingered all the way to the checkout lane.

But it was long gone by the parking lot, by which time she was annoyed with herself again.

Okay, so he was sweet in his way. But there was no way she could ever call him. Jesus Fuckin' Christ on a goddamn crutch, she had almost flirted with him at the end there. Her mouth had spoken without benefit of her brain. She would toss his card in the bin outside the automatic door. That's exactly what she would do.

But she didn't.

Instead it went into a jeans pocket.

Jordan sat on the couch with Kara in the St. Dimpna's sunroom, having just finished telling the slender, punky blonde about the grocery-store encounter with Mark Pryor.

"You are such a slut," Kara squealed, exploding with laughter as she gave Jordan a big shove, nearly knocking her over.

The two women laughed.

"Touching a guy's fingers makes me a slut, does it?"

"Honey, with your issues, that's like getting to third base on the first frickin' date."

They both laughed again. Neither did that very often, and seldom apart. But it felt good to Jordan, and to Kara, too, obviously.

"So," Kara asked, "*are* you going to talk to him? Sounds like he wants to help."

Jordan mulled that for a moment, then said, "Maybe."

"Good. Opening up might be good for you."

"Never mind that shit. What I need is to find out what he knows, if any-thing."

"That's the only reason? To get more information for your own . . . vendetta?"

"Yes," Jordan said, no hesitation.

"This Mark is definitely nutty enough about you to rate a bunk in here."

"Maybe."

"No maybe about it. He's a cop because of you. Because he wants to find the 'monster' who did all that bad shit to you and yours. He may be cute, and I get the distinct impression he is . . . but he's a whack job, too, honey."

"So I should avoid him then?"

"Hell no! He sounds like just your type."

They laughed again, not as hard. Too much truth in it.

Finally Jordan said, "There won't be anything between us. Mark is cute, and nice and sweet and everything. But there's only room for one man in my life."

"The one you're gonna kill, you mean?"

"That's right. Mr. Wrong."

"Damn straight," Kara said, with a grin that even Jordan knew reflected her friend's mental illness. They bumped fists.

Jordan spoke little at the support group meeting, her mind on other things. She did her best to seem attentive, but she was thinking ahead about sharing her encounter with Mark Pryor with the smaller spin-off group. Finally she decided it was best to keep that to herself, for now anyway. If she decided to talk to him, then she would share the result with the subgroup.

The coffee shop was becoming a popular place after support group meetings. In addition to their little investigative team, Jordan noticed an increasing number of other members relaxing there after every meeting. Little interaction, though—some sat as couples, others alone, none in a group as big as theirs. Postgroup, everybody went out of their way not to call attention to anyone else, as if they were members of a secret society, determined not to be discovered by the world at large.

To everyone's surprise (including herself), Jordan called the meeting to order.

"I've been thinking about Levi's geography theory," she said to the little circle gathered at its regular table, "as it applies to the two-year time frame."

"And the gap in that time frame," David said.

"Yes."

Levi said, "That could be the key. If we're able to fill in that gap, we'll have something to take to the authorities."

There were murmurs of agreement, and she felt oddly guilty withholding that she had turned away one representative of the authorities already, and had another on the string—Grant and Mark respectively.

"Problem is," Levi said glumly, "I've been digging into this for some time now and can't find a damn thing for those two years."

"Nothing?" Jordan asked.

David said, "Do I have to remind everybody that the lack of murder victims is a good thing?"

"Not in this case," the skater boy said.

Kay said, "Now, Levi *has* come up with a few possibilities, don't forget."

"But nothing that seems concrete," David said.

Jordan turned to Kay and asked, "What about your case?"

"*My* case?" Kay asked. "I don't have a case. Not in the sense that—"

"You never know," Jordan said. "In police terms, our killer has an MO that's all over the map. And what happened to your family fits into our time gap."

Taken aback, Kay glanced at David, who gave her a small supportive smile and nod.

The plump, attractive redhead sighed. "My *case* is . . . my brother-in-law shot my sister, then turned the gun on himself."

"What if he didn't?" Jordan asked.

"The police seemed so *sure*," Kay said, frowning, yet with something like hope in her eyes.

How sad to think that this nice woman might find solace in knowing that a loved one had not been a suicide, but a murder victim.

"The police can always be wrong," Jordan said. "Look at Levi's family and the care the killer took to stage it. Levi was their best suspect for a while, because of that."

No one said anything, though they were all clearly thinking that through.

Jordan pressed: "Isn't that why we're here, because we think the cops missed something, and that all our cases might be one great big case?"

Again, no one spoke, but eyes were moving with thought.

"David and I," she went on, nodding to him, "and now the Sullys, all suffered home invasions of one kind or another. But Levi's case was different, and other crimes we're looking for might not necessarily follow that pattern, either."

Nods.

Jordan pounded her fist on the high-top table just hard enough to make coffee cups jump. "What if we're looking for a monster who preyed on *all* of us, including Kay? If we're right, the cops haven't tripped to this bastard in at least *ten years* . . . and there's every possibility my family *wasn't* his first."

Jordan was getting wide-eyed looks around the table.

David, with an admiring half smile, said, "Jordan, for a woman who didn't speak for ten years, you are doing just fine. Very well said."

But Kay was shaking her head, obviously shocked. "I didn't even live with Kathy and Walt. All of the rest of you shared a home with the loved ones you lost."

"Brittany Sully's brother didn't live with his family," Jordan said. "He was in fucking Afghanistan, and still is."

Kay blinked at the harsh language, but she and the rest again lapsed into a thoughtful silence.

Finally Levi turned to David. "She could be right."

"She makes a good case," the writer said. "She's just what we've needed—a fresh pair of eyes, and a sharp damn mind."

Levi ran the fingers of one hand through his long hair, taking in and then letting out a deep breath. "Now I know what to do, anyway—go over every family-related homicide for the four years between David's family and the Sullys."

Jordan glared at him. "You haven't done that *already?*"

"Stay cool, Catwoman. We're all feeling our way in the dark here. Sure, I checked any case that fit our profile even a little bit . . . but *not* the ones marked solved by the cops. Those I threw out, like Kay's."

"Whether Kay's case is our man's work or not," David said, "you raise a valid point, Jordan. We never considered that a crime the police had marked as 'solved' might have been wrongly attributed."

Elated, Jordan asked, "How many cases are we talking about?"

Levi said, "I'd have to go over my research, but maybe . . . a dozen?"

"That sounds manageable enough."

Levi smirked humorlessly, then ticked off on his fingers as he spoke. "We have a dozen homicide cases usually involving at least two murders. We're looking for clues the police missed in what are not closed cases, which means no access, and maybe even false information in the papers and on the Net, because the police likely used the explanation most readily presenting itself."

Elation left Jordan like air from a punctured tire.

"Take Kay's case," Levi was saying. "The cops presented a perfectly reasonable solution based on facts available at the crime scene. But if you're right, Jordan, they overlooked or outright missed evidence."

David said, "It's a notorious flaw in too much police work—ignore any evidence that doesn't fit your theory of the crime. A theory often formed very early on."

Levi said, "A dozen cases could take years to look at properly, particularly considering we're working off the grid, with no PD support."

"I can pitch in," Jordan said. "No problem."

Levi gave her a wan smile. "No offense, but you've been off the street for, what? Ten years? How are your computer skills?"

"I'm amazing at Google," she said, then immediately realized how lame that sounded. Maybe she should tell them about Mark, after all. Putting Levi together with the detective might add up to something.

Only that might lead the police to the intruder before she got to him. . . .

But that was a risk she would have to take, a contingency she would finesse when the time came.

Levi was saying, "The Freedom of Information Act gives us access to certain records in these closed cases. Northwestern Law's Center on Wrongful Convictions has been using that kind of info to get innocent people out of prison."

Kay said, "But we're trying to put somebody *in* prison."

"That door swings both ways," Levi assured her.

"With that much information," David said, "we're going to need help to sift through it all."

Levi said, "I'm the only one here with the computer skills to get that done . . . meaning no offense to Jordan."

"Excuse me." The male voice came from the table behind Jordan. "But, uh . . . I'm pretty good with computers."

They all turned. Phillip, from group, was sitting at the next table, something approximating a smile on his lipless, alabaster face. He sat alone, a saucer under his coffee cup, a napkin neatly in his lap, his outfit brown and tan today. He wore a too-white shirt, tie brown with tan diagonal stripes, jacket a medium brown, slacks crisp and tan, loafers brown and buffed to a high sheen.

"You don't even know what we're talking about," Jordan said, nastiness creeping into her voice unbidden.

"I've heard enough to have a pretty good idea," Phillip said, the breathing through his noseless nostrils as loud as if he were deep asleep.

But he wasn't.

"What," Jordan demanded, "you think eavesdropping is cool?"

David raised a hand to intercede, but Phillip ignored him, his eyes on Jordan. "No. But you weren't exactly whispering—any of you."

He had a point.

"You're lucky I'm a fellow group member," he said. "A civilian might report you to the police. . . . May I join you?"

He pulled his chair around and sat between Jordan and Elkins. Any irritation or even anger she felt was trumped by curiosity.

"Okay, man," Levi said, and grunted a laugh. "What do *you* know about computers?"

"I've always taken an interest in technology," Phillip said. "I was on the Internet years before it was widely in use." Then, looking around to make sure no one else was listening, he added in a whisper, "But since my attack, I've learned to hack security video, and your odd state and local police system."

Jordan was impressed. "Now that *is* cool," she said.

"I am hoping," Phillip said, gesturing to his ravaged countenance, eyes traveling around the table, "to find the man who did this to me. You see, I have . . . anger issues. Issues that I would imagine are similar to your own."

Kay said, "You *really* think you can help us?"

"I do," Phillip said. "What you're proposing isn't that much different from what I'm already up to."

"Any questions?" David asked their new member good-naturedly. "Or did you pick up everything already, from next door?"

Phillip smiled in his friendly yet ghastly way and said, "I've got the general idea, but I missed a beat here or there."

They looked to David, who took on the task of bringing the teacher up to date. Five minutes later, Phillip let out a sound that Jordan assumed was the scarred man's equivalent of a low whistle.

"And the police have no idea," he said, "that one individual may be responsible for all or most of these other atrocities?"

"The police assumption is," Jordan said, "they're separate cases."

"Which is still a possibility," Phillip said, smiling that awful smile. "Listening to you folks talk, you might well be caught up in mini-mass hysteria."

Jordan bristled. "If you're not *interested*—"

"I said, 'might be.'" He had raised a lecturing finger; he was a teacher, after all. "And on the other hand, if you're right about this, you may have discovered a serial killer that the powers-that-be have completely missed. And such perpetrators are not the epidemic that popular culture indicates, no—they are rare. Quite rare. They are jewels of evil."

Was Phillip some kind of poet, Jordan wondered. *Or just nuts, like the rest of them?*

"Then you're in?" David asked.

"Oh, most definitely," Phillip said. "Right or wrong, it's a crusade, and I'm always up for a good crusade. But I have to admit—and you need to know this—that if I have the opportunity to remove this cancerous creature from God's earth, I will. If the police get there first, well, good for them. But you all should be ready to live with what I might do."

Jordan liked Phillip more already.

But David said, "We're not vigilantes, Phillip."

"Oh, I understand. I'm not suggesting we go down that road . . . though if the opportunity presents itself . . . ? Well, I've said my piece."

They drank their coffee and made small talk while Levi and Phillip traded contact information. The pair decided they would get together to start going over the cases, and Jordan would provide them with what she'd recently culled from the Net about the attack on her family.

When the group broke up and left the coffee shop, she didn't notice Mark Pryor in his blue Equinox parked across the street, possibly because the detective was sitting on the passenger side, as a surveillance technique.

A good thing, too, that she didn't see him, because she had decided she would call Mark, and see what information she could glean from him.

And if she'd noticed him, maybe she would have changed her mind.

CHAPTER TEN

Mark watched as Jordan and several friends from her support group drifted out of the coffee shop. He hunkered down a little, making sure the young woman hadn't seen him. Then he used his cell-phone camera to take photos of her friends as they gradually went off to their individual lives.

He knew none of them (other than Jordan), but recognized the thriller writer David Elkins, who had some national fame and had been covered extensively in local media even before the tragedy that struck his family.

Of course, "tragedy" hadn't struck his family at all—a maniac had, very likely a maniac named Basil Havoc.

Despite his promise otherwise, Mark had followed Jordan home from the market the other day. He didn't feel wonderful about that, and hadn't made a habit of, well, stalking her. But now—on a rare day off—he had done so again, this time tailing her on a St. Dimpna's visit.

While she'd been inside, he had done a little investigating via his smart phone and discovered the facility hosted the Victims of Violent Crime Support Group meetings. That Jordan would, as part of release, be required to attend that group took no Holmes-like leaps of deduction. Nor was any leap required to figure that the little circle of friends with whom she left St. Dimpna's, walking over to the coffee shop together, were also members of that group.

Mark doubted they were just *any* members of the Victims Support Group, though, given what Mark knew about Elkins, and what happened to the man's family. The young detective had never interviewed the writer—like the Sully murders in Strongsville, the Elkins homicides were not his official concern. Nor were the Rivera homicides, at least not until Sergeant Grant had brought him in to try to win Jordan's cooperation.

But in the several days since he and Jordan had talked at the market, she had not called . . . and pressing her, he felt, would only make matters worse. Now, however, he had another way to go—next best thing to getting Jordan to talk might be getting her new friends to talk for her.

This would take precedence over pursuing Havoc. The exchange Mark had had with the gymnastics coach in that Italian restaurant's parking lot made it practically impossible to stay on the guy. This was a solo effort on Mark's part, after all, with only tacit approval from Captain Kelley—it wasn't like someone else could take over surveillance.

He would have to come at this another way.

Two hours later, a sports jacket thrown over (and a tie added to) the short-sleeved blue shirt and jeans he'd worn staking out the coffee shop, Mark drew his Equinox up in front of the writer's home. A broad two-story in need of paint, its front porch sagging slightly, the house itself had a melancholy cast, as if it hadn't weathered the atrocities that took place in these walls any better than its owner had.

Mark climbed the few steps to the porch, which creaked under his shoes, then rang the bell and waited. His fingertip was poised to try again when the door opened and Elkins stood before him.

Mark had seen photos of the writer, in the papers and in the case files; he'd watched interviews of the confident, even charismatic writer being interviewed about his latest book, before the world had crashed around him. This was a shell of that man, the navy polo and jeans loose on him, like clothes on a hanger.

"Yes?" Elkins said.

Mark already had the fold of leather out, open to his gold shield. "I'm Detective Mark Pryor."

Elkins nodded, barely. "Detective Pryor. How can I help you?"

"I'm doing some follow-up on the recent homicides in Strongsville, exploring some similarities to previous crimes in the greater Cleveland metro area."

"All right."

Man, this guy was making him work.

Mark said, "I'd like to talk to you about the perpetrator responsible for the loss of your family."

Elkins's eyes were unblinking and distant. "I don't think so."

"Sir?"

"Detective . . . frankly? I'd really rather not put myself through it again. Can you understand that?"

"Well, certainly, but—"

"I've told this story too many times over the years, to an endless succession of detectives, and it just never leads anywhere except to another sleepless night. I'm going to pass."

The writer started to close the door, but Mark gripped its edge, like a pushy solicitor, and said, "Mr. Elkins! I've been anxious to talk with you for a very long time. It took a devil of a long time for me to get the authority to do so. Please, sir, don't deny me."

The strained earnestness of that, the desperation, embarrassed Mark even as the words careened out; but at least it gave his reluctant host momentary pause.

". . . Look, son, I'm sure you're a real go-getter, but I am just not interested in the betterment of your career. And if your superiors refused to let you talk to me, maybe they had good—"

"Sir," Mark interrupted, and the words came out in a tumbling rush, "I'm convinced your wife and daughter were murdered by a serial killer, who is still at large, and very much active. You can't wish what happened to you and your family upon anyone else. Help me stop him."

Elkins just stared at the young detective—though Mark not getting the door shut in his face was a start, anyway.

"Give me five minutes," Mark said. "I'll share my theory with you, and if it strikes you as nonsense, just show me to the door. I'll go away and never bother you again."

And still the writer just stood there, with a poleaxed expression.

Then Elkins did something that Mark could never have expected: he smiled, just a little.

Then he stepped back, and motioned Mark inside.

"Thank you, sir," Mark said, "thank you."

The interior of the house somehow matched the outside, nothing really wrong, but something off-kilter. The living room was orderly. A television sat on a low stand to the left of the door; bookshelves rose almost to the ceiling on either side of it. On the far wall, a doorway led to the dining room, a formal table and a couple of chairs visible from the front door. The wall on the right was home to a sofa and a recliner, both facing a flat screen on a stand, an end table nestled between them.

Ordinary enough.

"Have a seat," Elkins said, gesturing casually toward the sofa.

"Thank you," Mark said, sitting.

"I can offer you a beer."

"No thank you, sir."

"Well, I'm having one."

And his host exited. For a moment Mark wondered if Elkins would return with a shotgun and run him off his property.

As he waited, Mark put together what it was that didn't feel right about this place. Though everything appeared neat enough, a thin patina of dust covered most surfaces—bookshelves, end tables, base of the TV, the stand itself. The carpeting, a high grade, hadn't been vacuumed in some time. The recliner nearby had regular wear patterns; the sofa on which Mark perched appeared barely used.

Like the exterior, the interior of the Elkins house remained in mourning.

Elkins returned with a bottle of Michelob and sat on the edge of the recliner, like a football fan studying an instant replay. The thriller writer had, on closer inspection, an even rougher look than had been obvious in the dim porch light. Dark circles camped under Elkins's blue eyes in a face drawn and pale.

"I'm very sorry for your loss, sir," Mark said.

Elkins managed an unenthusiastic nod.

Okay, Mark thought. *So much for sympathy. Down to business.*

"Mr. Elkins, I've followed your case from the beginning."

He frowned, half in irritation, half in curiosity. "You couldn't have been on the force back then, not unless you're older than you look."

"I'm twenty-eight, sir. I was a rookie, fresh out of the academy."

"So, then . . . you didn't work any part of the investigation?"

"No, sir," Mark said, well aware he'd gotten on the wrong end of the questioning. "My interest was because I was already looking—quite unofficially, I have to admit—into the somewhat similar murders of another fam-ily."

"Really. What family is that?"

"The family of a friend of mine."

"Don't be evasive, son. Not good interview technique. No way to open up a subject. What's your friend's name?"

Elkins was a thriller writer—he knew police procedure, even if only from research.

"Jordan Rivera," Mark said, not anxious to reveal that he had seen Elkins with her just hours ago, but having no choice, really.

Elkins was frowning again, this time in thought. "You and Jordan must be about the same age. Were you—"

"In high school together," Mark said, nodding, but wanting to finally get on the right side of this questioning, he added, "Sir, since I've never been able to question her about her family tragedy—she's reticent, as you must know—I thought talking to you about *your* case was, uh—"

"Better than nothing?" The writer was smiling again, a wry one this time, still barely enough to register.

"No! I, uh—"

"You could call not saying a word for ten years 'reticent,' I guess." He took a swig of Michelob. "Before I consider answering any of your questions, I've got a couple more for you."

"Okay."

"Have you seen Jordan since she got out?"

"Once."

"When?"

"A few days ago. We, uh, ran into each other at the grocery store."

"You mean, you tailed her there and arranged a meeting. I'll bet she saw right through it."

Now Mark smiled a little. "Yeah, she did."

"You really aren't very good at this, are you, son?"

"Not yet, sir. But I will be."

Elkins studied him. "Maybe. Maybe you will. You *have* tried talking to Jordan about her family?"

Mark shook his head. "She says she'll let me know when she's ready."

"The reason I ask is because she's in my support group."

This was delicate. If Mark pretended ignorance, and got caught at it, this interview—maybe *any* interview with Elkins—was over.

Mark said, "I thought you and she might be in group together."

"And why is that?"

"The Violent Crimes Support Group meets at St. Dimpna's. That's where Jordan was institutionalized, and she's a likely candidate."

"And I am, too."

Mark shrugged. "It's the only support group of its kind in Cleveland."

Elkins nodded. He seemed to be buying it.

"Detective, uh, Pryor, is it?"

"Yes, sir."

"We have a certain loyalty, you know. Group members. There's a confidentiality that's understood, like at an AA meeting."

"I guess that makes sense."

"And since Jordan hasn't talked to you, I shouldn't either." Elkins sat back in the chair, but did not push back to make it recline.

Mark felt he'd blown it—*gosh dang it!*

Then Elkins said, "At least not about *her* case. If you want to ask about *my* family, I might answer your questions."

"That would be very helpful, sir."

"So ask. Listen, how new at this are you?"

"I've been a detective a few months."

"So I should cut you some slack."

Mark grinned. "I wouldn't mind."

Elkins grinned back at him. "Well, I'm not going to. You said five minutes, and we're almost there."

No more stalling.

"You were gone when the attack occurred?"

"You already know that."

"And no one, none of your neighbors, saw anything unusual that night?"

"Come on. You know that, too. I thought you were going to present your theory."

Funny—he seemed testy and good-natured at the same time.

"Yes, sir. I started thinking about it back in high school, with Jordan's family. There just didn't seem to be any explanation for what happened to them, nothing beyond just . . . random evil at loose in the world."

"Nice phrase, son," the writer said. "But get to it."

"The more I studied, the more likely this seemed to fit the classic mode of a serial killer. I know, I know that they are rare, no matter what our pop culture puts out there. And there were problems—one was that he left Jordan alive. Another was that there was no even vaguely similar attack, at least not until your family six years ago. Some killers of this ilk will take a hiatus between episodes . . . but six years seems inordinately long."

"I don't disagree."

"As I got older, studied more, learned more, it finally occurred to me that this predator's hunting ground might be a far larger one than just the Cleve-land metro area."

Elkins set his glass down and sat forward again. "And where did that thinking take you?"

"Eventually, all across the country."

The writer's eyes widened. "Really?"

"Yes. Some here, in this region, but . . . well, I think I can tie together at least a dozen family murders to this one killer."

Now Elkins leaned forward so far he was almost off the chair, his prayerfully folded hands dangling between his legs. "And no one else has put these pieces together? The FBI has profilers and investigators working on just these kinds of rare cases."

"Maybe so," Mark said, "but there's no indication of that. My captain would be in the loop if the FBI was investigating the Cleveland-area homicides."

"So why hasn't the FBI noticed this killer?"

"Our predator is highly intelligent, maybe genius level. He knows not to have an immediately recognizable MO, so his methods vary—there's always extenuating circumstances that make the crimes look like something other than textbook serial killings."

"Such as?"

"Home invasions, primarily. One instance on the East Coast was made to look like a mob hit. He takes an approach that I would call diversionary."

"Where nationally have you tracked these cases?"

"Providence, the Bronx, the Midwest. So far, never the South, but with several out west."

Elkins was mulling it. "One man operating on that kind of scale—is it even possible?"

"For a suspect who travels a lot—with his business perhaps—it would be feasible, even fairly easy."

Elkins got up, leaving the beer bottle behind on an end table, and began to pace, to prowl.

"How would he go about targeting families?" the writer asked. "Ran-domly? My God, that's somehow more horrifying than think-ing your family *had* been targeted. Even a warped reason is, at least, a reason."

Mark had no answer for that. He asked, "No one ever found a commonality between you and the Riveras, did they?"

"Not really," Elkins said, returning to his chair, perching himself on its edge again. "We both had six-figure incomes, but that was about all."

"Didn't your daughter study gymnastics?"

"A couple of lessons—she was just a beginner. Why do you ask?"

"Jordan took a few gymnastics lessons, too. Just to build a foundation for her cheerleading. This never came up in the investigation?"

"Not that I know of. You seem quite conversant about Jordan, Detective Pryor. How well did you know her?"

"Not well, but we were friendly. The gymnastics aspect I learned from talking to several of our mutual friends from back in high school."

Elkins was no dummy. He wrote about crime, and the research that required gave him a leg up; and he created densely plotted thrillers, which meant he could put things together. Still, his next question jarred Mark.

"You've got a suspect, haven't you, Detective?"

"Well . . . suspect might be too strong a word. Let's say . . . person of interest."

"That's a stupid phrase," Elkins said, with a sneer that hinted at the man's underlying anger. "I hate that it's entered the law-enforcement lexicon. What the hell *is* a 'person of interest,' anyway?"

"A person who isn't a suspect yet, but is under consideration."

Elkins scowled. "I know that, Detective. It was a rhetorical question. *Mine* isn't—*who* is your 'person of interest'?"

"I'm sorry, sir. You're not a novice in these matters. You know I can't share that with you."

"Why don't I tell *you* then?"

"Sir?"

"Basil Havoc."

That didn't jar Mark—in a way, getting Elkins to identify Havoc as a suspect had been his intent, bringing up the gymnastics tie. But he was more and more impressed with the writer.

Mark asked, "Why would you mention Mr. Havoc as a possible suspect?"

Elkins returned to his beer for a sip and leaned back in the recliner, again not reclining. "Havoc was in charge of the gym where Akina went. He's a publicity hound and a prick. But not a killer."

"Why do you say that?"

"Why a publicity hound and a prick? He used my daughter's death to get on the news and talk about how much promise she had, as if she'd been his star student, which she most definitely hadn't been. It was nothing but a publicity grab for him and his gymnastics school."

"But he *did* coach Akina, right?"

Elkins grunted. "He may have worked with her once, maybe twice. Hell, he was barely ever at that 'school' of his. His flunkies actually trained the kids. Oh, he might have worked his magic with the best and the brightest, but the beginners' class? He might come over, say hello on the first day, give a little pep talk, then fade away."

Mark had watched video of Havoc's interviews again and again. The coach always made it sound like the girl was practically his protégé.

Elkins said, "He couldn't have picked my daughter out of a lineup of any six girls in that dump. If, as you say, Jordan wasn't serious about gymnastics, the chances of her having much personal contact with him are next to nil."

Had he singled out Havoc too soon, too easily? Mark wondered what he might have missed. *Who* he might have missed. . . .

"But maybe Havoc *isn't* your suspect," Elkins said. "Maybe it's one of Havoc's staff. You know, he was frequently out of town, judging tournaments and making personal appearances."

Mark sat up. "That kind of travel would be ideal for this killer."

"You've seen the case files, so you know CPD didn't look at Havoc very hard, if at all. He's *your* person of interest, not theirs."

"I didn't say that."

"Well, I don't find him a very interesting person at all."

Mark just sat there, the wind out of his sails.

"But maybe you're looking at Havoc's staff," Elkins went on. "Is *that* what you're up to?"

He hadn't been. Mark hadn't really looked into the staff carefully at all—didn't know who, or how many of them, traveled with the man.

But what about the encounter in the parking lot of Apollonia's? And Havoc's jab about the osso buco being "to die for"? Or had it been a jab? Could it have been nothing more than a guy spouting a cliché with an unfortunate, unintentional resonance, and Mark all too eagerly misinterpreting it?

"So is that it?" Elkins was asking. "You have a suspect on Havoc's staff?"

"I'm sorry, sir. Not at liberty to say."

"Then why did you bring up Havoc?"

"Actually, sir, *you* brought up Havoc. I merely pointed out that both girls studied gymnastics at his school, if briefly. It just demonstrates one connection I've found that was overlooked in the initial investigation of your family's murders. There might be others, and that's what I'd like to talk about."

"Maybe looking at Havoc and particularly his staff is worthwhile, and I wish you luck. But I have nothing to contribute."

"Sir . . ."

Elkins let out a sigh that filled the room. "Look, son. Detectives have come around every few months since this goddamn thing happened. They seem always to have some little new thread to pull on, but it winds up leading nowhere, and I have to revisit the . . . the *horror* of it all . . . over and over and over. And each time, it cuts off another little piece of me."

"I'm sorry you've been put through that," Mark said, "and needlessly. But those detectives, none of them have been pursuing the serial killer possibility, have they?"

"That's true. That is true."

"So they haven't looked for the kinds of connections that I have. Like your tragedy and Jordan's. And there are more, not just around here, but all over the map."

Elkins sipped more beer. He leaned back, rocked a little, thinking. Then a brusque laugh came out of him. "You know, Detective Pryor—it's funny."

"What is?"

"Some of my support group has been working on this very theory for a long goddamn time. Serial killer notion? And way at the beginning, when we first saw the pattern emerging, we took it to the police, and they basically patted us on the head and sent us on our way."

Someone else was investigating his theory? Victims of the killer, no less. Were they Jordan's circle of friends he'd seen exiting the coffee shop?

Mark gave his host a bitter grin. "You and me both, Mr. Elkins."

"Huh?"

"Sir, my investigation is strictly off the books. I've managed to be taken just seriously enough by my captain to secure permission to explore this on my own time."

"Are you *sure* you and Jordan weren't good friends?"

Mark ignored that. "What made you and those other group members think a serial killer might be behind these different cases? No one else did."

Elkins sent the question back: "What made *you* think this was a serial killer?"

"Families as victims. That's the common dominator."

The writer sat forward again, nodding. "That was our thinking, too. But they all seemed too different to be connected."

"The details vary," Mark said. "I believe we have a shrewd actor who knows all about MO. But underlying these assorted atrocities is a desire to destroy a family, leaving one family member alive to suffer."

Now Elkins was looking at Mark in an entirely new way. "Maybe I can get the group to meet with you. You could be our door into the police."

"I'm anxious to see what you've got," Mark admitted. "But I don't think I can share what I've found with you."

"That doesn't seem like much of an arrangement."

"I know. But if my superiors do finally accept my theory, my investigation will suddenly be a heck of a lot more official than it is now. I can't be seen as having compromised it by showing potential evidence to civilians."

Elkins was nodding again. "I can understand that. Perhaps . . . perhaps it's enough that we share the same goal."

Mark nodded back. "To put this monster away, yes."

Before they could go any further, Mark's cell chirped. He slipped it out of his jacket pocket, saw an unfamiliar number, and almost ignored it. But a hunch told him to answer—wasn't he waiting for a call, after all? He hit the button, knowing it couldn't be her.

Yet it was: "This is Jordan Rivera."

Getting quickly to his feet, Mark put a hand over the phone and told Elkins, "I need to take this."

Elkins waved permission and Mark excused himself to the front porch.

"Are you there?" Jordan asked.

"Sorry," Mark said. "I needed to step away from something."

"Okay."

"I'm, uh . . . a little surprised you actually called."

"Not as surprised as I am."

He thought of how she'd looked when he saw her at the grocery store, close-up for the first time in so many years, as beautiful now as she had been in high school—maybe more so. Not a lot of makeup, dressed casually, a baseball fan like him, apparently, judging by the Indians cap.

"I'm ready for us to talk," she said.

"When and where?" he asked, perhaps a little too eagerly.

"Whoa, big boy. I'm not looking to hook up or anything. This is police business. Right?"

"I know, sorry," Mark said, still too darn eager.

"Come over to my place at nine. Bring pizza. Thin crust. Sausage. See you then?"

"Sure. What's your address?"

"Your buddy Grant didn't give it to you?"

"No."

"Oh, I get it. You're asking because I'm not supposed to know you followed me home from the market the other day."

Busted.

"Sorry," he said automatically.

"Don't sweat it," she said.

"You mad?"

"Fucking furious."

"I'm really, really sorry."

"It's all right," she said. "The only men I've ever known I could trust were my father and my brother, and they don't seem to be around."

He was searching for something to say to that when she clicked off.

CHAPTER ELEVEN

Levi Mills was already doing research online when David Elkins phoned with a new name for him to start digging into; meanwhile, the writer would drive across the city to meet up with him.

Though this name meant nothing to Levi, he didn't question his fellow group member, just followed his instructions, looking forward to having David come over. The writer had sort of taken Levi under his wing, a year ago or so, and the younger man looked upon the older as a mentor, maybe even a father figure.

By the time he heard his friend's footsteps out in the hall of the Shaker Square apartment building, Levi had already amassed a pretty good pile of information on this new lead. David would be pleased, a reaction that always gave Levi a boost.

As for his apartment, it was nice enough, if on the small side— modest living room, one bedroom, half kitchen, fair rent, and no bugs, though calling the walls paper-thin wasn't as much an exaggeration as you might think. Good thing Levi liked his neighbors, that lesbian couple next door—in addition to friendly if quick conversations in the hall, he knew what TV shows they watched, what music they liked, what they argued about, and sometimes, deep into the evening, heard sounds that reminded him he hadn't had a date in a very long while. . . .

Life for a single gay guy in Cleveland wasn't always easy. But in Ashtabula, it would have been impossible, which was why he stayed in the closet till he moved, which had been right after high school. His parents had saved a little money and there'd been some insurance; still, if some very nice people from the PTA and Planned Parenthood hadn't raised funds to help him go to college, he would have been shit out of luck.

Leaving Ashtabula when he did gave him guilt pangs, but that little town just wasn't a place where he could be himself. Where he could grow. He still kept in touch with a few high school pals and some of his parents' friends who mounted that fund-raising drive; but the honest truth was: first chance he had, he split.

The siren's call he heeded took him not to France or New York or Hollywood, not even San Francisco, and not very far from home, at that. The ethnically diverse campus of Cleveland State University offered a place where Levi could be openly gay and nobody gave a toss. That wasn't always true in Cleveland itself, particularly in blue-collar areas, but overall a city that size offered possibilities way beyond what his hometown could offer.

For three years he dug in and worked hard and graduated early. He didn't find anything in the computer field, but at least he got a job, and quickly, working as a night desk clerk at a Marriott Courtyard. Nothing spectacular, but it paid the bills, and his computer skills had been noted by management. Who knew? Maybe he'd move up in the company.

The printer was spitting out the final page of his research as Levi opened the door for David. The writer wore jeans and a navy polo, dressed up compared to Levi in his ragged Chuck Taylors, jeans, and FREE PUSSY RIOT T-shirt. David lugged a laptop in a shoulder bag.

Moving through the living room with its secondhand array of sofa, three chairs, coffee table, and end tables, David went straight for the kitchen and took a seat at the old Formica table, the other end of which Levi's laptop, printer, and accessories dominated. This served as Levi's office (he regularly ate on a TV tray in front of his small flat screen in the living room).

David, unpacking his gear and plugging in, asked, "Find anything?"

"Hmm-hmm. But first, what brought this on? Where'd you come up with this name, anyway?"

"Havoc is somebody I dismissed early on as a suspect. Looks like I may have been hasty."

The writer told Levi about Detective Mark Pryor's visit, and their wary exchange of information.

Levi frowned. "So this Pryor guy didn't really cop to Havoc being his suspect."

"No," David admitted. "But he didn't deny it. And this opens up a whole new area for us—not just Havoc, but his coworkers."

"Sounds like it's reopening an *old* area."

David's shrug was elaborate. "Maybe I'm grasping at straws. We haven't had a glimmer of hope in . . . how long? Now this Pryor is actively investigating, and we've added Jordan Rivera to our team. . . . Maybe, at long last, we're getting somewhere."

"That's great. That's terrific. But, David, let's not set ourselves up for another disappointment. This needs to be a methodical process—"

"Skip it," David said testily. "Show me what you've got."

Levi was gathering the computer printouts when another knock came at the door. Both men turned, David with a nervous start.

"Damn," David said. "Did that cop follow me?"

"No," Levi said, "that'll be Phillip."

"Yeah?"

Levi was halfway to the door. "I called him after you called me. If we're going down a new road, even if it's another blind alley, we can use the com-pany."

"He does appear to know his stuff," David said.

Levi opened the door and Phillip paused until Levi gestured him in. As usual, the teacher wore a nicely cut suit, navy blue, with a white shirt, red-and-navy striped tie, and black loafers—a laptop bag slung over his shoulder.

"Welcome to the madhouse," Levi said as they shook hands.

David came over and held out his hand and the two men shook, with the friendliness of Phillip's smile making it not quite so ghastly. The plastic surgery repairs to the man's damaged features had so far worked no wonders.

David said, "Nice of you to come on such short notice, Mr. Traynor."

Traynor was Phillip's last name. Before their team meeting at the coffee shop had broken up late this morning, Levi had gathered the basic information—the last name of the support group member as well as his cell phone number.

"Glad to be included," Phillip said, his breathing clearly audible. "Levi said you had a new name for him to check."

"That's right," David said. "We may have a lead."

"Splendid," Phillip said.

Levi led the two men to the kitchen table, where Phillip set up his laptop, as well. Playing host, Levi fetched coffee for Phillip, a Michelob for David (Levi was not a beer drinker but stocked some for his friend), and a Diet Pepsi for himself. Meanwhile, his two guests chatted.

"Well," David was saying, "I know your last name now, and that you're a teacher, but the rules of the support group have kept us strangers in many ways. What kind of teaching do you do exactly, Phillip? You do prefer 'Phillip' to 'Phil'?"

"I do prefer Phillip, if that isn't too pretentious."

"Not at all. I prefer David to Dave. We'll be pompous together."

The two men exchanged smiles.

"Of course," Phillip said, "I know about you, at least the basics—I believe just about everyone knows David Elkins and his thrillers."

"I wish that were true. And who knows? Maybe someday I'll even write another."

Levi joined them, saying, "Phillip and I spoke on the phone earlier, got to know each other a little. His teaching gig is pretty interesting. Pretty cool."

Phillip shrugged, as he offered another lipless smile. "I teach online. Levi says he envies me, because my job pays fairly well, yet my time is my own."

Levi had not been surprised to learn that Phillip's current teaching did not involve standing before a classroom, not with his compromised countenance.

"Sounds like interesting work," David said. "What is it you teach?"

"Religion, actually. Of the Judeo-Christian variety."

"The Bible, then."

"I offer a course on the Torah, as well. I'm afraid my work is quite mundane compared to writing novels."

"Plenty of action, sex, and violence in those books," David said, and sipped his beer.

"Sounds very cool to me," Levi said. "But then I'm a night clerk at a Marriott. What do I know?"

Levi handed around his stacks of computer printouts. Then David repeated his story about his meeting with the detective.

Phillip was frowning, or at least seemed to be—the face reminiscent of a burn victim made it hard to tell exactly. "Why did you lead Detective . . . Pryor, is it? Why did you lead Detective Pryor to believe that you had dismissed the possibility that Havoc was a good suspect?"

"I knew it wouldn't dissuade him," David said, "and at that stage of the conversation, I was keeping from him that we were doing our own inves-tigation."

"But later you did tell him. And invited him to visit our little group within the greater group."

"Yes. You think that's a bad idea?"

Phillip shook his head. "No. Not unless he tries to shut us down. Judging by what you say, I doubt he will—after all, his investigation is only lightly sanctioned by his superior. He can use all the help he can get."

"That's my take on it," David said, nodding. "And I think he'll loosen up about what he knows."

Levi then shared the basic background information on Havoc that he had dug up while waiting for the others to arrive.

"I'm afraid," Levi said, finishing up, "I couldn't ascertain whether Havoc was in the area when the Riveras were killed, or your family, David. He appears to have been in Cleveland for the Strongsville homicides."

"That information," Phillip said, "is somewhere . . . even if it's only on the school's computer, or Havoc's home one."

David asked, "Levi, what's the size of Havoc's coaching staff?"

"Seven," Levi said. "Two more are strictly office workers . . . I printed out all of the information available at his website."

The two men paged through the material Levi had provided.

Phillip said, "Any one of those seven . . . perhaps even all nine . . . could be a viable suspect."

David nodded. "Yes, but Pryor is concentrating on Havoc."

"Why?" Phillip asked. "It strikes me as thin—that David's daughter and Jordan took gymnastics at Havoc's school may be a simple coincidence."

"Pryor did mention," David said, "that he believes the 'predator,' as he calls him, may have committed murders in New York and Providence, and several others out west."

"Where out west?"

"He wasn't specific."

Now Phillip's frown was definitely able to be discerned. "And he didn't say how Havoc might be connected to any of these homicides?"

"No. Frankly, he didn't even imply it."

Levi said, "I think finding out the dates Havoc was out of town, and his whereabouts . . . where he was lecturing or judging or competing . . . may be vital."

Phillip said to Levi, "If he was making public appearances, there should be plenty of mentions online."

"Phillip," Levi said, "Havoc is something of a minor celebrity. His name gave up over half a million hits. Sorting through them is going to take awhile."

"Understood," Phillip said. "But worth doing."

Levi nodded.

"In the meantime," Phillip said, "I'll look into Havoc's staff."

"Where do I come in?" David asked.

Levi could tell David was taken aback, just a little, at the way Phillip had asserted himself—before, David was always clearly the leader.

"If I may be frank," Phillip said, "what skills do you bring to the party?"

The question obviously irritated the writer, and Levi stepped in: "David's Internet skills are adequate at best, but he is one badass researcher. He doesn't let go, once he latches onto something, dog-with-a-bone kinda deal. And he has contacts, including cops and forensics experts, all over the country."

Phillip unleashed a grotesque smile. "David, my friend, I meant no offense. May I suggest a plan of attack?"

David, just a little stiffly, said, "Certainly."

"Those cases out west? Search online for murders, say, west of the Mississippi that may present a similar MO to our predator's."

"If I may be frank," David said, "that sounds like needle-in-the-haystack stuff."

"And time-consuming as hell," Levi said.

Phillip shrugged. "If it were easy, the FBI would be on the trail of this madman already."

David sighed, nodded. "No argument there."

Over the next hour, silence prevailed, as they dug into their respective tasks at their respective laptops. Levi continued sorting through the Internet mentions of Havoc, and then ran checks on two of the family homicide cases that were on his own list of possibles by their man.

Finally, he spoke up. "*Guys!* Those two East Coast murders that Detective Pryor thinks Havoc is tied to? I think I have them. And something more."

The other two were looking up from their keyboards at him expectantly.

"I've found gymnastics meets that put Havoc—or one of his staff—within driving distance. One in New York, one in Providence."

"Very good, Levi," David said, smiling.

Phillip said, "We really need a list, going back as far as possible, for the gymnastics meets Havoc and his people attended out of state, to track other crimes."

Levi turned to David and said, "All right, David, you and I will switch tasks."

"Why?"

"I've almost certainly pinpointed Pryor's two murders out east. Now that I have the details, you go over those. You're better qualified for that. And now that *I* know how to track what we're looking for, I can tie any other murders to Havoc's travel history."

"But we don't have that yet."

"We will. Now those half-million hits don't seem so overwhelming."

Phillip was nodding. "No, they don't."

Levi went on: "Granted, this assumes Havoc goes to all or most of the big gymnastics meets, and takes his staff with him, at least some of them. If that assumption is correct, we'll soon know where Havoc's traveled, and I can look for crimes within, say . . . a hundred miles of a possible related homicide. We can broaden the search from there."

Phillip was nodding. "Excellent work, young man. Stellar work."

They went back to their individual tasks.

Half an hour later, Phillip raised a hand, as if stopping a unit of soldiers trudging through a jungle. "Havoc may not be our predator."

Levi sat up, rolling his head around, rubbing sore neck muscles.

David leaned forward, squinting in interest. "Why do you say that?"

"Let's start with the fact that Havoc's assistant—one Stuart Carlyle—has been with the man from the very start of the school."

"How in hell did you find *that* out?"

"I hacked Havoc's payroll records," Phillip said, as casually as if reporting the time.

David frowned in astonishment. "And you managed that *how?*"

Phillip shrugged. "It's not terribly difficult with some of these small businesses. Really, their security is laughable. Figuring out the password is always the hardest part. The rest is strictly rote."

"You figured out *Havoc's* password?"

Phillip waved that off, as if batting away a bothersome gnat. "Most people who aren't computer savvy use something they care about, something easy to remember. In Havoc's case, it was something that applied to both gymnastics and money."

Levi and David traded a look that said they had no idea what that might be.

"Balance," Phillip said.

David blinked at him. "Balance?"

"Balance sheet, balance beam. Not exactly NSA-level encryption."

Levi, impressed, immediately started searching Havoc's travel history. Within minutes, he said, "Oh yeah."

David and Phillip's eyes were on him.

"In 2008 in Boston, and 2010 in Hartford, Carlyle had a room in the same hotel as Havoc. With homicides in Providence and the Bronx, easy enough transits."

"So instead of one suspect," David said, "there's at least two."

Levi said, "We need to know how *many* possible suspects we have, out of Havoc's staff."

"That may not be as difficult as you might think," Phillip said. "The two office workers have been with Havoc for eight and ten years, respectively." He gave Levi their names.

After a few moments, Levi said, "Neither is on the hotel register for either Boston or Hartford."

"Which means," David said, "we can probably eliminate them."

"Of the remaining six trainers," Phillip said, "four were hired in the last two years."

David asked, "Has Havoc been having trouble keeping help?"

Levi said, "He must be hard on the trainers. Anyway, they're all ruled out because they weren't employees when the two East Coast murders occurred."

David asked, "What about the other two?"

Phillip said, "Bradley Slavens and Patti Roland."

"A female trainer in the mix now."

Levi said, "Both were on the Hartford and Boston trips."

"Jordan's family was attacked by a man," David reminded them.

"If one killer is responsible for these atrocities," Phillip said, "the woman is eliminated, as Jordan tells us the Riveras were attacked by a man. But ruling the Roland woman out entirely would be a mistake."

David cocked his head. "Why's that?"

Levi, who followed Phillip on this line of thought, said, "Bradley Slavens or Patti Roland could be working with Carlyle or Havoc."

David frowned. "A killing team? Like the Hillside Strangler pair? That's rare. Particularly a male-female duo."

"But not unheard of," Phillip said.

"No," the writer said. "There's Doug Clark and Carol Bundy, Karla and Paul Bernardo, Gerald and Charlene Gallego."

"You do know your stuff, David. Yes, such teams go all the way back to the Honeymoon Killers, the notorious Martha Beck and Raymond Fernandez, and undoubtedly long before—Ahab and Jezebel, perhaps, in First and Second Kings."

Nodding (though he knew none of these references), Levi said, "Other than Jordan, no one has gotten so much as a glimpse of the murderer—why can't *he* be *they*?"

David nodded. "So, it could be Havoc or Carlyle or Slavens working alone . . ."

". . . or," Phillip continued, "any one of them working with the help of one or more of the others. They were all in the right cities at the time of the murders in question."

David's eyes were tight. "*Finally* we're making sense of this."

"Are we?" Levi asked. "I still don't get it. The *why* of it."

Phillip asked, "How so?"

Levi floundered for the words. "It's just that . . . killing families, de- stroying families . . . *why?* There has to be a motive—these may be insane acts but they are not random fits of rage, they are planned, they are stage-managed, and what the hell motive could Havoc, or *any* of them, have?"

"An insane act," David said, "by definition lacks a rational motive."

"But not *a* motive," Phillip insisted. "To a madman, an irrational motive would seem quite sane."

"I mean, Havoc's enjoyed success," Levi said. "He came to this country, built something, made it thrive—what would possess him to attack families as a sort of . . . sick hobby?"

David said, "There are individuals among us who are both highly intelligent and deeply insane. A sociopath, for example, essentially mimics behavior, like compassion and love, he witnesses in others. And plays that against those others."

Phillip said, "This is no sociopath."

"No. But he's smart *and* he's crazy. That much we know." David sat forward. He got his cell phone out and gestured with it. "I think we should share what we've learned with Pryor, and right away."

The teacher was shaking a lecturing forefinger. "Your young detective is very inexperienced and prone to jumping to conclusions. If we don't ground him in sufficient information, he'll foul this up, and worse, he'll turn his superiors against him and they'll never listen to him again, much less us. We have to keep digging until we can give Pryor something more substantial than a longer suspect list."

Clearly, David didn't like that, but Levi could see the writer's face moving from irritation to acceptance. It was like watching someone go through Kübler-Ross's five stages of death right in front of you.

"Okay," David said. "Let's start with motive. How are we going to find that?"

Phillip asked, "How would you shape a motive planning one of your thrillers?"

David let out air. "I would determine what my villain was after, what he would do to achieve it, and what he had been through to get him to that point."

Phillip's lipless smile was something Levi couldn't quite get used to. "Is that what we're up against?" the teacher asked. "A 'villain'? Evil, in the Old Testament sense?"

"Yes," David said. "I guess so."

"Evil *born* that way? Or created by circumstance and experience?"

"What's the difference? Does it matter how a fire starts, once it's raging?" Then David realized what he'd said, and apologized.

Levi waved that off, then David said to him, "Are we going to find our villain on the Internet, do you think?"

"Maybe, but we'll start by digging into the lives of four people instead of just one."

David shook his head, smiled ruefully. "Fellas, you don't suppose we're in over our heads, do you?"

"I don't *think* it, I *know* it," Levi said. "But nobody else is stepping up."

"Except one lone rookie detective," David reminded him.

Phillip said, "I admire you, and all the rest of our little team. It takes a lot of strength, and a good deal of tenacity, to do what you're doing."

"Same back at you," Levi said. "And we're not the only ones with tenacity—our 'villain' has it, too. He's been working at his 'hobby' for at least a decade."

David was staring into nothing. "You really have to hate people," he said, "to be able to do what this predator does, for as long as he's been doing it."

Phillip let out a raspy sigh. "The poor soul probably doesn't even see them as people anymore. They likely became something else to him a long time ago. Something less than human."

"If not people," Levi asked, "what *are* they to him?"

"When we figure that out," David said, "that's when we'll have him."

"Tall order," Phillip said.

"But we've made progress," Levi said. "The three of us, a trio damaged by him or the likes of him. Sitting at computers, fighting back."

"True," David said. "I'm something like encouraged. If our prey ever gets wind of us, though, it may take a very different kind of fighting back."

CHAPTER TWELVE

The moment Jordan ended the call with Mark Pryor, she knew he'd think she was stalling. But she'd told him she was on her way out, and that was true, throwing on a denim jacket over her T-shirt and jeans, pulling on her cycle helmet. Soon she was climbing onto her scooter, laptop computer in her backpack, ready to head to Kay Isenberg's place.

All the members of their support group spin-off team had long since exchanged last names and addresses. Having Kay's address had given Jordan a new lead, and she had already done some preliminary research into the alleged murder-suicide of Katherine and Walter Gregory, Kay's sister and brother-in-law.

This allowed her to switch gears, gain a different angle of view, getting her out of her own head and away from the deaths of her family, and the lost loved ones of Levi and David. Although going from those tragedies to another was hardly a change of pace, it did provide an opportunity for her to look at something new that was possibly related, and with fresh eyes.

Kay's house was a modest bungalow in a clean, quiet neighborhood. Painted a light blue with flower beds crowding the porch, a tiny tree providing almost no shade to its side of the postage-stamp lawn, the place exuded a warm, homey feel that belied any turmoil within. Jordan took off her helmet, shook her hair free, and strode up the short front walk.

She rang the bell and Kay opened the door almost at once, a hint of a smile on the careworn face. She looked typically neat but not prim in a denim skirt and a pale blue blouse, her white-touched red hair in a loose bun.

"So nice to see you, Jordan, away from group. Come in, come in."

"Nice seeing you, too," Jordan said.

Kay led Jordan into a smallish living room dominated by rows of shelved Hummel figurines covering most of one wall, the overflow in glass curio cabinets that straddled the archway into the dining area. Little eyes stared at them.

Slightly embarrassed, Kay said, "I see you noticing the Hummels."

Jordan nodded. How could she not?

"They were Katherine's children, in a way. I say that because she and Walt never had any kids—they couldn't have any . . . but she made a sort of family out of them."

"Oh."

"They kind of overwhelm my little place, don't they? They looked nicer in Katherine and Walt's place."

"I'll bet."

"Funny thing is, I've kept buying them, you know, each year's issue, since. . . ."

"Well," Jordan said, "they're very nice."

"Let's sit down, shall we?"

The hostess gestured toward the small floral sofa and matching chair, near a coffee table across from a low-slung stand with a flat-screen television and cable box. A peace lily in a vase perched on another tiny table.

Jordan sat on the chair, more comfortable than it looked, and set her backpack and helmet at her feet.

"Something to drink, dear?"

"I'm fine, thanks."

Nervously, Kay sat at the near end of the sofa.

Jordan said, "We don't have to do this. It can wait. Or we can never do it."

Kay sat silent for a long moment. Had Jordan's bluntness offended the woman?

Jordan said, "It would be good if you *could*. I just mean, we don't *have* to. . . ."

"I *want* to," Kay said. "No. That's not right . . . I *need* to. If we can talk about this, and find an explanation for why Walt would do such a thing to himself and Katherine . . . or even learn that perhaps he *wasn't* responsible . . . then maybe I can start to understand . . . or to *process* it, or at least . . . accept it."

Yanking her laptop from her backpack, Jordan said, "Cool. Then let's get started."

Kay, clearly apprehensive, nonetheless nodded.

Logging on, using her cell phone as a hot spot, Jordan said, "Levi showed me how to access the police file. I've read it and there's not a lot to it."

Shaking her head, Kay said, "I tell you, they were happy, Walt and Katherine. I *knew* they were. Walt had no reason to do *anything* like that."

"The only thing that really jumped out at me is the lack of any sign of struggle. If the police assumptions are correct, your sister just stretched out on the bed and let her husband shoot her."

Kay shuddered. "I can't imagine that happening. I don't think it's possible Katherine would do such a thing. The police insist these . . . these complicit murder-slash-suicides are more common than you'd think."

Jordan nodded. "That sometimes people just give up."

"Yes. But even so, to die by gunshot? I always thought a couple that decided to die together took sleeping pills and maybe went to their garage and turned on the engine and. . . ."

Kay began to weep. Tissues were already waiting on the coffee table—the woman had prepared for the occasion. Jordan waited politely, feeling uncomfortable but resigned.

Finally Jordan said, "Is it possible they were having some sort of trouble—like you said, health or money or something—and Katherine just never told you?"

"Katherine told me *everything*." A sad smile touched the tortured face. "Too much, sometimes. I had to hear all about how Walt was such a great lover and how big he was and this and that that they did in bed. You can't un-hear such things, you know."

Tell me about it, Jordan thought.

"But that's something positive in their lives," Jordan said. "Maybe if it was something negative, she wouldn't be so quick to bring it up—like . . . an affair?"

"Never."

"Or a terminal condition?"

"Katherine enjoyed sharing any medical woes, her own or those of her friends. No, I've racked my brain for a cause that might be behind it. If it's there, I haven't been able to find it."

"Okay. Financial problems?"

"No. Walt had a brother who is pretty well-off and would have helped out, in any case. And after we sold the house, Walt's brother and I split up everything."

She obviously got the Hummels, Jordan thought.

Kay was saying, "There were hardly any outstanding bills. Just utilities, that kind of thing. They were a rare couple who lived within their means."

Jordan changed tactics. "Let's go back to the beginning. Sorry to ask, but you need to take me through this again."

Kay told the tale of going into the house and finding the two bodies. By the finish, tears had returned, and the box of tissues proved handy. But Jordan didn't know any more than she had before.

"They were on the bed," Jordan asked, "side by side?"

"Yes." Kay was winding a tissue around her index finger, as she had at the group meeting where she'd shared the same story.

Jordan had the police report up on the laptop screen now. "The autopsy indicates no sign of drugs in their system."

"They took good care of themselves. No recreational drugs, no smoking, very little drinking. Even very little prescription medicine, just over the counter. And if there was an autopsy, wouldn't any terminal condition, like cancer, show up?"

"Probably, but not necessarily. They would be looking to make sure Walt and Katherine weren't deceased *before* the gunshot wounds."

Kay blinked at her. "How would that be possible?"

"If someone killed them by some other means, poison maybe, and tried to cover it up as a faked murder-suicide."

"I never thought of that."

Jordan was scrolling down the screen. "No crime scene pictures on the site, just the final report. That's standard."

Kay was just listening.

"So," Jordan said, sighing, smiling, "I'm afraid I need you to re-create the scene for me. Are you up to that?"

Kay drew in a deep breath, let it out slowly, and nodded.

"You need to picture it in your mind. I know it's nowhere you want to go, Kay, but please. Put yourself there. Shut your eyes, if it helps."

Kay nodded again. Closed her eyes.

Jordan said, "You're in the doorway."

"Yes."

"Is it a big bedroom?"

"Master suite. King-size bed."

"Where's the bed?"

"On the wall, opposite the door."

"What else is in the room?"

"Bookshelves to the right. Left of the door, a double-wide dresser with a TV on top. Facing the bed, and beyond that, bathroom door. Wall on the left has a narrower bookcase and a big window onto the backyard."

"The window's locked, right?"

"Not sure."

"The police report says no sign of forced entry."

"The room's clean, pristine. Katherine is an immaculate housekeeper."

"Do you look in the bathroom?"

"When I realize what's happened, I go in there, not to look. To be sick. Before I call the police."

"But do you see anything else in the bathroom? Unusual or out of place?"

"No. I just go in and get sick and flush it and come out to call the police."

"Do you see anything unusual in the bedroom? Is there anything else that strikes you as odd?"

"I see nightstands on either side of the bed. Nothing unusual about them."

"Katherine and Walt are on the bed, holding hands?"

"Yes. They are."

"You're facing the foot of the bed from the doorway, right?"

"Yes."

"Where are Walt and Katherine?"

"On the bed."

"No, their relative position from where you're standing."

"Katherine is on my right, Walt on my left."

"Can you see the gun?"

"No, no . . . *yes.*"

"Where are you standing now?"

"I've walked around to Walt's side of the bed."

"Is that Walt's usual side?"

"What?"

"Is that the side he usually sleeps on? Or is that something you don't know?"

Kay was thinking, and then her eyes popped open.

Jordan asked, "What is it?"

"They were on the wrong side of the bed. I never *thought* about it before . . ."

"Keep going."

"Walt always slept on the *other* side of the bed, near the phone, to take work calls that could come in at all hours. He was left-handed. Katherine slept on the opposite side from where I found her, near the alarm clock. Even as a little girl she always slept next to the clock."

"How long had they been married?"

No hesitation: "Seventeen years."

"Can you think of a reason why, after seventeen years of sleeping together, that they would change their accustomed sides of the bed on the very day they decide to kill themselves?"

"Well, of course, there isn't one," Kay said, excited. "It doesn't make any sense."

"What about this for a reason—Kay had no need for a clock, and Walt wasn't concerned about a work call. Not at the end."

"Jordan, that's just stupid. That's silly. Habit would override such thoughts, even if they had them."

"I agree. Yet that's the only explanation for it—a bad one." She scrolled down the screen. "The police report says they were both shot in the right side of their heads."

Kay, shaken by the wrong-side-of-the-bed information, didn't pick up on the significance of Jordan's comment.

Jordan tried again: "Why would a left-handed man shoot himself in the right side of the head? The gun in his left hand doesn't preclude him from shooting his wife on her right. But . . . was Walt ambidextrous?"

"No," Kay said firmly. Her expression turned oddly hopeful. "Does that mean Walt didn't do this thing?"

"Not necessarily. Not definitively. But it is definitely weird. And I don't see any gunshot residue test in this report, which would tell us which hand he used."

"That's sloppy police work, isn't it?"

"I would say so, but with investigators who didn't realize that Walt was left-handed? And that he and his wife were on the wrong sides of their bed? They would just see the convincing surface of a murder-suicide."

"Jordan, this is a breakthrough. You're wonderful."

She ignored that, scrolling farther. "The report says that the pistol was unidentified, serial number removed. Says here your brother-in-law was a parole officer."

"Yes."

"Dangerous work. Did Walt carry a gun?"

"No. He didn't own a gun, not a licensed one, at least. The police said he probably bought that from one of his . . . uh . . . clients after he decided to. . . ."

Jordan would ask Levi if there was a way to track when the gun was stolen and from where. Nothing in the report on the Gregory "murder-suicide" indicated the police had tried to pursue that.

"Wrong side of the bed, right-hand wound by a left-handed man," Jordan said. "There are things here that simply don't add up."

Kay looked hopeful. "Enough to get the case reopened?"

"Possibly," Jordan said. She shook her head. "Where's the motive? If it's not health or an affair or money."

Kay shrugged. "There just isn't one."

"There's nothing in the report about motive, other than 'Male victim known to have suffered depression.' What did the police say on that score?"

"They found an old bottle of Xanax that Walter had in the medicine chest. He'd been treated for anxiety attacks once, and his doctor gave him that for it. An officer named Grant, I think it was, told me 'confidentially' that the police assumption was that Walt had been deeply depressed and didn't want to live, and Katherine didn't want to live without him."

"And you've never bought into that?"

"It's ridiculous. Walt wasn't ever depressed—anxiety attacks aren't clinical depression! Jordan, I'm a nurse at a women's health clinic. They would have talked to me. They would have gotten help."

The doorbell rang.

"Excuse me, won't you?" Kay asked, rising, dabbing away tears and straightening her blouse and skirt.

Jordan gave her a small nod. While Kay disappeared to the front door, Jordan continued studying the police report. She didn't know what she was looking for, but they'd already found enough out of whack to keep reading.

Voices at the front door were too muffled and faint to be audible, but Jordan sat up straighter as she heard the screen door open and someone enter the house. The door closed, and Jordan rose as she heard two people approaching.

Kay's voice grew louder as she said, "Coincidentally, I was just discussing my sister and brother-in-law's case with a friend . . . *Jordan!* This—"

"I know who it is," Jordan said, looking into the blue eyes and boyish smile of Detective Mark Pryor. "Detective, we were just discussing the inadequacies of the Cleveland PD."

Kay, at Mark's side, looked from one to the other in surprise. "You young people know each other?"

She gave him a smile that had her upper lip curling over bared teeth. "I thought we had an understanding that you were gonna stop fucking *following* me?"

"Oh dear," Kay said.

Freezing in midsmile, Mark's eyes went almost comically wide, though Jordan remained unamused. "No, Jordan, please. I . . . I was coming to see Ms. Isenberg."

That slowed her momentarily, then she went on the attack again. "Why?"

"Why do you think?" he said. "To talk about her case." He shook his head. "When I saw your scooter parked at the curb, I knew I should have come back another time. . . ."

"That's right. You should have known that." She was in his face, and not in the way he might have hoped. "What happened to Kay's family happened long before you made detective—how did you even *know* about her case?"

Obviously, Mark didn't like being on the wrong side of flying questions. "I heard about it from a source."

"*What* source?"

"A *confidential* source."

Kay said, "You two should get a room."

That stopped them; they both turned to her.

173

"The chemistry is simply palpable," Kay said with a pleasant smile. "Whether Detective . . . Pryor? Whether Detective Pryor followed you here, or if this was just a happy accident, does it really matter? Jordan, this is an opportunity to discuss with a police detective what you've come up with this afternoon. . . . Detective, this is a remarkable young woman. Really quite brilliant. Let's sit down. Coffee? Iced tea? Soft drinks?"

Jordan and Mark declined the beverage offer, but the wind was out of their argument and they followed the older woman's instructions and sat, Jordan back in the chair, Mark with Kay on the couch. Jordan, with a few helpful interruptions from Kay, shared what they'd discussed, in particular the wrong-side-of-the-bed and left-handed victim issues.

When she had finished, Jordan looked expectantly at the young detective.

Mark only shrugged. "This is very interesting. It's what I'd call . . . suggestive. But I can't go to my captain with that. At least not yet."

Jordan frowned. "Why not?"

"Because it's a closed case." He gestured with widespread hands. "With our current caseload, he's not going to let me reopen it on the grounds that the shooter was left-handed, and what side of the bed each was on."

"What *would* be enough?"

"Something concrete. Something that puts someone else in that house at the time of the shootings."

"What about the gun? That might put someone else in the *room*."

"The gun was the weapon in the murder-suicide, and was near Mr. Gregory's hand."

"But there was no gunshot residue test!"

"Just because it's not in the report, that doesn't mean there wasn't one. And even if not, it's too late. Even an exhumation wouldn't . . . I'm sorry."

Kay had begun to cry again. She waved it off, as if they shouldn't be concerned, but she *was* crying, and Mark and Jordan exchanged concerned glances, on the same page for once.

Mark said to them both, "This isn't to trivialize what you've come up with. I would encourage you to keep digging."

"Gee," Jordan said, "thanks."

"I'll help you where I can," Mark said. "But the department just isn't going to allot resources for a closed case."

"You can use a phrase like *allot resources*," Jordan said bitterly, "when we're talking about what happened to Kay's family?"

"I don't like it any better than you do. That's why I'm looking into your family's case on my own time. The CPD has a budget like every other city service. Money's only going to get spent on open cases."

"And my family is an open case?"

"Jordan, you know it is. The case is unsolved. Kay's sister and brother-in-law is a closed case."

Why was he talking to her like she was a child? She wanted to kick him. Or slap him. Or something.

"The major problem remains," Mark said, "that there were no signs of a struggle."

Kay, confused, said, "Why is that an issue?"

Mark didn't answer her directly, instead turning to Jordan. "You are obviously more conversant with the file on this than I am. Is there any mention of them being drugged in the police report?"

"No," Jordan said.

He glanced from her to Kay and back again. "Then, for the new information you've found to be impactful, we must assume that two healthy, sane people let a third person march them into their bedroom, go along with instructions to lie on the bed, and simply hold hands and allow themselves to be . . . I'm sorry, Ms. Isenberg . . . to be executed, one at a time, without either victim putting up any kind of fight."

Mark put a hand, very gently, on Kay's shoulder.

"Ms. Isenberg," he said, "does that seem possible to you? Does it sound like Walt and Katherine?"

With a tiny shake of her head, Kay said, "No. No, it doesn't. But I suppose, at gunpoint, it's hard to know what someone might be able to force you to do."

"Did Walt love your sister?"

"Yes?"

"Would he have sat still for that?"

". . . No. No, you're right, young man. Absolutely not."

Mark shrugged. "And, actually, anxiety attacks *are* a form of depression—perhaps not severe depression, but in this case severe enough for a doctor to prescribe medication."

Kay said nothing.

Mark turned to Jordan. "Sometimes the simplest explanation is the correct one."

She wondered if she'd be dragged back to St. Dimpna's or maybe tossed in the county jail, should she bonk this obnoxious dipshit with her cycle helmet.

Restraining that impulse, she asked, "Why did you come to see Kay?"

"I'm sorry," Mark said. "That's police business."

Seething, Jordan closed up her laptop and dropped it into her backpack. "Then I'll leave you to it."

Mark smiled sickly. "Are we . . . still on for tonight?"

The question made Kay smile.

Jordan said, "Yes, goddamnit!"

Climbing onto her Vespa, Jordan wished she could be a fly on a Hummel's nose in that living room. Mark had not come to talk to Kay about a closed case, that much was obvious.

So was one other fact: he had better bring her one hell of a pizza tonight, and if it wasn't sausage, she would kick his ass.

CHAPTER THIRTEEN

On this clear, cool spring night, an apprehensive Mark Pryor approached Jordan's apartment building, his only defense a Salvatore's jumbo sausage thin-crust pizza and a six-pack of Coke Zero. He knew she was unhappy with him, the way she had stomped out of Kay Isenberg's place this afternoon. If the two women had spoken since then, she might be ready to stomp all over him.

He let out a breath, then pushed the intercom button next to her apartment number, its name slot empty.

"Yes?"

"It's, uh . . . Mark," he said into the intercom.

"You have to think about it?" came the sharp reply, then a buzz that sounded equally irritated with him.

She was waiting in the corridor when he got to her floor—jeans, Westlake High T-shirt, hair tied back in a ponytail, pissed as hell. Gorgeous as hell.

"Why the fuck should I let you in," she asked, arms folded, "after what you pulled today?"

Nice to see you, too.

"Sorry," he said. He held out the flat box and soda in offering like a Pilgrim trying to appease a cranky Indian. "I come bearing sausage pizza. Best in town."

Did she almost smile? He wouldn't bet on it, as she snatched the box and the soda, then retreated into her apartment, leaving the door ajar for him to follow, should he feel he'd had enough SWAT training to dare.

He went into her almost shockingly bare living quarters. On the kitchen counter, to his right, the pizza box and the soda had been deposited. Jordan stood there, arms still crossed, with the coldly accusatory glare of a trooper who caught you doing eighty in a school zone. One sneakered toe tapped to a beat only she heard.

"You think I followed you to your friend's place," he said. "I told you—I didn't."

Her eyes and nostrils flared, and the words flew out, loud and hard, in what would have been a blur if she hadn't bitten them off.

"No, but you followed David Elkins *after* group, didn't you? What, did you think he wouldn't tell me? And that's how you knew about Kay. And how you know about our team without me sharing that yet, and you're just generally out there fucking working behind my back, aren't you, Mark? *No* to the prom, by the way. We won't be going together this year."

"I'm sorry," he said again, knowing how lame it sounded.

"I thought maybe," she said, her voice much softer, perhaps a tiny waver in there somewhere, "you were one fucking person on this sorry fucking planet I could trust."

"Some mouth you've got," he said, trying to kid her a little.

Mistake.

Her eyes narrowed and her pretty face contorted in ugly rage. "You really want to talk about my fucking language now? Or is this just a joke to you, Detective Pryor?"

He patted the air with both hands as if trying to hold back an invisible wall closing in on him. "I take this very seriously. There's nothing more important to me than this."

"Than what?"

"Than helping you. Helping you find the monster who did that terrible thing to you and your family. What do I have to do to prove myself?"

She screamed: *"Be* honest *with me!"*

Then she stood there, eyes averted, clearly embarrassed, hugging herself, shivering but not with cold, and he wished he could take her in his arms and soothe her, but he knew—despite whatever stupid moves he had already made—that that would be the stupidest move of all.

Then she began to speak in a voice so soft he had to strain to hear. "What happened to my family, what happened to the families of the other members in the support group, has taught me a valuable lesson. And that is that no matter how hard you try to be good and do the right thing, in the end, it just doesn't matter because truly bad shit can happen to anyone, at any time, and there's nothing you can do to stop it."

"Jordan . . ."

"There are only a few things you can try, when the world is a fucking minefield. You can stay inside. You can carry a mine detector with you, everywhere you go. And there's one other thing—you can find people you can trust, who can lend you support, like the little coffee shop team we've put together."

"I understand."

"Do you? I trusted you the way I trust them . . . no, more, because you're someone I knew before, back in my other life, and you are like a . . . a little window onto who I used to be, and that was comforting if scary. I was ready to let you in, Mark. I was ready to let you in."

He nodded. Then he gave her his smallest smile, but a smile, and gestured to the pizza and soda. "You did let me in. Let's sit and eat and talk. Like the old friends we are."

"We weren't friends, we—"

"Please don't start that again. We *were* friends. We did like each other. And I still like you. I know I let you down. I won't again. *Jordan?* I won't let you down again."

Her body language had shifted into something more relaxed, her weight on one leg now, though her arms were still folded. Her rage had dissipated into a sullen, hurt expression, though her eyes were clearly trying to forgive him.

"I went behind your back," he said. "To talk to your friends. Why? Because you wouldn't talk to me about that night. About what happened to you and your family."

She stiffened a little, but the rage was gone, or anyway tamped down.

He went on: "So I talked to your friends. They didn't tell me anything that you'd shared with them. I tried, I used my badge and everything, I couldn't pry anything from them that you told them in confidence."

In a voice small enough to remind him of how she'd sounded in high school, she said, "That's because they're my friends."

"They are your friends, yes. And I know you've been working as a team, to try to put something together that proves one predator is responsible for what happened, not only to you, but Levi's folks and David's family. We're all working toward the same goal, Jordan. I am your friend, too." He was trying not to choke up but not having much luck. "I swear to God I am."

"Okay," she said, with a smaller smile than might seem humanly possible.

It was enough to make him grin at her as he wiped some moisture off his face with his sleeve. "Now, can we frickin' eat before I starve and the pizza gets completely cold?"

That widened her smile. "I suppose we could eat. Get the plates." She nodded toward the cupboard by the sink. "And a couple of glasses."

While he did, she broke two bottles of soda off the six-pack and put the rest in the fridge. He glanced around the apartment and its sparse furnishings—not even a TV; a mattress with a box spring on the floor, a desk with a laptop and a chair. It was a sort of cell—a nice cell, but he couldn't help thinking that the Rivera murders had consigned the wrong person to jail.

She was getting ice cubes from the freezer when he noticed a colored-pencil sketch of a male face held to the door by a Cleveland Indians refrigerator magnet, a rare personal touch in the apartment. The portrait wasn't of her brother Jimmy or her father, or even him for that matter. It was someone he'd never seen.

"Who's this?" he asked as she dropped cubes into the two glasses.

Her hesitation was brief, only a second or two, and she didn't turn toward the picture. She simply said, "Some guy I met once. Thought he had an interesting face. Just a sketch I did."

"I didn't know you could draw," he said.

She shrugged. "A little. Old hobby. Maybe I'll pick it up again . . . I thought you were starving? You want to eat or play art critic?"

He accepted the plate she thrust at him along with a napkin and a glass of Coke Zero. They sat at a black-topped kitchen table with two chairs.

Surprisingly, the pizza had stayed fairly warm. Sitting opposite, the two ate in relative silence for a while. She was on her third slice and he on his second when he finally couldn't stand the silence any longer.

"I really should have asked you out in high school," he said.

"Oh, were you thinking that we finally got around to our first date? Well, this isn't it."

"Too bad. It's memorable."

She laughed a little. Actually laughed!

"I was just scared you'd turn me down," he said.

"You should have just asked me," she said, matter-of-fact.

"Yeah?"

"I would have been a hell of a lot more fun back then."

"Maybe. But not as interesting."

"Oh, you like 'interesting' in a woman?"

"Not particularly."

That made her laugh again. Just a little, but coming from her it seemed huge. "I don't believe I've ever heard you swear."

"I don't."

Now she was grinning. "Is that why you made the remark about my 'language'?"

He smiled as he started a third slice. "Maybe. You do swear like a stevedore."

"Wow, that's an old-fashioned expression."

He nodded. "Something my dad would say."

"*Why* don't you swear? Are you religious or something?"

"I go to church, but it's not that." He finished the slice, sipped some Coke Zero. "There's a story behind it, if you want to hear it."

"I think I do."

Mark told her about Kyle Underwood, the bully at school, and how he'd stood up to the kid, with fists but also with defiant dirty words, which his dad had heard him shouting out at school. How his dad had grounded him for a month and told him never to swear again.

Her eyes were large. "And you never have since?"

"Well, I'm not perfect. If I hit my thumb with a hammer, maybe."

"I don't think so. I think you say *shoot*."

That made him smile. "Yeah. I can't remember the last time I slipped."

"You're not grounded anymore, Mark. You can swear up a storm if you like."

"It's no big deal. Just a habit. Maybe it's a way of just . . . still paying respect to my dad."

"He's gone?"

"Of a heart attack, when I was in college. He was really young, in his forties. I still miss him. You never stop missing . . . oh, I'm sorry. So thoughtless. . . ."

She put her half-eaten third slice on the plate and said, "You really want to know what happened that night?"

"I don't *want* to know, Jordan. But I need to know."

She nodded. "Help me clean up first."

They were at the sink, and she was running cold water on her plate and she smiled over at him to hand her his. The scent of her shampoo filled his nostrils, and he leaned in and kissed her.

Or tried to. His lips had barely touched hers when she shoved him back so hard, he almost lost his balance and got dumped on his ass.

"You have lousy timing," she snapped, and she swallowed and her eyes brimmed with tears.

"I'm an idiot," he said, and he swallowed and felt tears trying to come.

"You are, kind of. An idiot. Get us a couple more glasses of that diet shit, and I will still talk to you. Don't ask me why. By the way, I don't kiss on the first date. I don't kiss on the tenth date, either. Got that?"

"Okay."

Then the damnedest thing—and that was the word that sprang to his mind: *damnedest*—she touched his cheek, just briefly, but it was warm, so warm, and so gentle.

"Someday maybe," she said.

"Eleventh date?"

"We'll see."

They returned to the table—it was really the only place where two people could sit and talk in this cell. For maybe a minute, Jordan sat there staring into nothing, or maybe the past; but at any rate, saying nothing.

Finally, in a voice small and emotionless, she said, "It was after dinner. I was up in my room doing my homework."

Her hands were folded as if she were saying grace, and she looked down at them. She would tell her story in her own time, her own way.

"That's not true," she said after a while, shaking her head, her voice normally modulated now. "I was *supposed* to be doing my homework—algebra. What I was really doing was daydreaming. About a boy I liked who never had the brains to call and ask me out."

"Sounds like an idiot I know," he said.

They exchanged tiny smiles.

She continued, back in the emotionless manner: "I heard a crash downstairs, then a struggle, a fight. I got up, went to the door, and I had just stepped out into the hall when my mother screamed for me to run."

No tears. Perhaps she had drained the horror out of the memory, created distance, to be able to revisit the terrible night.

She seemed to be staring into the past now. "I saw a man in a policeman's uniform fighting with my father."

Mark sat forward. "A police uniform?"

"Yes."

"That's new. First mention of that."

She looked at him curiously, as if she'd forgotten he was there. "Maybe it was only that one time that he wore a uniform like that."

"Maybe not. It may be part of his MO. You're the only survivor who was actually home during an attack, to report this detail."

He wanted to reach over and pat her hand, but thought better of it. "Jordan, you're doing fine. Just fine. Go on."

But she wasn't ready to let go of the previous point. "Is it possible he is, or *was* a cop?"

"Unlikely. The CPD canvassed all the neighbors at all the crimes and no one reported seeing a police car until the first-response units arrived."

She seemed skeptical.

He continued: "There was nothing in the police report that indicated any of the neighbors noticed a police car at or near your house that night, either. Wearing a uniform might be a way to get someone to open the door for him."

Again, she was staring into the past. "The badge, the emblem on his shoulder . . . he wasn't from Westlake. He was from somewhere else."

Sitting way forward, he reached his hand near hers, not touching. "Jordan, what was on the badge? What did it look like? Was it star-shaped? Did it have sharp corners? Did it—"

"It was oval," she cut in. "Silver. A sort of . . . shield. Like on that old show on Nick at Nite, *Dragnet*? It had a number."

"What was the badge number?"

"Sixty-nine."

"What about the shoulder patch? Did you get a look at it?"

Jordan thought about that. "A triangle, tip down."

"Jurisdiction?"

"Well, this is going to sound weird," she said. "I don't remember ever seeing the name, but when I think about it? The patch is blue with silver letters and it says . . . I'm sorry, but what I see is *funky town*, all in capital letters."

"Funky Town," Mark said.

She shrugged. "I told you it was going to sound weird."

"You're remembering it wrong, but are probably close. Frankfort, maybe? Fullertown? Fultonham? Funk? There *is* a Funk, Ohio, south of here."

She shook her head. "I just don't know."

Mark thought out loud: "Two-digit badge number—small town, maybe. This might be a real cop from a small town, who drove his own car to the big city."

But what about Basil Havoc? Had he been zeroing in on the wrong guy all this time?

One way to find out. Finally, just this one way to find out, though it was a risky breach of prodecure. . . .

On his cell phone, Mark brought up a photo he'd snapped of Havoc, surreptitiously, the night he'd followed the gymnastics coach to the Italian restaurant. "This is a recent shot, but look at it hard. Have you ever seen him before?"

"Yes."

"*Yes?*"

"He's that stupid full-of-himself gymnastics coach. If you mean, is this the man who attacked us? No."

"You barely looked at it."

"It's not him."

"You seem sure. It *has* been ten years."

"How old is that creep—fifty?"

"Around there."

"Meaning ten years ago, he was forty."

Mark shrugged. "Yeah."

"The intruder was in his twenties, young, strong. This guy has dark hair. The intruder was blond."

Every word she spoke gave fresh information, but it also underlined that Mark had likely spent a very long time pursuing the wrong suspect. In his head, he was reeling.

"Should I go on?" she asked.

"What?"

"Am I boring you?"

"I'm sorry, I just . . . I was . . . go on, please."

In straightforward language and in an emotionless manner, she told Mark about watching her mother die, getting pulled out from under the bed, being forced to group her family's bodies together. She never cried, but Mark wanted to.

Then she stopped and frowned, looking beyond him, into the past, but her eyes were moving quickly.

"You've remembered something," he said.

"He made me take pictures."

"Pictures?"

"Photos. He had a digital camera." Her eyes dropped to the table and she rubbed her forehead, as if it were a genie's lamp and she could wish her life into something else.

She sprang to her feet and began to prowl the apartment, talking more to herself than him, as if she had forgotten he was there. "Why *photos*? And where are they? Did the police find a camera?"

"No. Jordan . . . come sit back down . . ."

She didn't. "If he'd posted them on the Net, the sick fuck, we'd know, wouldn't we?" She whirled and planted herself and pointed an accusatory finger. "Did he send them to the police? To brag? Do you people have them? Is that one of the things the cops held back? They always hold something back, they always hold *something* back . . ."

She was prowling again. Searching the floor for answers.

"Are they still on the camera?" she asked. Not him. The floor. "Did he print them so he can jerk off to them or some other sick thing?"

"Jordan . . . take it easy."

She came over and leaned on the table and, eyes wild, demanded, "I want those photos! Those are the last photos of my family and I want them, and they are for me to have and for me to destroy. If *you* people have them, goddamnit, I *want* them!"

"We don't have them. Jordan. Sit down. We really don't."

"It's not your case. You don't know—"

"I know. I have access to the file. Sit. Please."

She did.

He said, "Serial killers often keep souvenirs of their atrocities. Mementoes."

Her eyes disappeared into slits. "They're evidence. Mark, Jesus, Mark, he must have some kind of horrible scrapbook, and monstrous as that is, that's great!"

"It . . . it is?"

"Find that scrapbook, and you've found him."

"True. And that book, or maybe data file, will put him on death row."

They sat in silence for what felt like a very long time, to Mark at least. She was staring at her folded hands or maybe the tabletop. Anyway, not at him.

Finally, still looking down, she said, "What David and Kay wouldn't tell you? That I had told them?"

"Yes?"

"That's the reason I reacted like that. When you tried to kiss me."

"Wh . . . what is?"

Her eyes lifted from the table and they were clear and lovely with no sign of tears. As if telling him what tomorrow's weather would be, she said, "He raped me."

Mark felt like he'd been struck a blow to his stomach, so hard a blow that the wind was knocked from him. His vision blurred, and he felt very sick.

"Where," he said softly, "is your. . .?"

She pointed, and he ran, and he knelt over the stool and threw up the pizza and the cola. It came up hard and wrenching and he was still kneeling over the stool when she entered, flushed it for him, knelt by him, and slipped her arm around him, patting his shoulder. *There there, there there. . . .*

She helped him to his feet and then slipped out and let him wash up. He threw water on his face, looked at himself in the mirror and saw an exhausted, emotion-ravaged wreck. *You're really showing her some great support, pal,* he told himself, and toweled off his face.

Then they were sitting at the table again. Now she was watching him until he was ready to speak.

"Sorry," he said.

"Did he do that to anyone else?"

"Huh?"

"Rape anyone else?"

"Not . . . not that's been reported."

"I never told anyone."

"I know." *You didn't talk for ten years.* "They didn't examine you?"

"I bathed and changed my clothes before the police came. A doctor looked at my bruises from the struggle, but that's all."

"I'm so sorry, so sorry you went through that. All alone."

"Don't start crying. If you cry, Mark, I'll cry, and I don't want to fucking cry. Get it?"

He nodded.

She was frowning. "I don't understand why he did it to me."

"Power. Rape is about power."

"I know that! But I'm the only one, seems like, that he did it to.

He killed my family. Power? He could have killed me at any time. How much power does one fucking asshole need?"

"He . . . he wanted to *own* you, to show you that whether you lived or died was *his* decision."

She grinned at him. How could she grin? "Wonder why I was silent all those years? Why I haven't talked to anyone about this until lately?"

"Tell me."

"Because he said he *wanted* me to tell his story."

"Wanted . . . ? His story?"

"That's right. Well, fuck him. That was my attitude, from that first night on. I wasn't going to say anything about him—ever."

He frowned at her. "Why break your silence now?"

"The Strongsville homicides. I saw it on the news. I *knew* it was him. I had to stop him."

"You had to . . . stop him?"

"Yes. And I've let you and the support group in, because I don't think I can find him on my own."

Mark was studying her. "And if you find him? What then?"

". . . Turn him over to the police."

It almost sounded like a question.

He said, "I hope so. Because I can't help you, if you're looking for revenge."

"I want revenge, but I'll settle for justice."

Mark put his hand on hers. She started to draw it away, then left it there. Their eyes were locked as he said, "Do I have to tell you how dangerous this individual is? You cannot deal with this yourself. Tell me you won't try to deal with this yourself."

"I'm not. Who was it said, 'I get by with a little help from my friends'?"

"Stopping him is what's important. Getting even . . . you can't get even with a lunatic. You can only stop him."

She sighed. Nodded. "There is one other thing about that night. . . ."

"Yes?"

"When he was . . . done? He said some very weird shit to me."

"Weird how?"

" 'Thou shalt not wear a garment of different sorts, as of woolen and linen together.' "

"Deuteronomy 22:11," Mark said.

"You know the *Bible*?"

"Some. Enough to recognize that's not the King James version."

"No?"

"King James uses the phrase 'divers sorts' instead of 'different sorts'."

She was frowning. "What the hell does it *mean*?"

Mark said, "What it means to us isn't important. What it means to the killer, and his twisted take on it, could be vital."

"So . . . where do we go from here?"

"If you'll allow it, I'll meet with you and your team. They can show me what they have, and maybe I can bend a few rules and share some of what I've learned."

Her half smile had a wry tinge. "Isn't that better?"

"Better?"

"Than going behind my back?"

"Much," he said, and grinned at her. "It's, uh . . . getting late. I really should go. . . ."

He hoped she'd have a different opinion, but instead she just walked him to the door.

"Trust me, Jordan. We'll catch this SOB."

She smiled at him. "Pretty salty talk."

"Maybe you're a bad influence on me," he said, and as she closed the door on him and her own small smile, he found himself wishing she'd be a much worse influence than that.

CHAPTER FOURTEEN

"He *kissed* you?" Kara said, gawking at Jordan.

"More like he tried," Jordan said, shrugging. "I about knocked him on his ass, and that shut him down."

"You *want* him 'shut down'?"

"One thing I don't need is a man in my life. There's *already* a man in my life."

"A man in your life that you want to kill." This time Kara shrugged. "Maybe there's room for one you want to kiss."

Jordan shook her head. "No. Anyway . . . no."

"Anyway what?"

She sighed. "I doubt he wants to even touch me now. After what I told him."

"What did you tell him?"

". . . About what the intruder really did to me that night."

Kara leaned forward. "You *told* him?"

She nodded. "And it made him sick."

Kara shook her head and the punky hair bounced. "He got sick because he cares about you. Not because you sicken him or some shit. Girl, you need to screw that head on tighter."

"Moot point."

"Yeah?"

"I don't want to kiss him. I don't want to fuck him either, okay? All he is to me is a resource."

"A resource. A very cute resource who brings you pizza and Coke."

"A resource who can help me nail the son of a bitch I'm after. Got a problem with that?"

"No. I'm all over that, sweetie. I only wish I was out of this craphole so I could help you slice and dice the motherfucker."

Jordan smiled. "You are a good friend, Kara."

They bumped fists.

Kara said, "So what now, honey?"

"I told Mark he could stop by our little postgroup team meeting."

"You think he will?"

"Oh yeah. He'll be there. He's almost as fucked-up about this thing as I am."

Jordan was one of the last to arrive at the support group meeting, at its regular late Saturday morning slot, and she took the empty seat, next to Phillip. Typically, he wore the long-sleeved white shirt, tie, and cotton vest, shades of gray today except for the navy blue tie.

Across the circle, David sat with Kay and Levi on either side. They each acknowledged her with a nod, but without a smile. Not even Kay smiled at her, and Kay would smile at anybody or anything.

Were they mad at her?

David and Kay had both talked to Mark, so they might know that she hadn't shared with them that she'd already been talking to a CPD detective about the case, without cluing in the team.

After Dr. Hurst called the meeting to order, the first speaker was a new member of the group, a woman who had been mugged on a bike path, her wounds so fresh she still sported the black eye and the swollen jaw earned for having the temerity to jog in a mugger's wonderland.

After the woman had told her tale, Jordan asked her—her name was Alice—if she would describe the two muggers. Everyone looked at Jordan curiously, but when the woman said the two men were African-American, and then went into a defensive, anxious spiel about not being racist, Jordan stopped listening. She'd only wanted to make sure this wasn't that same pair of muggers from a few nights ago. If that had been the case, there might have been significance to it. But this was just more random violence in the minefield.

Jordan paid scant attention throughout group, not offering anything else, caught up with thoughts about what she would do if she were ostracized from the team. She would continue her mission alone, of course, but she'd lack the insights and help of the others. Levi and his computer expertise would be especially missed. But she could always hire somebody, couldn't she?

As the meeting continued, no one else on the team participated and that only served to feed Jordan's suspicions that they were displeased. Even Dr. Hurst seemed to notice their silence, but did nothing to draw them out, apparently content to let other voices be heard.

Afterward, Dr. Hurst stopped Jordan near the door. "May I speak to you for a moment?"

Jordan just nodded and they waited for the rest of the group to file out.

When they were alone, Dr. Hurst asked, "You didn't have much to say in group today, Jordan."

"Lot of people didn't."

"You've spoken about your family these last few weeks and that's such a fine start. I'd hoped you might continue to express yourself here in front of—"

"I was just giving everybody else a chance to talk."

Hurst nodded. "Are you feeling better?"

Jordan had called in sick for her recent one-on-one session with the doctor.

"Just terrible cramps. You remember, Doctor. I have very hard periods."

"So I can expect you next week?"

"Absolutely."

Jordan was losing time; she wanted to get to the coffee shop and talk to the team before Mark arrived.

"You're settling in to your new apartment?"

"Yes. Nice. Very homey."

"And your college plans . . . ?"

Jordan was supposedly planning to start college next semester, but she had done nothing about it.

"Haven't decided which school yet," Jordan said.

"There are some nice local options."

"Can we talk it about at our session next week?"

"Certainly. Would you like me to round up some pamphlets on your possible choices?"

"That'd be great."

Then Jordan was out the door, moving quickly.

When she walked from the hospital into blinding sunlight, she almost bumped into Phillip milling there, smoking.

"Jordan, are you all right?" he asked, pitching the cigarette, his breathing painfully audible through his Phantom of the Opera nose. "I saw Hurst waylay you. She can be a pain sometimes . . . but she means well."

"Tell me about it. Anyway, thanks, Phillip, I'm fine. Walk with me?"

They headed down the sidewalk toward the coffee shop.

"Beautiful day," he said. He was taller than her, his wispy brown hair tossed by the breeze.

"Is it? Yeah, I guess it is."

"What are you worried about?"

"I'm worried?"

"Oh yes. I'm afraid it shows."

"Maybe I am . . . a little."

He smiled that ghastly smile, which she was actually getting used to. "It's about Detective Pryor, isn't it?"

She smiled back, mildly. "So you've heard? Yes. I am worried. And yes, it's about me not telling the group about my contact with . . . Detective Pryor."

Brown eyes twinkled mischievously in the ravaged face. "Why the hesitation before his name? Had you forgotten it?"

"No."

"You went to school with him, didn't you? Old boyfriend?"

"Yes I went to school with him, no he wasn't my boyfriend. Who told you, anyway?"

"The detective mentioned it to both Kay and David. They don't keep anything from the rest of us."

"Is that a dig, Phillip?"

"Maybe just a tiny one. You've got to learn to trust again, Jordan. I speak from experience. After the senseless violence I endured, don't you think I've had to grapple with that?"

"Yes," she said.

"Anyway, you needn't be concerned. Everyone in group . . . everyone on our little spin-off team . . . understands that we each have to deal with things in our own way. It took time for you to share with the group what happened to you and your family, didn't it? We all understand. It will come. It will come."

She managed another smile. "Thank you, Phillip."

He shrugged. "Anyway, the detective has already helped, hasn't he?"

"He has?"

"Well, yes. He gave David the name of a suspect that we're already looking into."

Jordan wondered if that suspect was that gymnastics coach, Havoc. Great—Mark had provided them with a dead end to waste their time on. Jordan had already told him that Havoc wasn't the intruder.

"I must be getting paranoid," she said, as they strolled, her reason for hurry gone. "When I walked into group this morning, nobody smiled at me, and I started thinking all kinds of weird shit."

"We all have a lot on our minds," Phillip said, waving that off.

The other three were already seated and waiting when she and Phillip entered and ordered their coffee at the counter. Mark was not here yet. Good.

With cups in hand, they made their way to the high-top table in the crowded shop and took two of the three empty chairs, David on her right with Kay next to him, Levi on her left.

Immediately the writer got into it. At least there was nothing accusatory in the way he said: "We know you must have a reason for not telling us that a CPD detective was going down the same road we are."

Gently, Levi said, "We'd just like you to tell us what that reason is."

Jordan said, providing the alibi she'd spent much of the morning preparing, "I was waiting till we had something concrete to give him. Something the police would *have* to believe."

Kay said, "But why keep his interest from us?"

"Mark's an old high school friend. He's only able to look into this in his spare time. He has a sort of . . . impulsive side, and . . ."

David, God bless him, bailed her out: "Mark is on a very short leash with his captain. If he makes a misstep, he could get pulled off of even this semi-official part-time investigation."

"Anyway," she said, "I have to admit that . . . I've been alone for a long time. I was alone when I was at St. Dimpna's, even with a thousand mental patients all around me. It's not easy for me."

Kay leaned over to pat her hand, and Jordan didn't even mind. "Dear," the older woman said, "it's day at a time, step at a time, for all of us. We're not accusing you. We're just saying we're your friends. You can trust us."

"Can we skip the group hug?" Levi asked. "Because we may *have* something, and we might as well dig in—"

Levi was interrupted by Mark entering the shop without stopping to order anything, coming straight to the table and the waiting chair—Levi at his right, Phillip at his left. Jordan made introductions where needed, and after a brief exchange of pleasantries, David again took the role of spokesperson for the group.

"Good to see you again, Detective Pryor, though what we have to share may or may not please you."

"Such as?"

Levi said, "We think Basil Havoc may not be our man."

Mark just nodded—his demeanor, Jordan noted, was cool and professional. "I would agree."

Surprise widened eyes around the table.

Kay asked, "Why?"

"I'll leave that to Jordan to tell you," Mark said, and nodded at her with a businesslike smile.

She nodded back, then addressed the team: "Last night, Detective Pryor showed me a picture of Havoc, on his phone? I recognized the man as my old gymnastics coach—anyway, he was briefly."

David frowned and said to the young detective, "Jesus, man, was that wise? If she ever has to pick him out of a lineup, you've poisoned the well!"

"Beside the point," Jordan said. "I *saw* the man who attacked my family . . . who attacked me . . . and it wasn't Havoc."

"So anything you have to share," Mark said, sighing, "I'll appreciate. Because I'm feeling like I'm back to square one."

David said, "Maybe not. Levi and I thought you were on the right track with Havoc, but with the wrong approach."

Mark frowned. "How so?"

"You were concentrating solely on Havoc, right?"

"That's right."

"Did you ever consider looking at anyone on his staff?"

With a humorless half smirk, Mark admitted, "Not really. I've got a feeling you're going to tell me I should have."

Nodding, Levi said, "There were four people who traveled with Havoc extensively. You were looking into two cases on the East Coast, right?"

"Yes."

"I bring this up, because the National Gymnastics finals were in Boston, then Hartford, and there were family killings in Providence and the Bronx that coincide."

Mark shifted in his chair. "I can't officially confirm that without risking getting myself in dutch with my captain. But . . . let's say, hypothetically . . . yes."

Levi smiled a little, then the smile disappeared as he said, "I have the names of three staff members, other than Havoc, who were in both cities with him."

Mark held up a hand, got out a notepad and pen, then nodded, poised to write.

Levi said, "Bradley Slavens, Stuart Carlyle, and Patti Roland."

"Could you spell those?"

Levi did.

"Good," Mark said, writing. "Good."

"Roland and Carlyle are still working at Havoc's school," Levi went on. "Slavens left about two years ago, and as far as the Net is concerned, fell off the map."

Mark asked, "How did you get stuff on his employees?"

Phillip cleared his throat and all eyes were on him as he said, "The government may have repealed 'Don't ask, don't tell,' Detective. But we haven't. Any information you get from us, you need to consider confidential, like something you might get from a, uh . . . what's the television word? Snitch."

Mark grinned at the teacher. "Fair enough." Then he glanced around at everyone. "I just uncovered a case that might fit the loose profile. Near St. Louis, where the finals were in 2012. A family in the Hill neighborhood."

Phillip asked, "What makes you think they're victims of our killer?"

"The homicides were around the time of the finals. But I can't share anything beyond that—I'm sorry."

"We can be *your* snitch, but you can't be *ours*?"

"It's a matter of degree, Mr. Traynor, but . . . that's about the size of it."

"Levi," David asked, turning to the skater boy, "how does this fit in with the Havoc staff members?"

"Carlyle and Roland would have been there," Levi said, "along with Havoc, of course. Slavens was gone by then."

Phillip asked, "Is there some reason it couldn't be any other gym coaches that travel to these events? Or even a parent? Havoc's isn't the only school with a similar schedule—possibly not even in Cleveland."

David said, "These crimes started a decade ago. If it was a parent, his child would be long since off that circuit. Most kids have tossed in the towel, ten years down the road, or are in training for Olympic-caliber events."

Levi picked up: "The parent would have to follow the competitions after his child left the sport. Doubtful."

"I agree," Mark said. "Odds are better it's another coach. Serial killers are predators. They hunt, they kill. They start close to home, then branch out as their supply dwindles or they feel threatened. These crimes started here, they predominate around here. Remember, looking at Havoc's school began with Jordan and David's daughter both being students there. I believe this killer is local."

"Makes sense," Phillip said, and there were nods all around.

Mark turned back to Levi. "You seem to have narrowed it to two staff members at the school. How hard have you looked at them?"

Levi grinned, shook his head. "Detective, if I went beyond their Facebook pages, I'd be invading their privacy. You wouldn't want me to break the law, now . . . would you?"

Even Jordan and Kay smiled at that.

Mark said to Levi, "So, if I Google them, will I come up with all the information you have?"

There was a slyness to Levi's half smile. "Not completely."

"Care to let me in on what I won't find on Google?"

"As long as you don't ask me where I got it."

Mark's half smile was equally sly. "I never push a snitch for his source."

"Ha," Levi said. "Okay, for one thing, Patti Roland was accused by a parent of being a sexual predator."

Mark frowned and his pen was again poised to write. "When was this?"

"About three years ago. A mom claimed that Roland molested her seven-year-old daughter. She filed a civil suit against Havoc and his business."

"So this is in the public record," Mark said. "I can track this."

"Yes," Levi said, shrugging, "but the suit was dropped, possibly settled out of court. Mom and child left Havoc's center for another gymnastics training site."

David asked, "Money grab?"

"Maybe," Levi said. "That's not on the record, anywhere. Strictly closed-doors lawyer stuff."

Mark said, "But Roland stayed on staff with Havoc? He didn't fire her?"

"She's worked for him since the gym opened," Levi said. "Maybe she and Havoc are tight. Or maybe firing her would've given credence to that lawsuit. Anyway, Havoc has driven off plenty of trainers . . . but not her or Carlyle."

"What about Carlyle?"

"No criminal record. He did report a gun stolen about six years ago. But that's it."

"Nothing else?"

"Carlyle seems clean from the outside."

Jordan said, "Why are you even considering this Patti Roland? I *saw* the intruder—it's a *man*."

Briefly David explained that serial killers sometimes worked in teams, including male-female duos.

"Well, then," Jordan said, "she must have been waiting in the car or something. Because we were hit by *one* bastard."

Around them, the lunchtime cacophony had trailed off and the shop, which had been fairly crowded, was slowly emptying.

"The one thing," Levi said thoughtfully, "that still has me completely stymied is—"

"Motive," Jordan said.

"Exactly," Levi said. "I understand with this type of criminal we aren't looking at something as rational as wanting or needing money.

Or killing somebody you hate, like an unfaithful wife or a mean-ass employer."

Phillip said, "These are senseless crimes. They can't be analyzed for motive."

"No," Mark said. "There is, as the old saying goes, method to his madness. We just haven't figured it out yet."

Kay cocked her head. "I thought serial killers killed just to . . . kill."

Mark shook his head. "No, there's something behind this . . . but I grant you it's not apparent on the surface. Serial killers don't jump ethnic groups, as a rule—this one does. They usually have particular 'tastes,' for lack of a better word—this one doesn't. Men, women, young, old, even children, black, white, Hispanic. This guy is all over the place. Income-wise, too. Rich or poor, middle class, it just doesn't matter to him. Right now the family aspect is all we have."

David said, "*Something* is driving him."

"Or them," Phillip reminded.

"A killing duo doesn't seem likely to me," Mark said. "But we can't rule out anything, and knowing the killer's motive would be a big step in figuring out what he's up to. Figuring out why these crimes are dissimilar enough to not attract FBI attention. It might even tell us when he's going to strike next."

David said, "And there *will* be a next."

Silence.

Jordan broke it: "That's why I knew it was time to get the hell out of St. Dimpna's—the news coverage of the Sully family. I knew he was never going to stop killing unless someone stopped him."

Phillip said, "Surely you weren't planning to try to do that by yourself?"

"If need be, you bet your ass. I knew how *I* suffered, and now I know how all of you suffered. Someone has to stop the son of a bitch . . . and, all due respect to our guest, if the police won't, we have to."

Levi said, "Fine speech, kid, but we're still stuck at motive."

"Something Jordan mentioned," Mark said.

"Me?"

"Yeah. You. What you told me he said to you. Can I share that?"

"If you think it will help."

Mark told them the killer had recited a Bible verse after his killing spree at the Riveras': " 'Thou shalt not wear a garment of different sorts, as of woolen and linen together.' "

"Deuteronomy," Phillip said.

"22:11," Mark said.

Levi said, "Phillip teaches religion online. What's the meaning of that verse, anyway?"

Phillip frowning was not a pleasant sight. "I don't see that it is apropos of anything much. It may mean that one shouldn't give into the vain fashions of the world, and save their respect for the Lord. It might mean to maintain purity of heart and deed. I can give it some thought, and research it, if you like."

"Please," Mark said.

Then the detective pushed back his chair and stood, smiling in a businesslike way and nodding at them, one at a time. "Afraid I've got to get back to work. Keep digging for the motive. Meantime, I'll check up on those two employees of Havoc's."

Jordan walked Mark out.

"We *have* figured one thing out," Mark said. "Or anyway, my partner Pence did."

"What?"

"The cop uniform your intruder wore. Your memory is probably right. It *was* 'Funkytown.' "

"That's crazy!"

"No. Remember the badge number?"

"Sure. Sixty-nine."

"A crude sexual reference. That was a costume, a cop costume used by male strippers."

She frowned. "So your latest lead is male strippers?"

"No, I'm glad to say. That kind of thing is readily accessible on the Net or for cash at any number of sleazy sources, from adult bookstores to pawnshops. But that's helpful information."

"How so?"

"We can rule out real cops."

They were at his Equinox.

"Listen," she began, "I, uh . . . I want to thank you."

"For what?"

"For taking our little team seriously. I don't think you'll be sorry you did."

"I'm sure I won't. They're doing good work. This is the kind of support I wish the department was giving me."

"That's a relief to hear."

"Oh, no, this is fine. This is great. We keep this up, it won't be long till we'll have enough so that my captain will *have* to listen."

Mark grinned at her, gave her a little squeeze of the shoulder (she didn't mind), and got into his Equinox and drove off, obviously feeling he'd given her good news.

But if Mark was right, it wouldn't be long before the cops and the FBI would be tracking the intruder, and what she wanted was to beat them to the bastard. She didn't want him to spend the rest of his life in prison, or living out decades on death row, with appeal after appeal. She wanted to kill him. She wanted to watch him die.

Was that so wrong?

CHAPTER FIFTEEN

For four hours at his kitchen table, hunkered over his laptop, Levi had been figuratively banging his head against the wall and was at the point where doing that literally seemed like a viable option. Every time he had hold of something, it evaporated, as if he were chasing a ghost. He was starting to think that's what Bradley Slavens was— somebody who'd fallen off the grid and died and nobody noticed.

At least nobody on the Net.

An unnoticed death, however, was not as likely as somebody's concerted effort to disappear—if so, Havoc's gymnastics coach/assistant had done a hell of a job of it.

Up and vanishing was no easy task, in this world of forms and security cameras and voter ID. So much out there could give you away—an ATM card hung onto a little too long, a cell phone not thrown away, credit cards, car registrations, a forwarded check for a damage deposit . . . so many ways to slip up. To accidentally exist.

That meant Levi had to painstakingly track each such lead as best he could, and every time he hit a dead end, he recalled how frustrating it was to be a kid in an arcade who got killed on his last quarter.

Still, he had diligence on his side, and odds were Slavens had missed something somewhere—most everybody did. Chasing each lead down, Levi could only think, *We don't even know if this is the guy—I may be wasting my time, looking for somebody who isn't really even a suspect yet . . . just a potential one.*

He was about ready to hang it up for the night. Kick back with a Blu-ray and a Blue Moon. Then he tumbled onto it—chasing one of those many, many ways to look for somebody in today's America. . . .

Seemed right before he'd fallen off the planet, Bradley Slavens had sold his car. That little tidbit had come from the county clerk's office. Suddenly Levi had a date to work with, the dealership where Slavens sold the vehicle, and the figure Slavens had been paid.

Using that as a jumping-off point, Levi found four sales of cars that same day at various dealers where men had spent cash of about the amount Slavens had received for his car. Three of the buyers had been easy to track, through previous sales, and sales that occurred in the years since—all very simple to follow . . . and to rule out.

The fourth and final one, Kenneth Simon, seemed to have acquired no past before showing up at A-1 Used Cars the same day Slavens sold his vehicle across town at Forest City Motors. Mr. Simon paid cash for a late-model Dodge van.

Then a year later he sold it, right before he seemed to cease to exist . . . just as Slavens had.

One way a predator could avoid detection was to constantly change identities, a snake shedding skins. Since their man seemed to stay in the Cleveland area, that might seem less likely, although an area this size could possibly accommodate a shift or two in identities, maybe more. At any rate, this was a solid clue, well worth pursuing.

But all this digging had also opened the door on a lot more digging to do. On his cell, he got Phillip right away.

"You home, Phillip?"

"Yes, just sitting here reading," he said, his distinctive breathing echoing over the phone. "You sound excited."

"As excited as I can be," Levi said, "this exhausted."

Levi filled him in, then said, "I could use your help to dig into this 'Kenneth Simon.' Can you come over?"

"I can do that, but my home rig is more powerful than my laptop—can you come to me?"

"Be there in less than an hour."

"See you then," Phillip said, and they ended the call.

Rushing to pack all his gear, Levi felt his exhaustion disappear as his mind raced with the possibilities of what he was onto. If they could trace Kenneth Simon, they might be able to pinpoint where he resided now, and if Simon was really *Slavens*, then maybe, just maybe he was their man. . . .

Carrying his backpack with his laptop in it, Levi headed downstairs, tossed his gear into the car, then got behind the wheel. He put the key in the ignition and turned it.

Nothing.

Not even a whir. He pounded the steering wheel with a fist, though if he said he was surprised, he'd be lying. The only thing he could depend on with this car was that it was undependable. He could feel his exhaustion reasserting itself. . . .

Nothing a little Red Bull couldn't cure, and he had some upstairs.

He was about to call and see if Phillip could come to him, or if not, possibly come pick him up, when a low rumbling in the far distance made him look up. The Green Line train. He hurriedly got his stuff from the car, not bothering to lock it—if some thief could figure out how to start the damned thing, he could have it—and started hoofing it over to the train station.

Backpack over his shoulder, Levi trotted across the two westbound lanes of Shaker Boulevard. Not a lot of traffic this time of night, and he had heard the train from a good ways away, so when he hit the sidewalk on the RTA side of the street, he slowed to a brisk walk.

Though he was in pretty decent shape, running while carrying all that gear had left him a little winded. He was still a good twenty-five yards or so from the station, coming up even with a half-dozen trees intended to pretty up the station area. He could see the train's lights now.

Picking up the pace, he started to reach for his wallet, to be ready to buy a ticket. Then he smiled to himself—even in a hurry, he wouldn't do that, especially not near that shadowy area in and around those trees, which had long been a boon to muggers.

He was just past the trees and had only the barest sense of movement to his right as somebody grabbed him by the backpack and yanked him to a stop, an arm looping around his waist to drag him into the darkness of the trees. A hand gripping his head by his hair jerked back sharply, his chin rising, as if to provide a better access to the white flesh of his throat. Arms flailing, he caught a gleam of metal and then a burning sensation started just behind his left ear, moving swiftly across his throat and stopping just below his right ear.

His flailing slowed to a slow swimming motion as he saw the scarlet spray and felt hot wetness spilling down the front of him. He sagged to his knees. Tried to scream, but the only sound he produced was a raspy inhuman cough. *Fucking throat's been cut!* he told himself, as if some part of him should do something about it.

He knew he was going into shock, but he still remained aware, his hands clawing toward his neck, trying to keep the blood in; but it ribboned through his fingers. Already he could feel his extremities going cold.

His damp red fingers dropped. There was no fighting it now. Although he hadn't seen his attacker, someone had been waiting in the shadows, and not just a mugger. *It was their man.* They had found him! Or *he* had found *them* . . . These thoughts gave him an odd satisfaction as his strength and consciousness ebbed. Even as the killer hovered over him, Levi couldn't make out more than a distorted silhouette. The figure bent toward him and Levi, just for a second, thought he recognized something about the attacker, but the thought cut off as something sharp dug into his abdomen, and his insides began spilling out.

No pain now, just his parents calling to him from the end of a bright tunnel. Was his mind providing that fabled tunnel of light? Was he soothing himself in his last moments, or were his parents really waiting for him, in another, better place? Levi hadn't seen them in so very long. They were smiling, arms extended to hug him, looking just as they had the last time he saw them, before a fire and a fiend had taken them from him.

As they wrapped loving arms around him, a switch in his brain turned off.

My greatest thrill is watching as a sinner breathes his or her last, allowing me to bear witness as the Lord claims another soul. I never feel closer to God than when I have taken a life for Him and He is gathering one of his flock for final judgment.

Even the threat of a passing car or an approaching pedestrian is not enough to deter me as I stand transfixed at the exact moment the Lord is welcoming Levi's soul home. The boy won't be there long, I fear, as the likes of a sodomite like Levi would find his soul sent to Purgatory at best and more likely Eternal Fire. But even the worst sinner deserves a moment of grace, and a fair shot at the Lord's mercy.

I have kept close watch on Jordan because she is God's Reward to Me. But I have kept close watch on the sodomite Levi, as well, because he was blessed by God with a brain and of Jordan's friends is the one most likely to block the Lord's path. Without him, the others will dry up and blow away like fallen leaves, as his mind and skills are the tree to which they cling.

I gather Levi's cell phone and his backpack with its laptop, even his wallet. If the police believe it's a mugging gone awry, that may be all the distraction they need to go traipsing down the wrong path. They have shown themselves to be unworthy, stunted opponents in the past, and I have no cause to think they will do any better now. Certainly not the callow youth Pryor.

Even if they perceive the transparency of the mugging ruse, they will still never suspect that the real reason I have taken the laptop is to keep the information on it away from prying eyes.

Speaking of eyes, there's just one task left to perform.

"If thy right eye offends thee. . . ."

CHAPTER SIXTEEN

Doing his own Net research, Mark started digging into the lives of Stuart Carlyle, Patti Roland, and Bradley Slavens, stopping just short of violating anyone's civil rights.

As Levi had said, Slavens was off the grid. The guy had no online presence, neither Facebook nor Twitter, nor any other social website. A Google search had brought up next to nothing, not even a photo, which was frustrating—a simple photo shown to Jordan could either rule Slavens out or give them their man.

But there was nothing about this ghost—nothing in obits, neither local nor online, though in Slavens's employment history, a short post-Havoc stay at a rival gymnastics training center did turn up, then nothing. Aggravating though this was, Mark took solace in Slavens being the least promising suspect, not fitting the time frame as well as Roland and Carlyle.

He would concentrate on them.

Roland appeared to be a first-rate gymnastics instructor. The three-year-old sexual abuse charges had been a one-time thing, most likely brought on by a mother with a conservative background being offended by Roland's openly gay lifestyle. The out-of-court resolution may have been a cash settlement or a lawyer advising against further pursuit of a weak case.

Despite the matter being a civil one, the case began with a criminal complaint that, though it didn't get anywhere, resulted in a mug shot. Patti Roland had short black hair and a narrow, angular face; with makeup she might have been borderline pretty. Without it, she looked hard and her eyes stared at the camera lens in cold rage. Was she merely angry about the false charges, or was Mark looking into the eyes of a killer? Half of a killing duo maybe?

She had frequently traveled with Havoc and had been in every city that Mark had associated with a nearby murder. Was she as clean as her record (minus that questionable sexual abuse charge) appeared? Was she capable of violence, as her angry mug shot seemed to indicate?

But her gayness spoke against that. Few lesbian couples indulged in the kind of sick sexual conquest games that male-female serial killing teams pursued. And, anyway, there was no other woman on their very short suspect list.

Likewise, Carlyle had been in all the same cities at the same times. His record was even cleaner than Roland's. He had no mug shot. But surveilling Havoc, the detective had seen the tall, lithe Carlyle several times, coming out of the center into the parking lot—his name had been stitched to the breast of his windbreaker. Pushing forty, with short blond hair, he could be the monster Jordan had described.

Yesterday he had driven to the gymnastics school and used his cell phone to grab a parking-lot picture of Carlyle. Mark got a decent three-quarter front shot as the guy was getting in his car. Then he'd called Jordan and asked if he could stop by her place, briefly, to discuss a possible suspect.

They sat at the black-topped table near the kitchenette, as before, having some of the Coke Zero left over from his previous visit.

Mark brought the photo up on his phone and handed it to her. "Is this your intruder?"

She studied it awhile.

"I'm . . . I'm not sure," she said finally. "The blond hair and blue eyes are right, but a lot of guys have those. You have those. Ten years is a long time."

She'd had to barely glance at a cell-phone photo to dismiss Havoc.

"He has . . . isn't that a scar by his eye? His right eye? The intruder didn't have that scar. But he could have gotten it since. Ten years is . . . I said that, didn't I?"

"Take your time, Jordan. Could it be him, ten years on?"

"I think maybe his eyes are spaced wider. And his hair is parted. The intruder's wasn't."

"He could have changed his hair," Mark said.

"Is there any way to tell how old a scar is?"

"Somebody with more medical expertise than me might be able to approximate when he got it."

"He's around the right age. And you can put him at the scenes of the out-of-town murders?"

"He was traveling with Havoc to nearby cities. Is it him?"

"Maybe."

That was good enough to keep Mark going. He searched the Net for a younger shot of Carlyle that might enable Jordan to make a more definitive ID; but he got nothing.

And no mug shot. The only blip on the police radar that Carlyle ever made was when he'd reported his gun stolen six years ago. The missing piece was a nine mil, like the ones used in some of the murders. A coincidence? Lot of guns like that out there, particularly Glocks, many like this one with a polygonal barrel. Hard to trace.

Had Carlyle reported the gun stolen so he could more safely use it to commit murder?

At that point, the whole twisted scenario started over.

Friday morning, a day off that he intended to start by sleeping in, Mark was awakened by his cell phone on the nightstand.

He fumbled with the thing, then heard himself saying, "Yeah. Pryor."

Captain Kelley's voice. "Pryor, you don't sound awake. It's ten-thirty, man."

"I'm awake now, sir. What is it?"

"I got the results of the bullet-matching tests from the different cases you've been looking at."

Mark sat up. "And?"

"Not great news," Kelley said. "They're all nine millimeter, but because of the polygonal barrel, there's no matching the bullets. Those interchangeable barrels make it practically impossible."

"What about shell casings?"

"The shooter appears to've picked up his brass."

"Damn."

"Don't give up so easy, Pryor—he missed one casing. The family in the Bronx? Rolled under a low sofa and he missed it."

Kelley was sounding like he was accepting as fact Mark's theory that one killer was behind these family homicides.

"So we have a casing," Mark said. "Finally something solid."

"Solid, but with nothing to compare it to. Running it through NIBIN will take for-fucking-ever."

NIBIN—the National Integrated Ballistic Information Network of the Bureau of Alcohol, Tobacco, and Firearms—matched bullet and shell casing marks from cases nationwide.

Mark said, "I may have a comparison for you."

"Yeah?"

"Long shot, but still a possibility. One of the women in that little spin-off team from the victim support group—Kay Isenberg?

I spoke to her about the supposed murder-suicide of her sister and brother-in-law, Katherine and Walter Gregory."

"Supposed?"

"Captain, it was *ruled* a murder-suicide. . . ."

"That's my memory."

"But there are some . . . discrepancies."

"Enough discrepancies to open the file of a closed case?" The old irritation was back in Kelley's tone.

Mark pressed on: "There's a right-handed bullet wound from a left-handed supposed suicide, and the wife and husband were sleeping on each other's side of the bed."

"And you think that's enough to—"

"I didn't bring it to you, Captain," Mark said, "but I'm raising it now because there was a Glock at the scene. Might be worth comparison."

"This so-called serial killer of yours has the most fluid goddamn MO I ever heard of. It's almost like you were just stringing a bunch of unrelated homicides together to see how big a jackass you can make out of me. What the hell am I going to do with you, son?"

"Keep helping me?"

After a long sigh of exasperation, Kelley said, "You come up with anything else about any of these murders that might lead us somewhere?"

"We *are* making some strides, sir."

" 'We'? Don't tell me you've got Pence talked into helping you on your off-hours. He wouldn't help his grandmother across the street."

Mark smiled. "No, I haven't bothered Pence beyond using him as a sounding board. I've got one of the support group members doing some computer research on the case—kid named Levi Mills."

Suddenly the back-and-forth stopped and silence took the line—Mark thought perhaps they'd been cut off.

Then Kelley's voice returned, his voice soft: "What was that name, again?"

"Whose name?"

"The, uh, the computer kid."

"Levi Mills. Why?"

"You have an address on him?"

"Sure." Mark gave it to him, worry prickling his neck.

"Same Levi Mills," Kelley said, still soft. "Friendly with this kid?"

"Somewhat. Nice young man."

"Well, I'm sorry, but your nice young man was murdered last night."

". . . Shit."

"Call came in a couple of hours ago. An early morning dog walker found the body."

Mark practically swallowed the phone. "I want to go to that crime scene. And don't say I'm not homicide, Captain, because—"

"I *want* you over there. Damnit! This is the son in that Mills double homicide over in Ashtabula?"

"Yes, sir."

"You stay away from the media. Once they know that the only surviving member of a massacred family was murdered himself, this is going to blow up. You may get a lot of company looking into this thing. Multi-city task force, the works. But for now?"

"Yes, sir?"

"Get your ass over to that crime scene, and pitch in as needed. Grant and Lynch are over there. I'll let them know you're on the way."

Kelley gave him the location. Mark threw on one of his cheap, dark work suits and made tracks.

Driving over, thoughts fought for attention in his mind. Had they somehow attracted the serial killer's notice? Had Levi stumbled onto something and exposed himself? Were Jordan and the others in danger, too? Or was this all just a coincidence? A mugging gone wrong or something?

He used hands-free dialing to get Jordan on her cell.

"Morning," she said.

"You home?"

"Yeah. Why?"

"I need you to stay there until you hear from me again. Don't let anybody in but me, and find something to defend yourself with."

"What the fuck is going on?"

". . . Levi's been murdered."

"What?"

"I don't know the details. I'm on my way to the crime scene. When I know more, you'll know more."

"Pick me up. Take me with you."

"No. Call David, Phillip, and Kay and tell them to stay inside and not let anybody in. Please don't tell them about Levi yet. I'll tell them myself, when I have more to share. Got that?"

"Take me with you!"

"No."

He ended the call.

He made it quickly across town to the Shaker Square RTA station. Traffic in the westbound lanes was being swept over to the curb lane while patrol cars, Grant's Crown Vic, a crime scene van, and an ambulance were all parked in the lane closest to the station, which sat on an island between the east and westbound lanes of Shaker Boulevard.

Pulling in behind the others, Mark threw it into park, turned on the Equinox's flashers, and got out. The sun was high and a faint breeze announced the irony of a beautiful spring day.

A crowd of onlookers strained at the crime scene tape with patrolmen just beyond. Mark stretched to see over the small crowd—although the yellow tape line had been positioned near the station, the cops were grouped near a grove of trees a good twenty-five yards west, near the sidewalk.

With some effort, Mark edged through the crowd—he understood the mob mentality, but what did they hope to see at a murder scene, exactly? He showed his badge to the nearest patrolman, who raised the tape for him to crawl under.

Grant saw him coming and broke away from the rest of the cops to meet him halfway.

"Captain Kelley said you'd be joining us," the tall African-American cop said in that deep, commanding voice.

"You're okay with this?" Mark asked. He was well aware that homicide detectives, the rock stars of the force, did not like being encroached upon.

"I'll take all the damn help I can get. Cap says you knew this kid, and that he was working with you and some other civilians about the possibility these family homicides are related."

"That's right."

"I'm going to want you to fill me in about all of that, in detail. But for now? The Mills kid is over there."

The big detective pointed to a shady cluster of six trees, maybe ten or so yards west.

As they walked, Grant said, "Ask your questions, son."

"Anybody see anything?"

"No."

"Time of death?"

"No coroner yet, but from my experience and the amount of blood that's already dried? He got it sometime last night."

"Who found the body?"

"Old boy named Otto Stein. Dog walker. ID'd the kid, said they lived in the same building." Grant pointed to a seven-story brick apartment house a block west or so from their position.

"Mr. Stein say anything else?"

Grant said, "Mr. Stein got spooked pretty good. He never saw anything like this. Said that with the shadows, he might not even have noticed the body, but his schnauzer was licking at something. Turned out to be a pool of blood. That sent Mr. Stein running faster than I'd guess he has in some damn time. He went over to the train station and used his cell to call 911. That's where he waited for us."

"Where is he now?"

"A couple officers accompanied him home. Thought about impounding the mutt."

"Why's that?"

"Blood on its face. But, as you'll see, we got no shortage of that."

With the crime scene just up ahead, Mark took in the surroundings. At night this would be a quiet neighborhood—maybe the occasional walker, like Mr. Stein, or if it wasn't too late, workers from the strip mall and cinemas in the square, catching the train home. The Shaker Boulevard traffic would lighten and that dark patch of trees would be the perfect place for a mugger to lie in wait for a potential victim.

Reaching the shady grove, Mark and Grant put on plastic booties over their shoes. As he was snugging his on, Mark finally saw Levi. The young man was facedown, deep in the shadows, his battered Chuck Taylors pointed toward the detectives. His right leg and right arm were straight out from his torso, the left leg bent slightly, his left arm near his body.

Standing over the body now, the coppery aroma of blood in the air, Mark said to Grant, "He always carried his backpack, laptop in it."

"If he was just out for a walk, maybe not."

"If the bag's not in his apartment, then he had it with him, and somebody stole it." Mark shook his head. "This might just be a mugging gone wrong."

Grant shook his head. "No. Too many coincidences. A kid who was looking into his parents' murders, and a bunch of other homicides that might be related? This is who happens to be the rare mugging victim who buys it? I don't think so."

Away from direct sunshine, Mark waited a few seconds for his eyes to adjust to the much dimmer light. The crime scene team was already taking casts of the prints, and there were a lot of them in the soft earth—Levi's Chuck Taylors, another, heavier set about the same size . . . boots, maybe even combat boots. Nearer the sidewalk, Mark also noticed the paw prints of the schnauzer. Nobody was casting those.

"How did he die?" Mark asked, his gaze averting the huge area of black-caked blood that made him realize that he didn't really want to see Levi turned over. Right now, the kid was just Levi. Dead, but Levi.

"I need a look at the A side," Grant said to a crime scene guy, and the analyst gave him a nod. The African-American detective bent and gingerly eased Levi over onto his back, as if not wanting to hurt him.

Levi was way past hurting—the young man's throat had been cut, ear to ear, probably from behind, and then he'd been gutted like an animal, his shirt ripped to shreds, his insides spilled out like an overturned nest of snakes. That was vicious enough. But what had been done to his face managed to trump it.

His right eye had been carved out, none too carefully.

"The kid crossed Shaker Boulevard," Grant said, "hit the sidewalk, and somebody was waiting in the trees. Grabbed him from behind, yanked him back here, did his thing. We haven't found it, by the way."

"What?"

"The eyeball. So be careful where you step."

Mark was glad he hadn't taken time for breakfast before he left; right now, acid was burning his throat.

"Not a mugging," Grant said.

"Butchery," Mark said.

Every fear Mark had tried to keep at bay roiled up. He prayed that Jordan had followed his advice, and that she had called the others and they were being similarly cautious. Somehow, Levi had stumbled onto something and the killer had discovered as much.

Lynch trundled up beside him. "Weird shit, huh, the eyeball deal, huh?"

"His right eye," Mark said.

Grant said, "That's significant?"

"It's Biblical," Mark said, his voice steady, cool. "Matthew 5:29. 'And if thy right eye causeth thee to stumble, pluck it out, and cast it from thee.'"

Lynch wore a skeptical smirk. "What the hell does that mean?"

"It means I've been right all along—a serial killer has been running loose for years, and the CPD has done jack squat about it."

"I would tend to agree," Grant said. "Is there any sign of this perp taking souvenirs before?"

"Maybe," Mark said. But he didn't go into detail. "In any case, I don't think we have to worry about stepping on the thing. That it's gone is a message."

Grant asked, "How so?"

Mark ignored that, asking, "Was his cell on him?"

"No," Grant said, shaking his head. "Wallet's missing, too."

"That's funny," Mark said.

Lynch said, "Funny ha-ha, or funny fucked-up?"

"He tries to make it look like a mugging, a robbery, and then does this crazy eyeball routine."

"Maybe he was filling an order from an organ donor."

Mark wasn't sure if that was a dark joke or if Lynch was that dumb.

"It's another stabbing," Mark said to Grant. "That girl's picture you showed me—gotten anywhere with that?"

"The married boyfriend is cleared, but she had a lot of boy-friends, and a few johns. You're right that this has a few surface similarities, but that was a female victim."

"The Mad Butcher of Kingsbury Run had male and female victims."

"You know your history. But I don't see how that hookin'-on-the-side waitress has anything to do with this poor kid."

Unless that waitress's resemblance to Jordan had been some kind of perverted callout. . . .

The young detective stepped out of the crime scene area and removed the booties.

"Where are you headed?" Grant asked. "We need to talk."

"I have a class," Mark said.

A gymnastics class.

He followed Shaker Boulevard, State Highway 87, west. Even as the street changed names, Mark stayed on 87, weaving through traffic to its intersection with I-271, which he took to I-480, the Outer Beltway. He continued westerly, headed for Havoc's center. There, he planned to confront Carlyle and finally get some answers.

His tires squealed as he made the turn into Havoc's parking lot. To Mark's astonishment, Carlyle, blond hair bright in the sunshine, was strolling toward his car, probably headed for lunch.

Finally caught a break, he thought.

When he slammed on the brakes just short of Carlyle's car, the man turned, gave him a wide-eyed startled look, and ran.

Mark flew out of his own car, barely jamming the gearshift into park as he exited. "Cleveland PD, halt!"

That worked about as well as it usually did.

Flippin' criminals, did they *always* have to run?

Carlyle took off around the north side of the structure, between it and the credit union.

Mark took pursuit. This guy had less of a head start than Perry the Perv had, but Carlyle was in way better shape. Another parking lot waited on the backside of the building, and Mark was barely keeping up as Carlyle turned back south, going behind Havoc's business and heading for the woods at the far south end of the parking lot.

If the gymnastics coach made it into there, Mark would have a hard time keeping up, and might lose the guy in the shadowy landscape.

Kicking it up a notch, Mark sprinted after his prey. Slowly, the gap narrowed. Just as the first runner's feet left the pavement and hit a patch of grass at the edge of the forest, Mark leapt.

He caught Carlyle by the waist and the two men rolled to the ground. *Even a place kicker knows how to tackle,* he thought. As he struggled to his feet, Mark knew he had ruined another suit.

Carlyle got to one knee, but Mark was ready, pistol out.

"Stay *down*," Mark said.

Carlyle slipped back onto his stomach and, without being asked, spread-eagled.

"You're under arrest," Mark said.

"*Arrest?* What the fuck for?"

Cuffing the man's hands behind him, Mark said, "Resisting, obstruction of a police officer in the performance of his—"

"You're not workin' for my *ex-wife*?" Carlyle asked, twisting his head around, watching as Mark frisked him.

"No, Carlyle. I'm not private. Your tax dollars pay my freight."

He helped the suspect up.

Carlyle's eyes were wide and he was spitting as he talked. "I'm under arrest because I *ran*? How the hell was I supposed to know you were a cop? You didn't have a police car—how the fuck was I supposed to know you weren't sent by that bitch to serve me papers or beat the crap out of me, or—"

"I *said* 'Cleveland PD.'"

"That doesn't make you Cleveland PD."

"This does," Mark said, and read him his Miranda rights.

As Mark marched the suspect back around the building, Carlyle asked, "What's this really about? Never mind me obstructing shit, what's the *real* charge?"

"You're gonna love it, Coach Carlyle," Mark said, and couldn't hold back the grin. "First-degree murder."

CHAPTER SEVENTEEN

Though she had buzzed Mark into the building just moments before, Jordan remained jumpy as she peered through the peephole, waiting to see him fill her vision. And when he had, she flung open the door, ready to rip him a new one. Hadn't he essentially hung up on her, after hitting her with Levi's murder? Without providing any goddamn details! What the fuck?

Then, when she saw him with his disheveled hair, grass-stained suit, and torn suit coat and pants, she blurted, "Jesus, are you all right?"

"Hard day at the office," he said, and managed a small smile as he brushed by her into the apartment.

Jordan—in Indians T-shirt, jeans, and sneakers, her hair trailing down her back—had in her right hand the switchblade she had commandeered from that mugger out back.

"Where did you get that?" he said, eyeing the knife, frowning back at her.

"Didn't you know?" She clicked it shut, slipped it into her jeans pocket. "They issue these to all mental patients upon release."

He raised his hands in surrender. "Fine. I don't want to know. Truthfully, I'm glad you have something to defend yourself with."

"I don't need this to defend myself. What the hell happened to Levi? He's dead? He's *really* dead?"

He nodded solemnly, then gestured to the black-topped table. "Let's sit."

They did, and he filled her in on what he'd learned and seen. His delivery was understated, but he did not avoid the unpleasant details.

"Butchered," she said quietly. "Like my family."

"The use of a knife may indicate the same perpetrator, yes."

"You *think*? Mark, he knows we're looking for him. But he's found us, before we found him! *How* does he know?"

"That may come out in questioning."

She frowned at him. "What?"

He smiled and it was a self-satisfied smile of a sort she'd never seen from him. "I think I got him."

"What?"

"I *got* him, Jordan." He raised a fist chest high and shook it in a victory gesture. "This nightmare ends *now*. I only wish it could have ended sooner, before what happened to Levi, but . . . this is what you've been waiting for. It's finally here."

But it wasn't *what she'd been waiting for, was it? She'd wanted to find the intruder before Mark, before the police, because he had to die. This monster had to die, and at her hands. That was the only way. The* only *way.*

Proud of himself, Mark was saying, "I made an arrest before coming over here—that's why I'm so well-groomed." He gestured to his torn, soiled clothing. "I had to *tackle* his behind."

"*Whose* 'behind,' goddamnit?"

"Oh. Sorry. Stuart Carlyle."

"One of Havoc's coaches."

He nodded. "He's in custody now. That was whose picture I ran past you."

"But I couldn't identify him."

"No, but you said it *might* be the guy." Mark frowned. "By the way, you may want to forget I showed you that picture, when you're brought in to pick him out of a lineup."

"Bending the rules, Detective?"

"For you, I'd throw them all out the window."

All of them? Would you stand there and watch me kill the man, just as savagely as he killed my family? Because if you want to woo me, Mark Pryor, that's what it's going to take.

Her eyebrows went up. "What happens if it *isn't* him?"

His eyebrows furrowed. "Well . . ."

"If it's *not* him, when I get a better look at him, what then? I'll *tell* you 'what then'—it means the real killer's still out there."

"Yes," he said, though he was shaking his head no. "But the evidence indicates it is Carlyle. My work led to Havoc, and your team made suspects out of his staff. It's a joint effort we can all be proud of. We can all take credit."

"Credit! Who gives a fuck about credit?" She leaned forward. "We need to talk to the others on the team. I called them like you asked, but didn't tell them about Levi. Maybe we should call a meeting, and—"

Halfway through that, he had started to pat the air with his palms. "I'm ahead of you. I've already called David, Phillip, and Kay, and broken it to them about Levi. I've sent uniformed officers to watch Kay and David, as well."

"What about Phillip?"

"He declined police protection."

"Well, if you already have the killer in custody," she said openly sarcastic, "why bother with any of them?"

"Until you make your ID and all the evidence is in," Mark said, "we have to operate as if the killer were still at large. I could be wrong about Carlyle. You're right about that."

"I'm glad you grasp that. Because I'm not sure about that photo."
Or did she not want *to be sure?*

Mark shrugged. "As for Phillip, he's a survivor of a crime apparently unrelated to the family murders. Says since he didn't join the team until just recently, the killer probably doesn't even know he exists. He says he'll be 'extra-vigilant.' "

"That sounds like him," she said. "But you should talk him out of turning down protection. If there's any chance the killer is still out there, he needs that the same as the rest of us."

Mark was nodding. "I agree. If this killer has been watching you . . . and there's every indication that this is the case . . . then he knows all about your support group spin-off team. Might have intended targeting all of you."

"You'll talk to Phillip?"

"I will. You know, from what he said on the phone, he must be the last person alive to speak to Levi."

"Really? Why do you say that?"

"Levi was on his way over to Phillip's to work on the case. Apparently Levi had some kind of breakthrough. But he never showed. Then Phillip fell asleep waiting for him, didn't wake till morning, and . . . not surprisingly . . . got no answer when he tried to call." Mark shook his head. "Poor guy sounded shattered, hearing the news."

"I wouldn't have been surprised," Jordan said dryly, "if Levi called and said he was coming over, and then didn't show."

"Why's that?"

"We all knew that piece-of-shit car of his was a problem. Anyway, Phillip's going to be key from here on. He's the one with the computer skills."

Mark shook his head. "That shouldn't be necessary now. Even if I'm wrong about Carlyle—and I doubt I am—the one good thing that comes from Levi's murder is that a real police investigation is going to be mounted. Finally what I've been doing . . . what we've *all* been doing . . . will be recognized as valid."

She asked, "How did the killer—whether he's this Carlyle person or not—even *know* about our support-group team?"

He touched her hand and she drew it back quickly, but he reached for it, trying again, and this time she let him. He squeezed gently.

"Jordan," he said, "I'm afraid this predator may have been watching you since your release."

She frowned. "Why do you think that?"

He took a few moments, selecting his words. "There was a waitress killed in this neighborhood a few days after you got out of St. Dimpna's. She had a vague resemblance to you."

"God. How . . . how was she killed?"

"With a knife. Multiple stab wounds."

"You mean *she* was butchered, too?"

He nodded. "We can't be sure there's a connection. Sergeant Grant has a few suspects from the young woman's life—a married man, and she had her share of dates, some of them paying for the privilege."

"A prostitute?"

"Not hardcore, apparently. More casual than that, but yes. That she was found in this part of town, and that she had dark hair and your general build . . . her death may have been a message to you."

She winced in thought. "What, that he was still out here?"

"Yes. A kind of terrible, sick . . . 'welcome home.' "

Her eyes flashed and her nostrils flared. "How long have you known this?"

He put up his hands in surrender. "Hey, I didn't keep anything back from you. I knew about her death from Sergeant Grant, when he asked me to talk to you for him. But at the time, neither of us saw any connection. Now that Levi's been killed, in much the same way . . . well. It's still just a theory."

She shook her head. "What if you're wrong, Mark, and he's still out there? Watching us. *Murdering* us."

"Jordan. . . ."

And what if Mark was right, *and she would never get to bring the intruder to justice, to her very* special *brand of justice?*

She clenched her fists and shook them at the ceiling and howled in rage and pain. Then she began to sob, and she couldn't stop. She rose from the table and hugged herself and walked in weaving circles, weeping convulsively, for Levi, for her friends, for herself, and when Mark came to her and tried to put an arm around her, she pushed him away, not viciously, not on his ass this time, but away. Yet when he tried again, she did let him hold her, and she hugged him hard and cried into his chest, the tears bleeding out of her as if the blade that had punctured Levi had penetrated the wall that kept her emotions in.

He spoke soothing words, words she couldn't make out but their kind tone helped, as did the gentle pat of his hand on her back, and slowly control returned, sobbing ebbed, tears abated. He smelled good. Some kind of cologne, and it was warm in his arms, and she didn't mind being held, not at all, even if he was a man.

He brushed tears from her cheek and she backed away slightly, still in his embrace, and looked into those blue eyes, which were moist themselves, though he hadn't shed tears.

"Don't kiss me," she said.

"I won't."

"Don't you dare kiss me. It'll ruin it."

"I won't."

She kissed him.

Brief, sweet, moist with her tears, but a kiss.

"Don't get any ideas," she said.

"I won't."

"That was just 'thank you.'"

"You're welcome."

"This isn't the time."

"I know."

And she kissed him again, only not so brief, and the warmth was more than thanks on her part and the urgency of how he returned her kiss spoke passion not pity. He really had been doing all of this because he loved her. That was so obvious, and she had known it. But now she felt it.

Still in his embrace, she said, "Has to stop there."

"Okay."

"Let's go sit."

"All right."

They walked to the table, awkwardly skirting the mattress on the floor, a mattress that was a third presence in the room, silent but yelling at them. They pretended not to hear.

At the table, seated, they held hands, loosely. He looked vaguely embarrassed. He glanced back at the mattress, and she shook her head.

"Get that out of your mind," she said.

"Get what out of—"

"No."

He swallowed. Nodded.

"Maybe when this is over," she said, "who knows? Maybe after *he's* been taken care of . . . I'll feel clean again."

"You didn't do anything wrong."

"I know! But he was . . . inside me. Understand? He is a sickness and he . . . was *in* me. That's hard to live with. The idea of having any kind of . . . normal relationship, after that. . . ."

He was frowning. "Don't give him that power."

"What?"

"Jordan, he controlled you for a few minutes, a few terrible minutes. Don't give him any more than that. He doesn't deserve it."

She drew her hand away.

"Jordan . . ."

She raised a traffic-cop palm. "No. I'm not mad. I'm . . . I'm just coming to a kind of . . . realization. Having a . . . is the word *epiphany*?"

He wasn't following her. "Is it?"

Now she clutched his hand and squeezed it so tight, his eyes popped a little.

"Mark, you're *right*, you are so goddamn fucking *right*. He controlled me that night, but *I* let him control me for the next ten years. Well, that fucking ends now."

His smile was ridiculously boyish. "Jordan, I guess you know how I feel. You know I love you. That I have since—"

"Since high school. Will you stop? I'm not that innocent little girl anymore."

"I, uh, noticed."

"I am a bundle of neuroses and you need to know that and be ready to deal with it, if you want to find out if ten years later I'm worth knowing . . . never mind loving. No more kissing tonight, Detective Pryor. We have other things to do."

"You're right."

"But when this is over . . ."

When that miserable butchering bastard is dead.

"I think it *is* over," he said.

"When this is *over* . . . then we'll *start* over. We'll see if I'm anything more than some dream girl you wove out of your teenage fantasies, or if the reality of the woman I am now just isn't worth the fucking trouble."

He smiled a little. "I think you're worth the effing trouble."

"Even if I swear like a stevedore?"

"Even then."

She squeezed his hand. "We'll see. When the time comes."

"When the time comes."

". . . In the meantime, how about something to drink?"

"Sure."

"How about a sandwich?"

"I don't think I've eaten all day."

"I'll take that as a yes."

They wound up sharing the last two Coke Zero bottles from his pizza run. She made them both Swiss cheese and smoked turkey sandwiches on rye.

As the meal wound down, Jordan frowned in thought. "What do you think Levi's breakthrough might have been?"

With about two bites of his sandwich left, Mark said, "Maybe Carlyle will tell us. Otherwise, that'll be tough to figure, with Levi's laptop gone."

"It was taken?"

Mark nodded.

"Then," she said, "the killer knew there was evidence on Levi's laptop?"

"Maybe. But Carlyle also took Levi's cell."

"For now let's just say the *killer* took Levi's cell."

"Fair enough. But whoever did it took the time, just off a public thoroughfare, to make the killing look like a mugging."

"A mugger who collects eyeballs? I don't think so."

Her harshness made him blink, and he put down the remaining bite of sandwich.

"Anyway," he said, "that cell is not a great loss. I'm waiting on a warrant to get Levi's phone records now. Either our man didn't know we could get those, or didn't care. I'm guessing it's the latter."

"So he *was* after the laptop."

"I would say so." Mark used a paper napkin and had a last swig from his glass of Coke Zero on ice. "You'll have to take a ride downtown for a lineup, to identify Carlyle, tomorrow. Cool with that?"

She half rose. "Hell, I can do it right now."

He gestured for her to settle down. "The wheels don't grind that fast. I'll call you in the morning. Okay?"

"Okay. You're . . . going?"

"Yeah, I have a couple more things to do yet tonight." He rose. "There's a patrol car out front and it'll stay there all night, and tomorrow, too, till I say otherwise. You're protected. But just stay put till you hear from me, okay?"

"Okay."

She walked him to the door and she squeezed his hand. He looked at her like he wanted to kiss her, but she shook her head.

"Can't blame a guy for trying," he said, maybe a little embarrassed.

Then he was gone, and she was alone.

Shit!

She should be thrilled that Mark had apparently caught the intruder, and he probably thought he deserved more gratitude than she'd shown, maybe another kiss or even more.

Only she didn't want the intruder's ass in jail—she wanted his throat in her hands!

Maybe she could go down there for that lineup tomorrow morning and say he wasn't the guy, and they would release him, and she could . . .

Yes.

That would do nicely.

She curled up on the mattress and slept more soundly than she had in a very long time.

CHAPTER EIGHTEEN

Mark contemplated whether it would be more satisfying throwing his cell phone against a wall or pitching it off a high bridge. He'd been on the go all day, and had forgotten to recharge the thing last night, and now the g.d. battery was dead.

Had he been in an unmarked, he could have called in to the dispatcher to say he was on his way to see Phillip Traynor. But he was in his Equinox, and the trip from Jordan's apartment to Phillip's house at 38th and Chatham hadn't been enough for his phone, plugged into the cigarette lighter, to raise a single bar.

The neighborhood was a quiet one, and midevening, relieved only by occasional streetlamps, this area looked little different than it must have decades ago. Perhaps some of the houses seemed somewhat long in the tooth, peeling paint when their owners hadn't upgraded to siding. But the house on the corner, a twenties- or thirties-era two-story clapboard, sported a fairly fresh coat of white paint, and the smallish yard was immaculately well tended, lawn recently cut, bushes trimmed. No car parked out front, but an alley and likely a freestanding garage would be out back.

The physically and emotionally exhausting day seemed to press down on Mark as he trudged up the winding walk to a door at the far right side of the house. He climbed the five steps to the porch, and raised a finger to the doorbell, but before he even touched it, he was bathed in white by a switched-on porch light.

The door opened, framing Phillip there, the man smiling his rather horrible, lipless smile and nodding, looking oddly formal for this time of night. As had been the case at the coffee-shop meeting Mark had attended, Phillip wore a white shirt, a navy-blue cotton tie, and pressed navy slacks, his slippered feet the only sign of any at-home relaxation.

Then Phillip's smile disappeared and a concerned expression took its place. "Detective Pryor—I hope nothing else has happened."

"Sir, I'm sorry to just drop by—I realize it's getting late. I tried to call, but my cell phone is dead. I only need a few moments of your time." Mark gestured around the open porch. "We can talk right here, if you like."

"Don't be silly, Detective," Phillip said, gesturing graciously. "Come in. I'm anxious for an update."

Mark stepped inside and his host closed the door behind them. The foyer was small, with oak stairs and a heavy banister almost immediately rising before him, leading to a landing that made a quick left turn to the darkened second floor. A hallway to the left of the stairs led back to the white glow of the kitchen. To his left, separated from the foyer by a half wall and two oak columns, the formal living room seemed like something from another era. On the half wall nearest Mark, a baseball bat sat atop a short stand. He couldn't help taking a closer look—the darn thing was boldly auto-graphed by Albert Belle!

"Some collectible," Mark said.

Phillip's grin was unsettling. "Quite proud of that. Got it online—cost me something of a small fortune, I'm afraid. Are you an Indians fan, Detective?"

"That's an understatement," Mark admitted.

"What about this year? You think they stand a chance?"

"Little soon to tell. They've got some good young talent, especially the pitching. If everything falls together, who knows?"

"I like your optimism," Phillip said, and gestured for Mark to enter the living room, which he did, followed by his host. They walked across an area rug full of grays and maroons that looked antique but was so plush and clean, it might have been brand-new.

The large space recalled his grandmother's house, with its similarly massive fireplace, framed photos neatly arranged across the mantel in both cases. Separated by a curtained window onto the front lawn were a pair of Victorian-looking, deep red velvet-cushioned chairs. To his right, open pocket doors revealed a dining room with a long dark oak table with carved decorative flourishes, runner, and centerpiece.

The place had a certain "old lady" tidiness—did Phillip live with an elderly mother?

As if a barrier between Mark and the dining room doorway, a wide brown couch squatted, facing the chairs. On a low-slung coffee table, Phillip's laptop lay open, screen facing the sofa.

Phillip offered him one of the two chairs, then sat in the other. Mark sat. A tree stump would have been more comfortable.

"It's been a difficult day," Phillip said, sighing, shaking his head. "This is why I normally avoid getting close to people—it opens one up for sorrow."

The man's mode of speech was precise, but ragged breaths interspersed themselves between most words. Mark found it difficult to look at the man—he wasn't proud of that, but there it was. The damage that had been done to Jordan stayed within her; poor Phillip had to wear his for the world to see.

Phillip was saying, "I'd become very fond of Levi."

"He was a nice kid."

"He was a lovely boy, very intelligent. Such a senseless loss. Tragic." He nodded toward the laptop. "I tried to get some work done on the case, but I'm afraid I've been rather worthless today."

"You're apparently the last person to speak to Levi. Did he say what he was working on?"

"I just sensed that he'd had a breakthrough." Phillip's sigh was a rattling thing. "I wish I had more for you."

"You worked closely with him, this last week. What was he working on, do you know?"

Phillip was sitting with both feet on the floor, hands folded in his lap; there was something almost prim about it. "I know he was looking into that assistant at Havoc's gymnastics school—Stuart Carlyle? He was digging in deep, and that young man could make the Internet dance. I think to Levi, Carlyle was the chief suspect."

"That's something that I hope will give you some sense of relief, Mr. Traynor—I arrested Carlyle today. I believe he's our man."

He filled Phillip in on the details.

"Jordan will go down to the county jail tomorrow," Mark said, "and identify him."

"You sound confident."

"Well, she *was* somewhat hesitant to make a positive ID of Carlyle, based on a cell phone shot I grabbed of him. She said it *could* be the man."

"He surely changed over a decade. And it's been ten years since that attack, which left Jordan an emotionally overwrought young woman . . . literally a mental case, not to be unkind. If she identifies him, will she be taken seriously?"

"I think so," Mark said. "But she's only part of it. The department will be launching a full-scale investigation into all of these family murders. Very soon the FBI will be involved. It's all changing."

Phillip chuckled dryly. "No more off-duty investigations by a rookie detective? No more kaffeeklatsch amateur inquiries?"

"No," Mark said, with a serious smile. "The real detectives will take over."

"You seem convinced that Carlyle is your man."

"I am. But . . . frankly . . . I've been wrong before. Right now I'm operating on the assumption that our man may still be out there."

"You mean, you believe in the presumption of innocence. That Carlyle isn't guilty until the justice system, including a jury trial, says that he is."

"Well . . . not exactly. If he's not the guy, it will start with Jordan saying he isn't, and then the evidence will speak. We're still looking for that third coach—Slavens—and there's some very suspicious activity on his part."

"How so?"

"I'm not at liberty to give you the details. But let's say, suspicious enough that I don't rule him out—or the possibility that he and Carlyle were a killing duo."

And so much was left for this new official investigation—getting tests back on the shell casings for a start. If the Glock found near Kay's late brother-in-law matched the New York shell casing, and the gun turned out to be Carlyle's stolen pistol, then a slam dunk was coming.

Mark said, "I do think there's enough doubt that it would be advisable for you to have police protection. Let me make a call from here, and I'll get a patrol car out front. Right away."

Phillip shook his head. "Not necessary."

"If it means anything, Jordan sent me over here specifically to ask you to reconsider. I was at the crime scene. I saw what this monster did to Levi. Trust me, you don't want to take any chances."

The lipless smile made a terrible crease in the ravaged face. "Detective, meaning no offense, especially not to you personally— but we both know this individual certainly has the capacity to circumvent a simple parked police car. After all, he's been outsmarting the police for over a decade."

"I can't argue with that, sir. But that was before. This is all catching up with him. And, all due respect, I believe police protection can create a wall between you and this madman."

"I appreciate your concern, young man. I really do. But, no. I can protect myself." He gestured toward his flattened features. "I was attacked once. My guard has not been lowered since."

"I can understand that, but—"

He gestured vaguely around. "There are weapons salted here and there in my home. I am prepared for any contingency."

This was an extraordinarily dangerous attitude, but Mark had said his piece. Ultimately, it was up to Phillip.

Shifting in the uncomfortable chair, Mark said, "I understand you're a professor of religion."

"Well, an instructor." Phillip gave up a wry chuckle. "It's hard to be a 'professor' online."

"Still, that makes you an expert. Any other thoughts on that Bible verse the killer quoted to Jordan?"

"It's amazing that she spoke to you of that."

"Well, she did. Told me about that entire terrible night in detail."

Phillip shook his head and formed what Mark guessed was a half smile. "She must trust you, Detective Pryor. She held that in for a very long time."

"What about the verse?"

"Well . . . I can tell you that Levi thought it was the key. We spoke at length about its various interpretations, found opinions and even articles on the Net."

Mark sighed, nodded. "I've done that myself, not that I've gotten anywhere much."

"I'd be happy to hear *your* views, Detective."

"Okay. Well. Deuteronomy is a book about the law . . . *God*'s law."

Phillip chuckled. "That's a statement that could be made about most books of the Bible."

"There was a theory the coffee-shop team flirted with, early on, Jordan said . . . but that got tossed by the wayside. It might apply."

"What theory is that?"

"That these were hate crimes."

A ghastly smile appeared on the lipless lips. "You think this individual has appointed himself, what . . . God's sheriff?"

"Couldn't it be that simple? Take Jordan's family. Her brother, Jimmy, was openly gay. Many conservative Christians consider that a sin, though I don't believe it's really in the Bible anywhere."

"Leviticus," Phillip said, correcting him. "20:13. 'If a man also lie with mankind, as he lieth with a woman, both of them have committed an abomination: they shall surely be put to death; their blood shall be upon them.'"

Mark smiled. "I thought I knew my Bible pretty well, but I'm out of my league talking to you."

Phillip shrugged. "Bad habit teachers have—correcting everyone, even outside of class."

Mark sat forward. "No, I appreciate the help. Like . . . I'm still having trouble with Deuteronomy. What the heck does this mean— 'Thou shalt not wear garments of divers sorts; as of woolen and linen together?' Any ideas?"

Phillip leaned back, gathering his thoughts. Mark watched him, the lipless mouth, the smashed nose, the loud breathing, all so hideous, and yet the vibe he got from Phillip was one of peacefulness. The man seemed . . . what word best described it? Serene.

When Phillip spoke, it was as if he were tasting each word before uttering it. "What if it's a racial interpretation?"

"Racial? But it's about clothing, isn't it?"

"Different kinds of cloth . . . different races? Not to be mixed?"

Mark was nodding. "The Riveras were a mixed marriage. David Elkins's wife is African-American. You might be on to something."

Phillip raised a gently lecturing finger. "But I would hesitate before I went looking for a racist, some Ku Klux Klan nincompoop. This would not be an individual who considered any one race superior— just someone who respected God's law that racial lines not be mixed."

"But that falls apart with Levi."

Phillip shrugged. "Levi was gay."

"That might have been a partial motivation for Levi's murder. But he was deeply closeted, as to his sexuality, back when his parents were killed. And they were both white, so the racial motive is out."

Phillip frowned. "I thought he mentioned that his mother was Jewish. And I believe his father was Catholic."

"I believe you're right. You think religious differences might constitute a mixed marriage in this madman's mind?"

His host gestured with an open hand. "Being Jewish is also an ethnicity."

"Hadn't thought of that."

"Ethnically, I'm Jewish myself."

"But not by religion?"

"No. Christianity is a better fit for me. But being raised a Jew has been helpful in my profession—I have a better grasp on the Old Testament, for example, than most Christians."

"Interesting," Mark said, but felt they were getting off the track. Still, Phillip was a godsend as a resource for Biblical interpretation.

"For the sake of argument," Mark said, "let's say you're right. These families have in some way broken God's law, and he's going to fix it. How does he find these sinful families? Does he stalk them? If so, for how long?"

"Theology is my business, Detective. I'm afraid you're going well beyond my skill set."

"Right. Right, I'm sorry. Well, there's another Bible verse to explore. This one is only implied, but it's there."

"Which is what?"

Realizing he might be revealing confidential police information, Mark nonetheless told Phillip about Levi's eye having been carved out by the killer.

" 'If thy eye offend thee,' " Phillip said. "There are any number of interpretations of that one."

"I'll just bet. Listen, are you up for digging in yet tonight? Or should I come back tomorrow?"

Phillip glanced at his wristwatch, then shrugged. "We could spend an hour or so, yet tonight. I'm up for that if you are, Detective. But if I may be frank? You look a little tired to me."

"I could use some coffee," Mark admitted.

"I'll make some," Phillip said, rising. The lipless smile managed to seem pleasant. "Give me five minutes. You just relax . . . if you fall asleep, I'll nudge you awake."

Alone in the living room now, Mark got up, stretched, walked around a little. He would need that coffee. At the mantel, he paused at the framed photos.

He started at the left end, working his way right. The photos went back decades, to Phillip's childhood, probably, although Mark didn't recognize a young version of him in any of them. First in the row was a family portrait, everyone blond, their attire conservative, not unlike Phillip's preferred fashion now. The man and two young boys in shirts and ties, the woman and a girl in long, high-neck dresses. They stood in a yard, in front of a white crackerbox, not unlike the anonymous midcentury modern houses in the Sully family's neighborhood.

The next photo was just the kids, the three of them in a park, sitting on a playground bench in their Sunday best, not playing despite the setting. They rarely seemed to smile in these oddly joyless pictures. The family in these photos seemed to consist of two adults and three little adults. Nothing like his own family's smile-filled photos.

A shot at the end of the mantel stopped him cold—was this portrait of a blond young man in his twenties that of a pre-disfigurement Phillip? It might have been Phillip—it was hard to tell, though the thin-lipped straight line of his non-smile seemed to foreshadow the lipless future.

Yet there was something familiar about this face, something that had nothing to do with Phillip. He had seen that face before.

Where?

Then he had it—*this was the face Jordan had drawn, the face she kept magnet-pinned to her refrigerator,* and in a flash he knew why she did that, and in that same flash he knew exactly who Phillip was, and in the next moment, he broke a very old promise.

He said, "Oh shit."

He was going for the pistol on his hip as he spun, and there Phillip was, and he was swinging something, it was blurring toward him, though the bold signature ALBERT BELLE told Mark exactly what he was being hit with, before the world exploded in shiny, tiny stars against a black background, as if a firecracker had gone off inside his skull.

He crumpled to the floor. Though the pain centered in his head, his body burned as if his every nerve ending had fired simultaneously.

"Sentimentality," Phillip was saying, from somewhere in the room, "is not a sin, but it's probably a failing, particularly for a man with my calling."

Mark tried to get to his feet, but couldn't make his legs obey. His eyes were half open, the world a distorted blur.

"Those family photos should probably go," Phillip said, thoughtfully. "That one you were admiring is from back when I was Brad Slavens. I was Brad a rather long time."

On his back, Mark tried to roll to one side, vaguely aware that Phillip was pushing on him, then pulling at something. The detective's right hand managed to find its way to his hip holster, but the gun was gone.

He fought to keep his eyes open, which were swelling shut at an alarming rate, his vision filling with a curtain of blood. His face burned so hot that he thought Phillip might have set him on fire after hitting him with that bat.

Reality came back with a painful vengeance as the bat crashed down into his ribs. He actually felt them splinter. The pain burned like spreading flames. His breathing became a ragged, labored thing, not unlike Phillip's.

His host brought the bat down on Mark's leg, crushing his shin, pain exploding through him again, white-hot and everywhere.

Mark tried to roll into a ball, but could not. Again the bat, this time on the other side, struck Mark's ribs. Breathing was impossible now. Short, tortured gasps, each weaker than the last. To his surprise, the pain settled into the background. Still there, powerful, constant, but not at the forefront of his consciousness. That honor went to Jordan. He loved her so. On the floor, helpless, life leaking quickly away, he fought against the worst agony of all.

That he would never see her again.

Stabbing pains all over his body brought him back. He was in his car, in the driver's seat, with no memory of getting there. Barely able to see, yet looking through the windshield, he somehow knew the Equinox was perched atop Ninth Street's notorious Suicide Hill. Car running . . . but not in gear?

The driver's side door opened. Mark, eyes nearly swollen shut, could still make out the hideous countenance of Phillip Traynor.

Mark's broken lips somehow carried one word out to his tormentor: "Why?"

Phillip ignored him, leaning way over him, jamming something in next to the detective, and the engine began to race.

The driver's side door closed, and a moment later, the passenger side opened. Phillip leaned in again. He took Mark's chin in his hand.

"I *will* possess her again," Phillip said, his noseless breathing audible over the engine noise. "She is my reward, you see, for serving a merciful God."

"You . . . sick . . . fuck," Mark moaned, trying to move, not moving.

Phillip laughed, jammed the gear shift into drive, and jumped clear.

The Equinox roared down the hill toward Lake Erie. In the forties, Suicide Hill became famous for cars hurtling down its steep incline and intentionally flying into the lake. So many times had this happened that the city fathers installed concrete pylons at the foot.

Speeding down the hill, Mark helplessly hoped that cross traffic might stop him before he hit bottom—getting broadsided would be better than crashing into those concrete pylons! At this hour, though, no other cars were around, just the Equinox making its inexorable journey.

Too many things were broken in him, the pain too great, for him to move his legs to get to the brake pedal. He looked down at the gear shift . . . if he could just put the car into park. That would slow it down, stop it dead. . . .

His hands would not move. He felt glued to the seat. The speedometer read over eighty now, the concrete pylons waiting, unmovable, practically beckoning him.

His cell!

If he could just get to the phone, it might be charged now, and he could warn Jordan, save Jordan. He saw the thing, sliding back and forth across the passenger seat, as if playing keep-away. With all his remaining strength, he reached for it. His fingers touched the cell, barely, then it slipped away.

When the Equinox slammed into the concrete, Mark was aware of the sound of tearing metal, breaking glass, and his own pitiful scream, a scream so weak even he couldn't hear it. Hardly feeling the sharp shards tearing at him, Mark was thrown backward when the airbag exploded in his face, hitting him with nearly as much force as had Phillip's bat, a lifetime of minutes ago.

The last thing he said, before blackness took him, was "Jordan." Soft as a whisper, urgent as a prayer. Heard by nobody at all.

CHAPTER NINETEEN

Jordan sat in the ER waiting area next to Captain Kelley, Mark's boss. Kelley had called her about Mark's accident and asked her to join him at the hospital. He'd told her nothing more than that Mark was still alive. It had still been dark when the Vespa took her to top-rated Cleveland Clinic on Euclid.

Whether that was encouraging or a sign of the seriousness of Mark's condition, she could only guess. That was one of a thousand thoughts that careened through her mind as she raced through a chilly predawn city in a fresh sweatshirt and last night's jeans. Was it the cold that made her feel so numb? No tears, though her heartbeat was accelerated, providing a percussive beat for her reckless ride through mostly empty streets.

Kelley had met her outside the ER, where he stood smoking. Despite the early hour, the commanding-looking captain was unmistakable, though she'd never met him before, impeccable in a dark gray suit and darker gray tie, a lanyard badge identifying him with photo ID.

Mark was in surgery, his condition critical.

The circumstances of the accident, as reported to her by Kelley, were mystifying to Jordan—she knew all about Suicide Hill, and its history of accidents and suicides, but how Mark—apparently in the middle of the night—had been at that location, speeding and losing control of the Equinox, made no sense. Unless . . . unless. . . .

She said to Kelley, "You said you couldn't give me any details. I understand this is a police matter. Obviously that's what it is."

"It's good you understand." His half-hooded eyes in that African mask of a face had a brooding quality. This man could explode, and somewhere in there, his fuse was lit. Why?

She made an educated guess—ten years around mental patients gave her certain insights.

"You approved Mark's off-duty investigating, didn't you?"

He nodded.

The hustle and bustle of the ER, the dings of periodic bells, intercom voices, provided a backdrop of urgency as they sat enveloped in a bubble of quiet.

She asked, "Why would you do that?"

Fire flared in eyes that, momentarily, were not hooded. "What do you mean, Ms. Rivera?"

"I mean you either believed he was on to something, or you had a special regard . . . maybe even, affection? For Mark." She shrugged. "Maybe both."

Kelley shrugged. "He's got a lot on the ball. Also, he's impetuous. Naive."

"Yet you let him poke around out there alone."

He frowned at her. "What are you saying, Ms. Rivera?"

"I'm guessing you know all about our little support group spin-off team. Victims who've gathered together to, well . . . to do *your* job?"

"Ms. Rivera, I understand you're upset—"

Calmly, she said, "You would never dream how upset I am. I might be upset enough to go to your superiors and ask why you allowed a young, inexperienced officer to go out by himself into harm's way."

Kelley shifted in the plastic chair. "I called you, Ms. Rivera, as a courtesy. Because I know you and Mark are friends."

"That's nice of you. And I think you do like Mark. He sure spoke well of you. Looks up to you. He lost his father at a fairly young age—not as young as *I* did, but . . . well."

"What's your point, Ms. Rivera?"

"My point is, I can be an adversary, Captain, or an ally. I'd rather be your ally."

"I'd rather you were."

"Good. Then stop fucking around and fill me the fuck in."

He frowned, then smiled a little. "I could use another smoke."

"Let's step outside."

"You say that like somebody about to give somebody else an ass whooping."

"No. I just did that. *Now* we can talk."

Outside, where it was still chilly, though the sun was climbing, Kelley exhaled smoke and said, "A witness said the car never slowed down—no brake lights. Said it looked like Pryor intentionally ran into the pylons."

"*Suicide?* Well, that's bullshit. Not Mark."

Kelley shrugged. "He's a sensitive kid. He may have blamed himself for the Levi Mills murder."

"Mark was with me, Captain, just a few hours before this travesty happened. When he comes out of that operation, you'll see. He'll tell you. But for now, you'll have to take my word for it."

Kelley sighed. "I already do. That kid was happy. High as hell that he'd hauled that suspect in—Carlyle."

She shook her head. "I don't think Carlyle's your man."

"Ms. Rivera, you haven't been in for the lineup yet."

"Mark showed me his picture—hey, I didn't *tell* you that. I'll deny I told you that."

"You never told me that. Go on."

"I told Mark that Carlyle *might* have been the guy. There were things that were off about him, and I allowed that somebody could change in ten years, and . . . I think Mark kind of heard what he wanted to hear."

"I don't know—Carlyle seems right for this."

"Not now he doesn't. He was in behind bars, wasn't he, when this 'accident' went down?"

Kelley frowned. "You think this . . . this family killer did this?"

"Don't you?"

"We have a witness . . ."

"Your witness is full of shit."

Kelley grunted a laugh. "Probably. It was a guy on foot, half in the bag."

"Well then."

"Anyway, I only mention that Mark *may* have done this intentionally as it's a possibility we have to rule out. Our crime scene team has just started investigating, and we need to cover all the bases."

"What does Phillip have to say?"

"Phillip? Phillip who?"

She frowned at him irritably. "Phillip *Traynor*. Recent addition to our support-group team? Mark was heading to Traynor's house when he left my place. Why, didn't he make it there?"

Kelley tossed his cigarette and it sailed away spitting sparks. "You got contact info on this Traynor? Phone? Address?"

"Sure," she said. She got out her cell. "What's your number? I'll text it over."

Soon she was sitting alone in the ER waiting area, Kelley off dealing with this new information. She checked her watch—it was six. Fucking early, but she had to do it. She started making the calls, David first.

"What's up?" David said. Obviously he knew if she called this early, there was a good reason.

She quickly filled him in.

David said, "But it's *not* an accident, is it?"

"No. And the suspect Mark arrested yesterday is a dead end. Either that, or he's half of a team."

Kelley was coming back over.

"Can't talk," she whispered. "Just stay inside, and keep alert."

"I'll call Phillip and Kay for you."

"Thanks. But just Kay. The police are getting in touch with Phillip, 'cause Mark was heading over there last night. All I can say."

She ended the call.

Kelley was sitting down next to her again. "Who was that?"

"David from our team. He's calling Kay. Also on our team. Didn't Mark tell you anything?"

He ignored that. "Well, Phillip from your 'team' isn't answering. I've got officers on the way there. Should know something soon."

Jordan nodded.

"Ms. Rivera, with Mark sidelined, I need to meet with you and your friends as soon as possible. I want to be filled in, in depth, on everything you've shared with Mark, and frankly anything you haven't."

She nodded again.

"As a show of good faith," he said, turning almost sideways in his chair to really look at her, "I'll give you some information we're withholding, for now. Thanks to Mark, we've matched a shell casing from a family killing in the Bronx to the gun found at the Walter and Katherine Gregory crime scene."

She squinted at him, as if she were reading fine print. "So Kay's sister and brother-in-law . . . that *wasn't* a murder-suicide?"

"No. And it's now linked to the *other* family killings. Almost certainly the same perpetrator."

"Have you told Kay?"

"Not yet. We need to get our ducks in a row, first. Please keep that to yourself for now."

"All right."

"I have a call in to the FBI," he said, "and I anticipate they will be getting involved—maybe taking over—very soon. Perhaps yet today."

She gave him another nod.

"You should feel good about what you've accomplished," he said. "But I'd suggest you accept that from here on out, you're going to be on the sidelines."

"Like Mark."

"I hope not like Mark. If you're right, and we have a serial killer who is accelerating and devolving right in front of us, you and your friends are in danger, until we've either determined Carlyle is indeed our man . . ."

"Unlikely."

". . . or find the son of a bitch who is. You'll be kept under top-level police protection, and so will your friends."

She cocked her head. "You think Phillip is dead?"

"No reason to think that."

"Yet."

He nodded, and admitted, "Yet. I don't mean to be unkind, Ms. Rivera, but there's been a high cost to what you've accomplished. You've flushed out a killer, yes . . . but Levi Mills is dead, and Mark is in the operating room. Are you ready to leave this to the professionals?"

"Sure."

This seemed to satisfy him. "Good." He rose. "I have a few things to check up on. I've instructed the nurses at the station to let you know when Mark is out of surgery, if I'm not back first."

"Thanks."

He nodded, gave her a tentative smile, perhaps not entirely trusting her, and left the waiting area.

Was Phillip dead? If so, had she caused it? Was Levi's murder her fault? Mark's accident?

She almost flew into the little restroom nearby and leaned over the stool and threw up, or rather tried to—there was nothing in her stomach, and the effort was as wrenching and pointless as she suspected her investigation may have been. She sat there and cried and cried, for how long she wasn't sure. Then she rose, threw cold water on her face, dried off, and looked in the mirror at the blank countenance that she provided the world.

About five minutes after she'd returned to her chair in the waiting area, David and Kay blew in, two uniformed cops trailing in behind them, then lingering near the nurses' station.

Jordan got up as Kay came up to embrace her. The urge to push the woman away came and went in the same breath. She didn't mind being touched, being held, not by this good woman.

And not by Mark. Never again would Mark's touch be anything but welcome.

David, aware of her boundaries, gave her shoulder a quick squeeze and nodded and smiled, somberly. "I know you said to stay put. We just couldn't."

"For once," Jordan said, with a weak smile, "I'm glad you didn't listen to me."

Kay sat on her left and David on her right.

Despite her promise to Captain Kelley, Jordan immediately told the woman about the new ballistics evidence that disproved Kay's brother-in-law and sister's "murder-suicide."

Kay covered her mouth, as if stifling a scream, then began to cry. Jordan slipped an arm around the woman, and David came around and did the same thing. Then Kay slipped away from Jordan and threw herself into David's arms and he comforted her, smiling past Kay at Jordan and shrugging a little.

So they were an item, after all. Well, good for them.

Perhaps three minutes later, Kay excused herself and went off to the restroom, almost running.

Vaguely embarrassed, David said, "It just kind of happened. Two lonely people. You know how it goes."

"I'm happy for you. This is over, anyway. Our part of it."

"I suppose it is, with the police all over the investigation finally. We accomplished something, didn't we, after all?"

"I don't know. Levi's dead, Mark's fucked-up, and I'm almost positive the guy the cops have locked up isn't my intruder."

David leaned in intently. "What's your thinking on that?"

"You're so right—what happened to Mark was no accident. That was a murder attempt. Unless you think maybe Mark tried to kill himself."

David shook his head. "Utter nonsense."

"Absolutely. Your job now is make sure you and Kay are safe. Either stay in tight police custody, or take a quick vacation and don't tell anybody where you're going. Follow the news and come back when it's safe."

Frowning, David said, "Shouldn't we stay around and help the police?"

"Take your laptop with you. Forward anything you've got to Captain Kelley. I'll get you his contact info—he's Mark's boss."

Kay came back, tidied up, smiling, with only her red eyes betraying anything. She took her old seat, putting David on one side, Jordan on the other.

"I have no idea how I'm going to process this," the woman said. "Knowing the truth doesn't change anything, exactly—Walter and Katherine are still dead. The horror of thinking they'd been a murder-suicide is gone . . . but now, who knows what they were *really* put through?"

David, patting her hand, said, "You'll work through it."

"They were his victims, weren't they? The family killer's? Here I thought I was just along because I needed a ride home from David . . . but turns out I was a full-fledged member all the time."

Kay smiled bitterly and tears welled, but kept their place. She was twisting a tissue in her time-honored fashion.

"It was my intruder, all right," Jordan said. "The gun used to murder Walter and Katherine was allegedly stolen from the man Mark thought was his main suspect."

David frowned. "But that suspect is in jail."

Jordan nodded. "Yes, but who could most easily steal a gun from a coach's desk at Havoc's school?"

He nodded, smiled. "Another coach."

"Right. And Mark was looking very hard at Bradley Slavens, the third coach, the one who dropped out of sight two years ago."

Footsteps like gunshots were coming their way, and they turned toward Captain Kelley, walking briskly toward them. Almost running.

Jordan quickly identified Kay and David to the detective—handshake-type introductions did not seem called for, particularly judging by Kelley's intense manner.

He said to Jordan, "Traynor's not in his house and there are signs of a struggle—lots of blood, but nobody there, alive or dead."

Kay sat forward. "Then the killer has Phillip!"

"Apparently," Kelley said. "This means the three of you are going into protective police custody, preferably away from your homes. We have several hotels we use as safe houses."

David said, "What if I don't care to do that?"

"Then I'll arrest you as a material witness." He turned to Jordan. "Ms. Rivera, I know you want to wait around to see how Mark does. But when you're ready to leave, you call me. I'll arrange a police escort home for you to gather your things. We're going on full lockdown."

David said, "What about us?"

"You may stay here at the hospital as long as you like, if you care to keep Jordan company on her . . . vigil. Whenever you like, the officers who accompanied you here will take you home to prepare for some time away. A little vacation on Cleveland's taxpayers."

Kay said, "That's really necessary?"

"Your friend Levi is dead, my detective is in surgery fighting for his life, and your other pal Phillip may well be dead, too. So you will follow instructions. Understood?"

Everyone nodded, including Jordan.

Kelley stalked off.

Kay shuddered. "Awful to think that Phillip . . . poor Phillip . . . may be dead, too." David slipped an arm around her.

Jordan said, "I suppose that's one way to look at it."

They all turned to her.

David asked, "What other way is there?"

"Phillip could be my intruder. Our family killer."

Kay goggled at her. *"What?"*

"Levi was on his way to see Phillip," Jordan said, "when he was killed."

"But . . . wasn't Phillip at home when Levi called him?"

"He probably told Levi that. And that's what he told the police. But he might have been outside Levi's place. Watching. Waiting. He seized the opportunity when Levi called. Possibly jimmied Levi's car to send him to the train station, to waylay him."

"That," David said, frowning in thought, "is actually feasible. But, Jordan, you *saw* your attacker!"

"Maybe I saw Phillip . . . *before* his face suffered damage. And what do you want to bet he *wasn't* an innocent victim of senseless violence? Some victim fought back and did that to him."

Kay said, "But he's been nothing but helpful . . ."

Jordan said, "He insinuated his way onto the team. He watched from the outside, and he watched us from the inside. He's clever."

"Or *innocent*," David said. "You should share these thoughts with Captain Kelley. But for Godsakes, Jordan, don't do anything on your own."

She smiled blandly. "How could I? We're off the case now, right? We'll all be in police custody. Maybe in the same hotel, huh? We'll sit in the whirlpool evenings and talk about old times."

David was studying her. "You expect me to believe that horse-shit?"

"Believe what you like."

"Believe this, Jordan, and I love you like a daughter. I am *out* of this. Kay and I are out of this. We are going to do exactly what Captain Kelley asked of us. Right, Kay?"

Kay nodded. "Sorry, dear. We've done what we set out to do— get the police involved."

Jordan laughed and said, "What are you two talking about? We're *all* off the case."

And she gave them a smile that even she didn't buy.

Wearily, David rose and helped Kay up. He gave Jordan a hard, sharp look, and said, "Stay out of trouble, kid."

Jordan nodded, and her friends went off down the hall and linked up with the two uniformed officers waiting there.

For over an hour, she stared aimlessly at the talking heads on the muted television, leafed through magazines that might have contained blank pages, checked her cell for messages that weren't there. Anything not to think about what was going on in surgery. Finally, like the old days at St. Dimpna's, she simply detached.

She had no idea how much time had passed when sharp footsteps again caused her to look up at an approaching Captain Kelley. She snapped back, alert, returning from the empty place where she had been.

Kelley said, "He's out of surgery."

"Is he all right?"

"He made it through."

"When can I see him?"

"We can look in on him now."

She fell in step with Kelley and they left the waiting area and went down a corridor through some automatic double doors. The next set of doors was locked. On the wall above it said INTENSIVE CARE.

Kelley said, "I've got to use a key card to get us in."

She nodded.

"You're not next of kin, but I've cleared you."

"Thank you."

"Ms. Rivera . . . Jordan. He's in pretty rough shape. Are you prepared for that?"

She had seen her family slaughtered, and then been raped. What wasn't she prepared for?

"I am," she said.

Kelley passed the key card over a black plate and the doors swung open.

At right, a semicircular counter enclosed the nurses' work station—eight desks, currently occupied by five nurses. Opposite were eight glassed-in areas—the patients' rooms. Six were occupied, the first five with apparently slumbering patients. The sixth of the occupied rooms, at the far end, was Mark's. A nurse was in with him.

Other than a towel across his loins, he was uncovered and naked, except for the bandages, which seemed to be everywhere, particularly on his upper torso; he had a cast on his right leg to the knee and a huge gauze pad wrapped around his left thigh, stained pink. A skullcap-like head dressing was bloodstained and, most distressing of all, he was on a ventilator. His eyes were closed. But for the beep of his heart monitor, he might have been dead.

"Two minutes," the nurse said, and stepped out.

Kelley put a hand on her shoulder. She didn't fight it. She didn't even mind it.

He said, "There's no way to sugarcoat this. Mark's in trouble. In a coma. That machine is the only thing keeping him alive. . . . I'll give you some privacy."

Kelley stepped out where the nurse waited.

Jordan was able to keep her face impassive, not a twitch, barely a blink, but could not stop the tears. They flowed down her cheeks like rain down a statue. She swallowed, rubbed the moisture away with a sleeve, then moved closer. She touched Mark's hand, and it couldn't have felt colder if it had been a corpse's. His fingers—scraped and bandaged—were icy. She choked, emotion backing up, its acrid puke burning her throat.

She leaned near him. "Mark? There are two things I need to tell you. Can you hear me?"

His eyelids seemed to rustle, but it was probably just a spasm. He couldn't hear her, could he? But maybe he could. . . .

"First," she said, whispering in his ear, "I love you."

Another spasm.

"Second," she said, "I am going to kill his ass."

Such imbeciles, these police. All day long, they troop in and out of my house, carting out box after box of what they think is evidence, when it's not worth its weight in scrap. Yet all along, I am right next door, watching them. Never once do they glance in my direction, at the second-floor window where I stand on lookout.

Fat chance of them finding anything. After disposing of Detective Pryor, I wiped the house down for prints, not that mine were on file anywhere. And I removed anything that might carry DNA, like a toothbrush or hairbrush. But the blood by the fireplace I left for them—they would initially think it was mine. And when it turned out to be Pryor's, they could only wonder if I were victim, too, or perpetrator.

Did they imagine I wouldn't know that this day was coming? Phillip Traynor is nothing more than a character I portrayed, a costume I threw on. Like Kenneth Simon before him, and Bradley Slavens before that. Shed one identity, then slip into a new one. As Shakespeare said, "What's in a name?" This is what is in a name, friend William—a little thought and rendering that-which-is-Caesar's, which is to say hard cold cash.

My next identity, Isaiah Mentor, owns the house I'm standing in. I like that name—it's closer to my Jewish roots (I hadn't lied about that to Pryor), and—like "Traynor"—"Mentor" suggests my role as one who teaches, who gives lessons.

So handy owning the house next door to the Traynor home. Or should I say how handy that Isaiah Mentor owns it . . . yet another identity the fools won't be able to track. So-called computer whizzes like Levi Mills—bring them on! How nice it's been, having a vacant house between me and my neighbors. Considering my calling, a little privacy is appreciated.

All I will take with me from this life is my laptop and my family photos, including the nice little one of my once handsome face, before that sinner bashed me with that shovel.

Oh, and that sinner who smashed my face? In all honesty, that was my fault. I was arrogant and God made me pay for my hubris. Never again. Now, I am more careful. I plan ahead. Still, who would imagine that a sodomite raising a child with another sodomite could have the presence of mind to fight back? I thought I'd hit him perfectly hard enough, but when I turned to lift the unconscious form of his "partner" (intending to bury him alive in the hole I'd dug in their cellar), the unregenerate faker grabbed my shovel and smashed me with it! Fortunately, through my pain and the blood in my eyes, I was able to dispatch both sodomites (with the gun that would eventually be left behind with that Gregory couple) and crawl out of there and make my way to an emergency room.

That was where I first spun the story about the man on the bridge who struck me and stole my dog. The dog was the touch that made anyone who heard the story believe it. I would call them sentimental fools, but I admit sentimentality is a weakness of my own—like keeping the family photos I snap after every lesson (stored on my laptop for perusing at my pleasure).

Unfortunately, the Mentor identity must be discarded before it really begins. I will jump to another identity, already waiting, everything in place, everything prepared, in Seattle. My fondness for Cleveland is overridden by the necessity of survival. To stay, I would need to remove not just those on the "team" but everyone in the entire support group (sinners all, but such an ambitious program). Seems I have interacted too much with too many to stay much longer.

The only burden of this bold geographic move is my emotional tie to this city, because the monetary aspect is no burden. While every lesson I teach has a purpose, a good number profit me as well. God helps those who . . . surely you know the rest. Those drug dealers in the Bronx, for example, made a hefty cash donation to help pay for their sins. They also left behind large quantities of the poison they sell. The cash and the drugs alike all came back to Cleveland, packed in gym bags, riding beneath the simpering, sinning little girls in Havoc's charge.

The drugs I sold to the big sinners who sell that evil stuff to smaller sinners, their joint unwitting contributions benefitting my cause. The Lord provides. If the sinners want to poison themselves, who am I to stand in their way? Didn't the Almighty give us all free will?

The Bronx lesson was not the only time God provided largesse for me, His devoted, sharp instrument. I work hard, and God shares His bounty with me. His grace is available to any of His children, but they are so blind. So very blind.

Sometimes I can only smile at the thought of myself, God's Instrument, sitting unsuspected in the midst of sinners, sinners so wrapped up in their greed and lust they don't see His vengeance biding its time in their midst.

My only sin has been underestimating the imbecility of the police, and young Mark Pryor is such a prime example. How could he settle upon that buffoon Havoc as his suspect? Hadn't I handed him Stuart Carlyle on a platter, just as Herod gave Salome the head of John the Baptist? Stealing Carlyle's pistol, using it several times, finally killing the abortion nurse's sister and brother-in-law and leaving it there, and still Pryor and the rest of them fail to make the connection. If I hadn't manipulated the sodomite Mills to feed them Carlyle's name, the morons might never have taken the bait.

I joined the support group to be close to Jordan, God's Reward to Me, and then became a part of their "team" to stay even closer, not just closer to her but all of them, feeding them information favorable to my position. They were sluggish with sin and needed my help.

So many steps ahead of the police am I that it is almost embarrassing—take, for example, the two they have left in a patrol car in front of my old home. When the time comes, and it will very soon, the simple fools will be eliminated without even knowing they were ever in danger.

For now, they can wait. And I will wait.

Until she comes to me.

Even before her release from the madhouse, I knew she would come to me one day. It is His will. Ongoing media coverage of my Strongsville lesson made mention of Jordan's release, and I knew that the Violent Crime Support Group at St. Dimpna's would be her next stop. So I enrolled, too, and she looked even more magnificent than she had on that great night when I repaired her family and we consummated our union in the Holy Church of my mission, and I spared her life so she could spread the news of my teachings.

But she had disappointed me in that. She never spoke of me. To anyone. For ten years, she never spoke at all. So she still needs my teaching, my mentoring.

Yes, the greatest reward for any teacher is a worthy pupil! Yet she has tried my patience, my Jordan. Upon her release, she all but ran into the arms of that callow Pryor—perhaps she could not overcome the frailties of her mixed-race birth. That she would speak with him in a public place, like a wanton hussy—after having lain with me!

Unthinkable.

Further schooling will repair that. She will be reminded that she is bound to one who is truly God's Instrument. She will be shown the way. She will finally learn the lesson that I gave the night I repaired her family.

The boy Levi had not interpreted my message either. Despite the clear lesson that his abortion-loving parents (Planned Parenthood indeed!) had been taught, he failed to learn and fell into the abomination of lying with men. *Raised by sinners, he might seem to have had little chance of receiving true learning. But that is why God gave us free will.*

It's so simple!

The sodomite's computer with the damning evidence lies at the bottom of the Cuyahoga, next to his cell phone. The eye, the eye that lured him into sinful practices with other men, I burned in the incinerator in the basement. It will offend God no more.

Can there be any doubt that God is my copilot when He sends that foolish boy Pryor to my door? I returned at the very moment that the young detective put the pieces together, but now he is in pieces. Still, this was a lesson for me to learn: time for Traynor to disappear, for Mentor to exist briefly like a flickering flame, and then a new identity, half a continent away, will begin schooling anew.

Night is descending now. Time. My time. Time to go to work. I walk down the stairs—they creak with age.

I have the framed photo of myself in my pocket; I need to return it to the mantel.

Outside, after exiting out back, I creep along the side of the house and peek around the corner. The two officers in the car are looking away. God's grace, watching over me. I will deal with them later. I walk to the rear of my old house. The fool police have locked it. I unlock it. Obviously, they don't know I'm expecting a guest.

She will come tonight. She will come and she will finally learn the error of her ways.

And at last my devotion to the Lord, and to her, will be rewarded, and she will be mine.

Hallelujah.

CHAPTER TWENTY

When Jordan rolled down 38th on her Vespa, she was not surprised to see a police car in front of Phillip's house. The street was dark and quiet, and the streetlamp nearest the Traynor place was out. She cruised on by, the two uniformed officers not even glancing her way, one slumped and apparently sleeping on the job.

So much for police protection.

She turned at the corner, then took a left into the alley, following it all the way to the far end of the block. No cops back here. She tooled her scooter around back to Phillip's garage and parked it in the shadows against one wall, out of sight.

Behind the old, well-maintained two-story house, the only sounds were a rustle of wind in trees and the rumble of distant traffic. She crept up the narrow sidewalk to the back of the house. The lights were all out, no sounds from within.

There wouldn't be—Phillip Traynor was gone, either a murderer on the run or the victim of one. David considered the latter a feasible notion, but Jordan was convinced Phillip was her intruder. She hadn't recognized him, thanks to a little hair dye, contact lenses, and that damaged face. She smiled. Someone else had given him his own medicine, in one instance anyway.

She would do much better.

In her left hand was a small flashlight, in her right the mugger's commandeered switchblade, but before she used it, she would break as many of his bones as her homemade martial arts training would allow. He was old. She was young. She would prevail.

Not that there was much if any chance he'd still be inside this house. This was merely where she would begin. The police had searched the place, and boxed up and carted off anything they thought might be evidence. But they might have missed something, and anyway, she *knew* Phillip, or at least the construct of Phillip that the madman had presented, and she might see something, understand something, that the police had missed on their first pass.

Phillip would not be easy to find, and it would be a challenge to get to him before the cops did. Her next stop would be Dr. Hurst, to find out what the psychologist knew about her fellow support group member. Hurst wouldn't want to cooperate at first, but Jordan had the leverage of Levi's death, and that this one twisted creature calling himself Phillip Traynor had single-handedly performed half of the violent crimes visited upon that entire support group of hers.

Of course, Phillip might be in the wind—might already be long gone from Cleveland, and yet . . . he had kept the city his home base through a decade of serial killing, and likely had gone through a succession of identities. That missing coach, Bradley Slavens, was surely one of them. Mark had been close. So very close.

If she was right—if this madman was an eccentric who considered Cleveland his personal killing grounds—then she might be able to get to him before the cops. She would have to be resourceful and clever, because in a matter of days, probably two at most, the juggernaut of CPD and FBI and the attendant media frenzy would roll over her and all her dark hopes, all her violent dreams.

Strips of yellow crime scene tape covered the screen door in back. She yanked them off, discarded them like a child unwrapping a present. The screen door was unlocked and, surprisingly, so was the inner door. The cops seemed to have a naive notion of the ability of crime scene tape to keep out intruders.

She stepped into a dark kitchen, leaving the door slightly ajar behind her. Should those officers sense somebody was in the house, she might appreciate having an escape route ready. Moonlight filtered through small windows above the sink, enough to reveal the kitchen's blankness—no appliances, no knife block, no personal items at all. She checked the cupboards. Nothing. The police had carted everything off.

This was already looking like a wasted effort, but she pressed on. The kitchen fed into a narrow, dark hallway that led to the front of the house. Inky darkness forced Jordan to move sideways, using a hand on the wall as a guide, edging along. She did not dare use the flashlight until she had determined if the police car out front might detect its use, needing to know where walls and curtains protected her search. Down at the far end, light from outside filtered in through sheer-curtained windows.

Finally, she reached the end of the hall and found herself in a small foyer, living room to her right, stairs to her left, kitchen hall behind her, front door straight ahead. That door, with multiple glass panes, was the curtained source of outside light. She peeked around the thin semi-sheer fabric and saw the police car parked out front. The officers sat in darkness, thanks to that burned-out streetlamp. The only significant light came from the moon.

Why couldn't they just drive away and leave her to her search? Did they really think their killer would return to the scene of the crime? To the home they had stripped of damn near everything?

God, cops could be stupid. Even Mark, so many missteps. . . .

She went up the nearby stairs, and they creaked under her sneakers. The natural spookiness of a dark old empty house could not be denied, and she felt uneasy going up, some goose bumps rising on her forearms, where the sweatshirt sleeves were rolled back. Couldn't help it. She was human.

But the upstairs, where she used the flash with care, was a nonevent. Three bedrooms and a bathroom. Only one bedroom seemed ever to have been in use, as it had a Victorian dark wood bed, a single with fancy carving and a matching nightstand. Nice braided rug, too, but otherwise nothing. No clothing in the closet. No books or photos or other personal items.

Even the bathroom showed no signs of use, its medicine cabinet empty, no soap in the clawed tub's dish. Had the police taken all of this stuff? Or had Phillip cleared some of it out himself? And had he really lived in a house with so many unused rooms?

A noise from downstairs startled her. Had she been wrong? *Was Phillip here?* Or was that just the kind of grunt and groan you could expect from a structure of this advanced age?

Carefully, flashlight switched off and in her left, the switchblade open and gripped tight in a fist, she went down, one step at a time, pausing to listen. *Step, listen, step, listen, step, listen. . . .*

Nothing.

Back downstairs, she made her way to the living room, operating only by whatever moonlight managed to infiltrate openings in the filmy curtains. Furnishings to navigate here, Victorian chairs, a matching couch, odd pieces in a sparse yet formal room. As she eased forward, she could make out dark patches on the floor, near the fireplace. Caked blood irregular and black in the moonlight—Mark's blood. Her stomach tightened. That acrid vomity taste was at the back of her throat again.

Forcing herself, she kept moving in the dim light. Like the kitchen, this room had been stripped of all human vestiges other than the furniture.

Skirting the blood, she looked at the fireplace, with its carved ornate wood trim and bare mantel. No knickknacks or framed photos, but wait . . . there *was* something, something the police had overlooked or that had just gotten accidentally left behind. One framed photo, small, not even three by five, facedown on the mantel. Easy to miss.

She took it and held it in the moonlight, and within the little gold-leaf picture frame was a face she knew very well. She knew it because she saw it every night before sleep took her, and she saw it every day when she went to the refrigerator for a bite or a drink, her colored-pencil drawing of the face held to its door by a magnet.

The face of the intruder.

The monster who had slain her family.

And she could see it now, see Phillip in the photograph, looking past the handsome face in the frame into the ravaged face from group, because (for one thing) the eyes, never mind the color, were the same. She should have seen that all along, but now she did, and now she had him.

Maybe she would lose him to the police, but now at least she could point to this picture and say this is *him*, this is the killer, the rapist, the man who played victim as Phillip, the madman who had murdered Levi, and who undoubtedly struck Mark down right here, when he made the same discovery.

A noise behind her made her turn quickly, and she had the knife tight in her hand. Her night vision was good, and the moonlight helped, too; but she lightsabered the flashlight around anyway.

Nothing.

Was Phillip here? Would he be waiting for her, in that hallway, when she stepped from the living room into the foyer? Was he crazy enough to stick around, lunatic enough to return?

Of course he was. She had so often thought of him as a madman—how could she question it?

And if the police had emptied every fucking item from the cupboards and the medicine cabinet, how could they miss this picture? Or had Phillip returned, and left it for her to find? To taunt her!

She moved slowly across the living room, thinking, *If I scream, those cops will come.*

But her scream might summon the intruder, only . . . *she* was the intruder. She was in his home. And on his turf. Where her cry for help might send him not scurrying away but toward her, and she might be dead, and he might be gone, before help could come.

She crept forward as she had coming down the stairs, taking a step, listening, taking a step, listening, taking a step, listening.

And when she reached the open space leading from living room to hall, she moved fast and low, in a crouch, knife poised to defend or attack as need be, the flashlight slashing the darkness . . .

. . . and revealing nothing but an empty hall and a similarly empty stairway nearby.

On her way back to the kitchen, she found the door to the basement, but by now she was rattled enough to think, *Fuck that shit*, and she just got the hell out of there. She wanted this bastard, but she was not going down into the dark, dank basement of the madman's house looking for him.

As she rode on the Vespa back to her apartment, the framed photo in one pocket of her jeans, the switchblade in the other, she argued with herself, logic and emotion rolling around inside her like a couple of sumo wrestlers, each too strong to do the other any damage.

Should she call the cops and tell them about the photo? If she did, she would be abdicating her role as avenger, and admitting that the police were better qualified and more likely to find and stop this bastard, and soon. Being alone in that psychopath's house, skirting the black, dried blood that had been inside Mark, had scared the shit out of her.

But today she had promised Mark, as she had promised herself long ago, that she would kill this evil creature, and she still wanted that, very much. She also wanted to stay alive and to start over with Mark. Yet just as much she wanted to see Phillip Traynor, or whoever the fuck he really was, stopped, and stop him herself. Finally, though, she had a responsibility, to other potential victims out there, to put aside her thirst for revenge, and make do with justice.

When she rolled past the police car parked in front of her apartment house—these two were at least awake, and one noticed her and gave her a tip-of-the-cap salute—she considered stopping to talk to them. Giving them the framed photo she'd found. That she gave this consideration represented the considerable journey she'd taken from Phillip's house to her place—when she'd left, she'd not even considered dealing with this with the two cops on watch outside there.

Inside her apartment, she tossed the framed photo with a clunk onto the black-topped table. She got out of her sweatshirt and jeans and panties, tossing them near the mattress, and went in the bathroom and took a shower, a long warm one, soaping every square inch of her body and trying to let the steamy warmth relieve the tenseness of her muscles. She didn't think about anything except how good it felt, but when she toweled off, her warring thoughts kicked back in, and then, finally, she knew what she needed to do.

She slipped into some gray sweats and got her cell from her wadded jeans. She sat on the edge of the floor-bound mattress, her knees high. Captain Kelley had given her his cell number and she called it.

She asked, "Anything new on Mark's condition?"

"Nothing's changed. Early yet."

She told him about going to Phillip's and of the photo she'd found.

"You got any idea," he said, his voice cold, "how stupid that was, going over there, entering a crime scene like that, this asshole on the loose?"

"Pretty stupid, I guess. Goddamn stupid?"

"Goddamn stupid is right. How the hell did you get in?"

"The back door was open."

". . . No, they locked up. There's no way in hell they didn't lock up."

Her voice was as calm as a grade school teacher telling her class it was time for recess. "Okay. So Phillip's still around. He went in, left that photo for me to find, and left the door unlocked to make sure I could find it."

"Why did he *want* you to find it?"

"He's fucking with me. What do you think? Captain, he's fucking with all of us."

"I want that photo."

"You can have it."

"I'll have one of the officers keeping watch come gather it. I'm going to circulate it immediately and see who recognizes him."

"You'll come up with several names, and one of them will be Bradley Slavens."

There was a nod in his voice. "The gymnastics coach who dropped off the grid. Man, Mark really *did* crack this thing."

"He did. Do me one favor?"

"Yeah?"

"Tell him you're proud of him, when he wakes up."

She ended the call.

She was opening the refrigerator to get herself a can of apple juice when the buzzer downstairs sounded. She returned the buzz, then went to the door, and had a sudden thought—*who the hell had she just buzzed in?*

This was no time to let her guard down, but when her doorbell rang, she looked out the peephole and saw the cap of a uniformed officer. She opened the door, just as her father had once opened the door for a cop, and Phillip Traynor looked up at her from under the black bill of the blue cap and his lipless smile was at its hideous worst.

He shoved her back, and she almost lost her balance as he slammed the door behind him. Then, in that way of his that inserted ragged breaths here and there, he asked, "Do you like my picture? I left it there for you."

He tossed the cap away. He wore a police uniform, though its blouse had a splotchy look, like a garment that had been hastily cleaned in a restaurant restroom after food had been spilled.

He saw her frowning, trying to put it together, and said, "I appropriated this from one of the officers in front of my house. They were already disposed of when you arrived, which you'd have noticed had you taken a closer look . . . but of course I knew you wouldn't. The officers out front, here? Those gentlemen I just took care of."

"You're a monster."

"I perform monstrous deeds at times, but I have a good heart. I think you sensed that, didn't you? In Phillip? You and Phillip hit it off well, I thought."

"What's your real name?"

"I'm known by many names. I am one of God's avenging angels."

"You're fucking nuts is what you are."

She backed off farther, as he made himself at home, strolling around, taking the place in. That he was dressed as a cop made it seem like he was looking for evidence.

"Simple, unpretentious," he said. "I like that. God's servants don't require worldly things. . . . You drew my picture!" He had paused at the refrigerator. "I *knew* you cared. I knew beneath the hurt and rage . . . that you cared."

"I care."

He gestured toward the pencil portrait, his smile a terrible rip in the ravaged face. "I was handsome, wasn't I? As handsome as you are beautiful. But you know what they say about beauty."

She took a quick step toward him, planted and pivoted, left leg coming around to deliver a solid blow, but Phillip was ready. He grabbed her by the ankle and knee and flipped her to the floor, hard, on her stomach, a belly flop without a swimming pool. She rolled, then swung her leg around and took his feet out from under him, and now *he* hit hard, on his back. She landed with an elbow in his stomach that sent air whooshing from him, his face contorting as best as its tight skin would allow.

Then she was straddling him and her hands were on his throat and she was choking and choking and choking and his face was turning red, redder, reddest, and she was grinning, drinking in his pain, but somehow he brought his legs up and caught her head between his knees and yanked her back, tore her grip free. He was damn near double-jointed! And then she remembered, how fucking stupid of her—*he'd been a gymnast.*

He was on his side, with her neck between his knees, not squeezing, just holding her there, and she flailed with small sharp fists, kicking with the soles of her bare feet, landing blows anywhere she could, until their force and frequency caused him to use his legs to fling her away. She lay in a pile of discarded limbs as he strode over and picked her up and threw her against the wall, like a piece of furniture he was trying to break. She felt a rib snap, and slid to the floor, the pain sharpening with her every breath.

She lay against the wall, trying to decide her next move. He was standing there looking down at her, like a confused traffic cop, not close enough for her to kick out at—she would have to rally for another attack. Her breath was ragged. So was his, even more so than normal.

"Foreplay has its place," he said. "So often, because of the solitary nature of my mission, I must pay for sex. And it is a perfunctory thing. A biological thing. Not beautiful. Not sacred. Like the act of communion we experienced those ten long years ago."

She knew that she could not defeat him, not physically. She had trained, but he was bigger and better trained. Still, he seemed to have no gun. *How had he killed those cops?*

In a soft, even gentle voice, she said, "I know what you were doing. What your purpose was. Is."

"You do?"

"You were teaching. That's what you do. You showed families the way of their transgressions. You . . . fixed them. If they intermarried. If one of them was gay. Kay works at an abortion clinic. Many reasons."

"Sinful. Sinful."

"But where do I come in? Phillip . . . should I still call you Phillip?"

"It will suffice."

"What makes me special? I am a sort of . . . half-breed. The result of a mixed-race union."

He waved that off. "Not your fault, my dear one. Not your fault. God made you perfect. He made you for me."

"Really?"

"You're my *reward*. So much hard work. So much planning. So much teaching. And I grew lonely. Terribly lonely. Then you came out of that asylum and back into my life. I sent you a message—but you didn't respond!"

He meant the dead waitress. He seemed suddenly worked up.

"I didn't know *how* to respond," she said. "But thank you for the gesture. Was she a sinner?"

The question calmed him, but anger remained under there, spiking up and showing itself in his eyes. "Oh yes. My dearest . . . have you . . . forgive me, but I must ask . . . have you lain with Mark Pryor?"

"No! Oh no. I've lain only with you. I have waited."

His face contorted as if tears were near. "But why didn't you tell my story? Why didn't you tell the world? Perhaps I would not have had to teach so many *lessons*, had you told my *story!*"

"I didn't understand," she said. "Please forgive me."

She rose. She held out her hand to him.

"Come," she said. "Come to bed with me, my love."

He swallowed. His eyes brimmed with tears. His chin quivered with emotion. His pants bulged with an erection.

He held his hand out to her. She thought of a very old movie that her father liked—the one where the Frankenstein monster held his hand out to his bride.

Unlike that bride, Jordan took this monster's hand. She walked him to the end of the mattress. She stood before him, perhaps three feet between them, and tugged off her sweatshirt. She put her shoulders back and thrust her smallish boobs out, hoping they would do.

He gasped and blurted, "'Thy two breasts are like two young roes that are twins!'"

"You're so . . . poetic."

He trembled. "It's the Song of Solomon. There is nothing sinful in the union of two who love as we do!"

She stepped out of the sweatpants.

"Thank you, God!"

She lay on the mattress, on top of the sheets and blankets, and spread herself open to him. Agape, he fumbled with the police officer's bloodstained shirt, and unbuckled the belt, and pulled down the pants. He stepped out of them and dropped them, and there was a clunk—some weapon, a folded hunter's knife, perhaps.

Skinny but muscular, with very little hair on him, he was tugging at his tented boxer shorts when she raised a hand. "Not so quickly. Come to my embrace. Let's savor these moments, shall we?"

He gulped, nodded, and dropped to his knees on the mattress as if praying between her spread legs, and then fell on her like a tree, which fucking hurt because of her broken rib, and then he was hugging her, lost in the moment, not noticing her reaching for her wadded jeans, sliding them over, her hand slipping in the pocket, finding the switchblade, and when she clicked it open, he backed away a little, curiously, as if to say, *What's that?*

Then she showed him what it was by plunging the knife's blade into his back, with great force, force that straightened him in pain and surprise. She plunged it in again, and again, each time to the hilt, releasing between blows little plumes of blood trying for the ceiling but failing miserably.

"Fuck you, fuck you, fuck you!" someone was saying. Her, apparently.

"Oh! Oh! Oh!" someone was saying. Him, apparently.

She stopped stabbing long enough to pull herself out from under his wiry frame, and when free of him, she knelt over him, flopped as he was on his stomach, and like Phillip when he'd knelt between her legs, she too might have been praying, but she wasn't. She was stabbing him, two-handed now, plunging the blade deep, penetrating the intruder until he stopped shuddering from the blows and then she did it some more.

Finally, she drew back, breathing heavy, an artist appraising her work. His back was a welter of punctures and gliding blood streams, an abstract painting no one but a maniac might admire. Satisfied, she let the bloody blade tumble with a clank to the floor.

"*Now* I'll tell your fucking story," she said.

She went back into the shower and got his blood off her, and she was trembling, even shaking, when she toweled off. The shower had been fairly hot, so she was a little cold, but not enough to justify this shivering. She did not cry. She would not cry.

The son of a bitch wasn't worth it.

She sat at the table and drank her apple juice until real cops, among them Captain Kelley, came banging at her door.

CHAPTER TWENTY-ONE

In a pink T-shirt and jeans, hair ponytailed back, Jordan sat in Mark's room, at his bedside, holding his hand, the regular rhythm of the ventilator oddly comforting.

She barely heard Captain Kelley come in.

The African-American detective asked, "How long have you been here?"

"A while. Here to arrest me?"

He grinned at that, though there was embarrassment in it. "No. I told you there'd be no problem. The only thing the district attorney wants from you is to shake your hand."

"For getting rid of a public nuisance?"

"Maybe. Or maybe he wants to shake the hand of the young woman who stabbed a man nineteen times in self-defense."

"I just wanted to make sure the prick was dead."

"Oh, he's dead all right." Kelley, looking typically sharp in a tan suit, stepped closer to Mark. "Is his color better? I think his color is better."

"He'll be fine."

Kelley said nothing. Then: "You're gonna love this. Your pal Traynor owned the house next door to his. That's where he was hiding out, after things got tense."

"Set the trap. Watched me go in. I'm lucky he didn't grab me in there. Don't know how well I'd have done."

He grinned again. "My money would still be on you, young lady."

"How'd you find out he owned *that* house, too?"

"Came up when we canvassed the neighbors. Traynor kept a low profile, but he was seen going in and out of both houses. He didn't hang on to much in the way of personal possessions, you know. We found some family photos. But the really key thing we found was—"

"On his laptop. More family photos. But not *his* family, right? Photos of the families he butchered. After he butchered them."

Kelley looked at her as if she had just told his fortune. "How do you know that?"

"I posed for one."

The detective's eyebrows raised. "Yeah. I guess you did." He sighed. "That hard drive is already in FBI hands. I have a good relationship with the head fed, and he says they estimate they'll clear over fifty unsolved homicides from the evidence on that laptop."

"Horrible as it is," she said, with a little shudder, "it'll bring . . . closure to a lot of people. That's what my shrink would say, anyway."

"I heard a rumor you've had some good news."

She glanced at him brightly. "Yes, my friend Kara's being released from St. Dimpna's. I'm picking her up Friday." *With a handful of Dimpna Dust at the ready.* "We're going to room together."

"That place of yours is pretty small for that."

She shivered. "I haven't been back there except to pick up my stuff. I don't need those kind of memories. For now, I'm at Mark's place. His mom likes the idea of me looking after it, till he's better."

Kelley frowned, then plastered on a smile, and looked toward Mark, a man in a coma wearing the earbuds of an iPod. "What's he listening to?"

"Stuff from when we were in high school."

He smiled a little. "Including 'your song'?"

"We don't have a song yet. Captain, we really *weren't* an item back in school. That's something that was stolen from us. But we're going to get it back."

Kelley nodded. He looked at her with an expression that was a mix of kind and sad. "Jordan, wherever Mark is, it's a very dark place. You've talked to the doctors. You do understand that . . . he might be in that dark place a long time. He might not ever make it back. You need to start dealing with that."

She shook her head. "He'll be back."

"How can you be so sure he'll find his way?"

She smiled and stroked her boyfriend's hand. "*I* did, didn't I?"

ABOUT THE AUTHOR

Photograph by John Deason

MAX ALLAN COLLINS has earned an unprecedented nineteen Private Eye Writers of America Shamus nominations, winning for his Nathan Heller novels *True Detective* (1983) and *Stolen Away* (1991), receiving the PWA life achievement award, the Eye, in 2006. In 2012, his Nathan Heller saga was honored with the PWA Hammer award for making a major contribution to the private eye genre.

His graphic novel *Road to Perdition* (1998) is the basis of the Academy Award–winning Tom Hanks film, followed by two acclaimed prose sequels and several graphic novels. He has created a number of innovative suspense series, including Mallory, Quarry, Eliot Ness, and the Disaster series. He is completing a number of Mike Hammer novels begun by the late Mickey Spillane; his audio novel, *The New Adventures of Mike Hammer: The Little Death*, won a 2011 Audie.

His many comics credits include the syndicated strip *Dick Tracy*; his own *Ms. Tree*; *Batman*; and *CSI: Crime Scene Investigation*, based on the TV series for which he wrote ten best-selling novels.

His tie-in books have appeared on the *USA Today* best-seller list nine times and the *New York Times'* three. With frequent collaborator Matthew Clemens, he wrote the Thriller Award-nominated *You Can't Stop Me* and its sequel *No One Will Hear You.* His movie novels include *Saving Private Ryan, Air Force One,* and *American Gangster (*IAMTW Best Novel Scribe Award, 2008).

An independent filmmaker in the Midwest, Collins has written and directed four features, including the Lifetime movie *Mommy* (1996); and he scripted *The Expert,* a 1995 HBO World Premiere, and *The Last Lullaby* (2009), based on his novel *The Last Quarry.* His documentary *Mike Hammer's Mickey Spillane* (1998/2011) appears on the Criterion Collection DVD and Blu-ray of *Kiss Me Deadly.*

His play *Eliot Ness: An Untouchable Life* was nominated for an Edgar Award in 2004 by the Mystery Writers of America; a film version, written and directed by Collins, was released on DVD and appeared on PBS stations in 2009.

His other credits include film criticism, short fiction, songwriting, trading-card sets, and video games. His coffee-table book, *The History of Mystery,* was nominated for every major mystery award, and his *Men's Adventure Magazines* (with George Hagenauer) won the Anthony Award.

Collins lives in Muscatine, Iowa, with his wife, writer Barbara Collins. As "Barbara Allan," they have collaborated on nine novels, including the successful Trash 'n' Treasures mysteries, their *Antiques Flee Market* (2008) winning the Romantic Times Best Humorous Mystery Novel award in 2009. Their son, Nathan, is a Japanese-to-English translator, working on video games, manga, and novels.